DATE DUE

	11/2		

WINGS OF HONOR

WINGS OF HONOR

Book Three of the Black Sabre Chronicles

Tom Willard

A TOM DOHERTY ASSOCIATES BOOK
New York

WINGS OF HONOR

Copyright © 1999 by Tom Willard

This book is printed on acid-free paper.

Maps and ornament by Ellisa H. Mitchell

A Forge Book
Published by Tom Doherty Associates, Inc.
175 Fifth Avenue
New York, NY 10010

Forge® is a registered trademark of Tom Doherty Associates, Inc.

ISBN 0-312-86967-3

First Edition: January 1999

Printed in the United States of America

0 9 8 7 6 5 4 3 2 1

Especially for members of the Tuskegee Airmen who became my friends during the writing of this novel:

Lieutenant Colonel James Hurd, Jr., Sarasota, Florida;
Lieutenant Colonel Nasby Wynn, Sarasota, Florida;
and Major Alvin Downing, St. Petersburg, Florida.

Thank you, gentlemen, for helping save the world, and in doing so, making our country a greater nation!

And, for Cynthia Whitcomb, who has been my friend . . . and knows what it takes to see her name at the top of the page.

And, of course, my editor, Dale L. Walker . . . who taught me how to keep my name at the top of the page!

But we . . . shall be remembered;
We few, we happy few, we band of brothers;
For he today that sheds his blood with me
Shall be my brother . . .

William Shakespeare
Henry V

European War Theater Nov. 1942

1) Northern Ireland
2) Netherlands
3) Belgium
4) Switzerland (N)
5) Denmark
6) Bohemia-Moravia
7) N. Transylvania
8) Serbia
9) Slovakia
10) Gulf of Trieste
11) U.S.S.R. (A)
12) East Prussia
13) Austria
    (Ostmark)
14) Portugal (N)

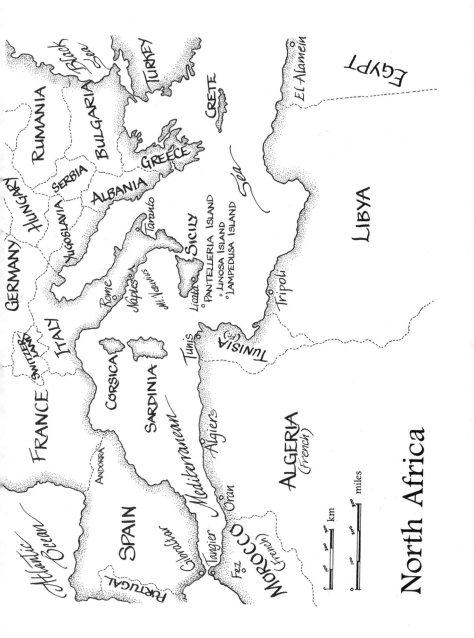

North Africa

Foreword

* * *

During World War II, the first all-Negro Army Air Corps fighter squadron was formed at Tuskegee, Alabama, under the command of Lieutenant Colonel Benjamin O. Davis, Jr., a Negro graduate of the United States Military Academy at West Point. Under Davis's leadership and strict discipline, what became known as the "Tuskegee Experiment" proved not only the Negroes' willingness and determination to fight for their country, but their exemplary courage and expert flying capability.

The first Negro squadron, the 99th Pursuit Squadron, was called the *Schwarzen Vogelmenschen*—the Black Birdmen—by the German aviators. American bomber pilots had another name for them— the "Black Red-Tail Angels"—for their brightly painted red tail sections. While flying bomber support from North Africa to Italy, from Yugoslavia to Berlin, the Red-Tails did not lose a single American bomber to German fighter attack.

Three more squadrons, the 100th, 301st, and 302nd would be formed, comprising the 332nd Fighter Group, which together with more than 450 Negroes trained as bomber pilots, bombardiers, and crewmen, would form the 477th Composite Group. Although the bombers of the 477th did not see combat, a fully trained and highly skilled Group had been formed in record time.

By the end of the war in Europe, the 332nd had suffered sixty-six of their personnel killed in combat, flown more than 15,000 sorties; destroyed over 1,000 German aircraft in the air and on the ground, received one Silver Star, numerous Bronze Stars, Purple Hearts, hundreds of Air Medals, and more than 1,500 Distinguished Flying Crosses.

These men should be remembered for their courage and tenacity to get into the fight during a period of segregated military. More importantly, these pilots, who called themselves the "Tuskegee Airmen," were the vanguard that would tear down the walls of segregation that had stood since the Negro military contribution to the United States began in the Civil War.

If we must die, let it not be like hogs
Hunted and penned in an inglorious spot,
While round us bark the mad and hungry dogs,
Making their mock at our accursed lot.
If we must die, O let us nobly die,
So that our precious blood may not be shed
In vain; then even the monsters we defy
Shall be constrained to honor us though dead!
O kinsmen! we must meet the common foe!
Though far outnumbered let us show us brave,
And for their thousand blows deal one deathblow!
What though before us lies the open grave?
Like men we'll face the murderous, cowardly pack,
Pressed to the wall, dying, but fighting back.

Claude McKay
If We Must Die

PROLOGUE

Fort Davis, Texas

⭑ ⭑ ⭑

In 1880, Selona Sharps was twenty-three and already stooped like a woman of fifty.

She had been scalped when she was younger and wore a piece of buffalo hide as a wig, now tied tightly with a scarf, which gradually worked loose from the wind and the heat of the laundry fires. Sweat ran from her forehead, until the hairpiece came to rest just above her eyebrows. She would pull the scarf back, resettling the wig, then hitch up her skirt and throw another piece of wood onto the fire burning on the dry, sunbaked west Texas ground.

The morning wind blew hot and dusty, wrapping around her tired legs and back as she stirred at a layer of white, gurgling lye soap foaming above the dirty clothes in the large iron kettle. She would pause from time to time and wipe at her forehead, then throw on more wood and step back as the froth hissed, then bubbled and popped against the heat of the day, which was nearly as punishing as the heat from the fire. Her long stick fished around the bottom, raised a pair of sky-blue trousers as another blast of hot dust swirled around the fire.

Looking down the line of boiling kettles on Suds Row, Selona could see the other laundresses buzzing about their kettles. At each of the eight iron cauldrons, the women held children, except Selona.

Nearby her two sons Adrian and David were playing beneath a

piñon tree by a swing fashioned from rope and an old McClellan saddle.

Adrian was tall, with deep ebony skin, like his father. He was a quiet lad, prone to sit for long spells on the back porch, his eyes scanning the desert, in search of the many types of animals that lived not far from their house.

David was short, with cinnamon-colored skin, a mixture of Negro and Mexican, like his mother and father. He had been brought to Selona the night of his birth for her to raise after his mother died. The mother had been a young prostitute in a local "hog ranch," the father unknown.

During the summer the boys lived in a small tent in back of the house on Suds Row, near the rabbit pens, spending their days scampering about half-naked like a pair of Apaches. They knew no fear, which terrified Selona.

She looked up as Vina Gibbs approached, pregnant with her fourth child. She had an armful of wet clothes and was wringing out the water with her powerful hands. She was a big-boned woman, the wife of Darcy Gibbs, Augustus Sharps's best friend and comrade in the 10th Cavalry.

That was when Selona, out of the corner of her eye, caught movement in a thick patch of sage twenty feet away. She eased to a wooden box stationed near one of the kettles, all the while talking, but not to Vina.

"David . . . jump up in that saddle with your brother."

David knew what that meant and was in the saddle as fast as her hand went beneath a white cloth lying on the box.

"Lord have mercy!" Vina moaned. She, too, had seen the movement.

Selona's hand whipped straight out, steady, and with a smooth move she cocked the Colt revolver and fired at the motion.

The "boom" shook along the Row, raced through the air, and ricocheted with dramatic echo against the caverns and crags of nearby Sleeping Lion Mountain, bringing Suds Row to a sudden silence.

The laundresses looked up and saw Selona step beyond the piñons, knew everything was all right, and went back to work.

The boys watched as she hiked up her dress, Colt horse pistol still in hand, and walked cautiously now from clear ground into the thick sage. She would bend, look, then step again, all the while watching. There was nothing but silence as she squatted, adjusting her eyes to the brown sage, then suddenly hurried a few feet forward and reached with her free hand into a thick patch of sage.

The rattlesnake was four feet long, and would have been longer had the bullet not blown the head clean away. She lifted the rattler, smiled, and stepped back, walking as though stepping on stones to cross a brook, careful should there be more rattlers.

"Good shot, Momma," David said.

Selona grinned as she handed the snake to Adrian, telling him, "Put this in the root cellar. Later on I'll skin it, clean it, then wrap it in a wet rag." Then she whispered as though conspiring, "We'll have it for breakfast in the morning."

David snatched the snake before Adrian's fingers could take it and ran off toward the house with Adrian in hot pursuit. Selona called to them, "Don't tear up that snake . . . I'm going to make your daddy a hatband from the hide."

That was when she realized it was the first time she had thought about Augustus since waking that morning in her empty bed.

The sun beat down mercilessly, relentlessly, and there wasn't the slightest sign of life west of Fort Davis, beyond the Alamita Creek, which was nothing more than a small stream that time of year.

Nothing could live out here except hard men used to hard times, thought Corporal Augustus Sharps, H Troop of the 10th Cavalry, as he led his horse at a walk. Now thirty years old, he had filled into a tall man, his facial features looking fuller within a ten-day growth of beard, the number of days he and his men had been on patrol.

Following in close trail were Private Darcy Gibbs and Trooper David Bane, a short, muscular young man who had been in the 10th for two months; a "young soldier," as new recruits were called until they finished their first year of service. A third trooper was out front, scouting for sign of ambush.

Augustus took his canteen and halted his horse, removed his kossuth hat, and poked the top inward, forming a depression. He poured water into the depression, then held the hat to the horse. The horse sloshed the water, which Augustus tried to catch with his fingers. He licked the wetness, forgetting the horse's saliva that mixed with the water. Water was more important than any thought of germs. A man might die from germs; the same man would surely die without water. The horse as well, and all soldiers knew it was better to be thirsty and riding, than to be a little sated and walking through the desert of west Texas. Then he took some buckshot from his pocket, shoved the lead pellets in his mouth, a trick he had learned to stave off thirst, and took a small sip of water.

"Tighten up," he ordered. The troopers tightened the cinches on their horses.

"Mount up." They threw their legs over the McClellans and settled their weary bodies into the saddles. Augustus led them out at a canter; sitting tall in the saddle, he could see a rising cloud of dust to the front. Beyond that he could see Davis Mountains.

The trail of dust grew closer and through the rising waves of heat he saw the familiar figure of Trooper Gabriel Jones approaching. Augustus pulled up as Jones drew to a halt.

Jones wiped the sweat from his forehead. He pointed toward the mountains. "Nuthin' ahead. Just a sweet stroll into the fort."

"We'll water the horses at the Alamita, then push hard for Fort Davis." Augustus started to say something else, but his mouth froze. To the east there rose such a storm of dust the very size of the cloud suggested a lot of riders.

"Patrol?" asked Bane. He was eighteen years old and had not yet developed the ability to mask his fear. That took more than two months; more than two years. Sometimes, it never came at all to some troopers.

"Don't rightly know," Augustus muttered.

"Could be Mexicans. Or Injuns," said Gibbs.

"We'll sit a spell," said Augustus. He motioned toward an outcropping of rocks some twenty yards away. To Bane he said, "Take the horses at a walk. Nice and slow. Don't throw up any dust."

Bane took the link attached to the left side of his horse and snapped it to the halter ring of the horse to his left; the others did the same, then removed their Springfield carbines from their saddle boots. This joined the horses, and Bane walked them behind the rocks and waited while the others selected a position in the rocks.

The boiling heat of the desert chapped their dry lips further as the dust drew closer; soon, they were able to make out the shapes of twelve riders.

"Ain't nothin' from a cavalry troop," said Augustus matter-of-factly. "The horses are many colored." All the horses in a troop were the same color; this gave their comrades a means of quick identification.

Augustus eared back the hammer on his Sharps. The others did the same and quietly removed their pistols and laid them at their sides. Augustus took fresh rounds from the cartridge case and laid them on a rock. He adjusted the rear sight. "We'll take them at fifty yards . . . if they be Mexicans or Injuns."

The riders approached in a group, and Augustus immediately eliminated the possibility that the riders were Indians. Indians generally rode in single file to deceive trackers about their numbers. That still left Mexicans, or any number of gangs of horse thieves and outlaws in Texas.

"Jason Talbot," Augustus breathed heavily, wishing the riders had been a threat. A physical threat. Jason Talbot, a local rancher, was more of a mental threat than physical.

Jason Talbot was the brother of the man who once owned Augustus and his family.

The Buffalo Soldiers stood, their Springfields resting on their hips, fingers lightly on the triggers.

Talbot, a tall man, slowed his horse to a walk and approached warily. His face was covered with dust; his gray mustache hung to his chin. His black-diamond eyes were like banked coals—fiery, gleaming, even in the heat.

Talbot reined in his horse; the others, all white men except for one Mexican, sat quietly in their saddles while Augustus and Talbot talked.

"You niggers seen any men running a string of horses through these parts?"

Augustus felt the chill streak along his spine as he had many times before. He spoke calmly. "I'm Corporal Augustus Sharps. My last name used to be Talbot. Do you remember me, Mr. Talbot?"

Talbot's voice was chilly. "I know who you are. I remember when you was a pickaninny over to my brother's ranch." Talbot spit. "I heard you was wearing Yankee blue."

The Buffalo Soldiers looked uneasily at each other, then to Talbot, who was undaunted as he spit again. "I asked you if you've seen any men with horses."

Augustus lofted the Sharps onto his shoulder. He shook his head. The hell with this man, he told himself. Then he laughed. "Lost the trail?"

Talbot's face hardened. "You army boys are suppose' to protect us ranchers from horse thieves and Injuns. Not doin' much of a job, are you?"

"We do just fine, so long as you folks stay out of the way and let us do our job." Augustus spit, which took all the moisture left in his mouth. But it was worth the dryness to see the look on Talbot's face.

Talbot wasn't a man to leave without the last word, especially if he could hurt a Colored man wearing Yankee blue. "I'm buyin' my brother's place. The crazy old fool has been evicted by the bank. I want you to know I'm goin' to plow the whole place under and plant cotton."

Talbot wheeled his horse and rode off without another word.

Augustus stood stunned; he thought he heard Gibbs cursing, but wasn't sure if he could hear anything except the great anger resounding from his very soul. His legs weakened for a moment, then he righted, squared his shoulders, and wiped at the perspiration clouding his eyes.

Or was it perspiration?

He took several deep breaths, then slowly walked to his horse, feeling the heat of the anger from his men. And he knew they still had a long way to go, and there was nothing that could stop him from reaching his destination.

"Mount up. We've got a lot of riding," Augustus ordered.

"Hadn't we best move slower, Corporal?" asked Bane.

Augustus grinned. "Talbot and his men will have scared off anything that might be waiting for us."

The sun was setting when the patrol reached the Talbot ranch, but Augustus didn't ride directly down. He sat on a hill studying the large adobe ranch house, which was in sad disrepair, watching with particular interest the various cross-shaped gunports cut into the closed windows and door.

One port at the door was open; the barrel of a rifle jutted through.

When Augustus rode down, he rode slowly, making certain they were seen in clear sight. Stopping at the front door, he spoke to the man he knew was holding a rifle trained on his heart.

"Mr. Talbot. This is Augustus. Do you remember me?" He always said that when the rode to visit the graves of his mother and father, knowing old man Talbot's mind now worked on a moment-to-moment basis.

The door opened and Talbot stepped out, wearing a tattered Confederate uniform. His left arm was off at the shoulder, but Augustus knew he could still shoot a rifle.

Talbot eyed him for a moment, then in a wild, crazy voice that sounded like the wind, he shouted, "The bank took my ranch. I ain't got nothing no more. Now you git! Git! I tell you."

Augustus spoke slowly, saying with a steady voice, "It's me Mr. Talbot, Augustus."

Talbot merely stared long and hard, then turned for the house, but paused at the door. "You was one of my nigras, weren't you?"

"Yes," replied Augustus.

Talbot's cruel voice barked, "I used to have a lot of nigras. Now the bank owns them." He opened the door, then called as he stepped into the darkness of the house, "Take them and be gone."

Augustus stepped down from his horse and took the blanket from his saddle and walked to the rear of the house. A small cemetery sat in hard open ground where wagon wheels half-buried in the ground marked the graves of his mother and father.

Gibbs spread a blanket on the ground while Augustus and the others took off their blouses.

Then, beneath the scalding sun, the Buffalo Soldiers took their sabres and dug into the hard, bitter ground, performing an act no human being should have to perform.

The following day the small patrol rode into Fort Davis and after reporting to the orderly room, Augustus dismissed his men and went to his quarters on Suds Row.

When she saw him approach, Selona dropped the stick she was using to stir one of the washing kettles and raced toward him. As she neared she suddenly stopped, and looked peculiarly at the blanket and blouse tied to his saddle in two bundles.

He dismounted, and she slowly stepped into his open arms and kissed him on the cheek. There was something in his eyes that was different, not like the times before when he returned wearing a big grin and swept her off her feet.

"I thought you would be here yesterday."

Augustus replied solemnly, "I had to go over to the Talbot ranch. Old man Talbot lost his land to the bank. His brother bought the land and said he was going to plow up the ground and plant cotton."

It took a moment before the reality made her eyes widen and she could only stand there and feel the depths of human shame. And the anger.

Augustus picked up the bundles and walked into the house.

Selona stood stone solid for a moment, then slowly walked into the piñons and sat beneath a tall cactus and wept.

That afternoon the heat was almost unbearable, but Augustus dug the two graves, smaller than any he ever dug before, each like a grave for a child. He took Gibbs's hand and was pulled out and faced the group of Buffalo Soldiers, the wives from Suds Row, and several officers from the regiment.

Chaplain O'Donnell stepped forward, read a brief prayer, then the remains were interred alongside the remains of scores of Negroes, many of whom who had died fighting to protect the white settlers and former slaveowners of the Texas frontier.

Colonel Grierson took his violin and began playing "The Old Rugged Cross," joined by a few troopers of the regimental band. The voices of the gathering joined the music and for a long moment, on the edge of the violent frontier, the remains were given the decency the bodies had not known in life.

Slowly the group broke up, leaving only Augustus, Selona, and the children to their private moments.

"I never knew them, Augustus. They never knew their grandchildren. Never knew they would even have grandchildren. But you know what's the most hurtful?"

"What?"

"They didn't even have a piece of ground where they could be buried and rest in peace."

Augustus walked off, stooped at the shoulders, followed by the boys.

Selona visited Marie's grave, as she did every day, and had brought along a gourd of water for the flowers she planted each spring. The grave was marked by a white board bearing Marie's name and the year of her death; there was no year of birth since Marie hadn't known it.

"Well, Grams, you finally got your piece of land," she whispered.

Some piece of land! Six feet deep, two feet wide, and six feet long. A flood of memories rushed as she thought of the craggy little woman.

"You got me that husband, and we've got children, but there's no piece of land in sight. I don't think I'll ever own any more land than what you've got, Grams."

How in the world could Colored people save enough money on army pay to buy land?

But it was her dream, one Selona felt gnawing at her with more intensity with each rising of the sun. As though Marie would never rest in peace until a part of the earth belonged to her.

"I'm going to own me a piece of land," she whispered. "Someday me and my family's going to have our own land. I don't want to be buried in some lonesome place like Momma, you, and Daddy. The children never knew any of you. Won't know what you looked like. How you sounded."

She sprinkled each of the flowers lightly, then stood and started back to her kettles on Suds Row.

Florida

☆ ☆ ☆

The morning found the bayou country of northwest Florida wrapped in a veil of low, clinging fog, painting the land an eerie purple. Through the mist, railroad tracks could be dimly seen rising above the swamp on a wide berm threading through the bayou like a snake. Minutes after the sun touched the dew-slick tracks, the rails burned copperish for a moment, then brightened to a soft silver.

Below, in the black muck, a lone alligator plied smoothly along the surface, his cruel snout thrust menacingly above the water, flagging his position while pushing forward a steady wake of rippling tide. To the creatures of the swamp, this signaled that the gator was awake, hungry, and on the prowl.

Near shore, the warning was respected in the tall reeds, where frogs plunged for the bottom and cranes lifted hurriedly into the air.

Then there was silence.

When the alligator had its fill, the swamp might have returned to normal had another presence not found its way into the bayou, breaking the serenity with a punctuality the animals had grown to accept as part of the morning ritual, like the rising sun.

A slow but accelerating vibration rumbled along the tracks: then the smoking engine boomed into the bayou, moving with funereal purpose from the darkness of the east. Behind the diesel trailed an endless caravan of open flatbeds stacked with lumber, their integrity uniform except for a single boxcar captured at the center of the shaking procession bound for New Orleans.

The train appeared as it always had: a dark and intrusive, noisy, shaking apparition pumping an ugly black cloud into the pristine sky.

To the alligator, whose empty eyes focused on the open door of the boxcar, instincts came alive at the possibility of fresh opportunity.

A young woman stood defiantly in the door of the boxcar. Her coal-black hair was whipped back by the wind, revealing a grime-coated cinnamon face.

Hannah Simmons saw no options and found no time to curse her dilemma, for another danger pressed from the dusty darkness three feet away. She gripped the knife in her long slender hands.

"Stay away from me, Billy. I'm warning you. Just leave me alone. Sit down and leave me alone!"

"You nigger bitch!" The man stepped from the shadows and nearly stumbled into her blade.

His name was Billy Turner and he too held a knife in one hand; his free hand pressed the dirty sleeve of his dungaree shirt to his cheek. Beneath the cut trailed a thin streak of blood that the wind shaped into a wet pool beneath the dripping lobe of his ear.

"Don't come any closer, Billy. I'm warning you." Her voice left no doubt that there would be a price to pay: She had cut him. Now Billy rolled the knife confidently through his fingers.

"I'm gonna cut off your ears," he said. "Then I'm going to feed you to the gators."

Hannah leaned back, glancing down the length of the tracks. There was nothing but the lurching framework of the flatbeds and jostling stacks of lumber, nothing that would offer a safer way out of the situation.

How did this happen? Her mind rocked with the question, but this was not the moment to reflect on the past. It was the present that mattered. Not the moment to wonder why she had boarded a train in Tallahassee with a stranger, a man who taught her two things: one, that he was from South Carolina; the other, learned shortly after dawn, that when he was drunk, he was mean.

She had learned that when the sun had drifted into the boxcar where she slept, using her rucksack for a pillow. When dreams of where she was headed had been suddenly interrupted by the nightmare of the present—him looming over her, swaying drunk, his words slurred but his intentions made clear by the knife he held in his hand.

She pulled her own knife from her back pocket, slashed the man across the cheek and raced for the door, where she waited for the right moment to jump.

Could she jump?

She had learned early in life that choices don't always provide a better answer, that choices merely provide a means of measuring the loss against the gain.

It was the result that mattered, and she knew what the result would be if she stayed aboard the train.

Then Billy made the choice for her, and regardless of the outcome there was only one choice.

When Billy stepped closer she kicked him sharply in his crotch.

The moment Billy screamed and doubled to his knees, Hannah stepped free from the boxcar. She glided into the muggy air and floated toward earth.

She felt the breeze in her hair and from behind heard Billy's trailing string of obscenities. Then she drew her knees up and exploded into the cool, green water of the bayou.

She relaxed and allowed herself to sink, shedding the heat of the boxcar; then she reached upward, pulling hand over hand toward the surface, where the light grew brighter, the temperature warmer, until, like a child breaking the embryonic seal of the womb, she reached through to the surface.

She was basking in her triumph, pleased there was no injury, when she spotted the alligator and swam to shore, threading her way through the reeds and paddies, through sea oats and cattails, where she found a small beach beneath the trestle. She stripped herself naked, first washing her shirt, then her overalls.

Hannah climbed to the top of the trestle, where she beat her clothes across the tracks to dislodge the dirt from the fiber. The tracks were still hot from the friction of wheels against steel, so to hurry the drying process she stretched her clothes across the hot tracks and went back to the beach.

She washed her body with handfuls of sea oats she pulled from the marsh, and was pleased when the rough texture scrubbed away the grime and gave her face a stinging glow.

Hannah found a tree branch and used her knife to cut the twigs along the branch's axis to form a row of teeth, then brushed her hair in smooth, easy strokes, taking care not to break the makeshift brush, nor cut her tingling scalp, which she had washed with mud from the swamp.

While drying her hair against the warm sea air coming in from the south, she began to realize where she was and recall where she was going. From the slow, steady breeze, which she calculated was drifting in from the Gulf of Mexico, she was reminded that she was in control again, and remembered jumping from the train, and though she was stranded in the middle of a wilderness, she was not lost. She knew where she was, knew that one part of her journey had ended and a fresh part, the most exhilarating, was about to begin.

She stepped naked onto the tracks and stared for a long moment to the south.

Hannah saw the blue, cloudless sky, and, in the distance, appearing like nothing more than a slit, lay a thin white fringe barely visible on the horizon where the sky met the green swamp.

Too excited to wait for her clothes to dry and enjoying her naked freedom in the isolation of the swamp, she tied the laces of her scuffed brogans together and threw them over her shoulder; she put the knife in the back pocket of her overalls and draped them and her shirt neatly over her arm.

She walked barefoot and naked toward the west, one of hundreds of thousands of Negroes working their way north toward the opportunity that had been created since the beginning of the Great War in 1914, just three years before.

Her destination was East St. Louis, Illinois, a city on the banks of the Mississippi, where she had heard there were jobs in the factories, meatpacking plants, foundries, and loading docks.

She didn't know what she would do to survive. She did know one thing: At the age of twenty-five, she would never again chop cotton!

Arizona

☆ ☆ ☆

On February 15, 1919, First Lieutenant Adrian Sharps arrived in Willcox, Arizona, aboard the Colored-only passenger car of the Southern Pacific Railroad. He rose slowly from his seat, stretched out the soreness in his back, and took the sabres and placed them between the handles of his valise.

His empty left sleeve was folded and pinned neatly just below the official symbol adopted by the 93rd Division: a round patch with a blue French helmet in the center. On the left breast of his tunic he wore the ribbons of the Distinguished Service Cross and the French Croix de Guerre with Palm; on his right sleeve he wore a narrow purple and white strip of cloth denoting that he had been wounded in combat.

He stepped down onto the platform and heard a familiar voice.

"Adrian!" Hannah's shout sounded like music.

He turned and saw her coming toward him, carrying a bundle in her arms. She stopped a few feet from him, looked for a quick moment at the empty sleeve, then rushed into his arm, baby and all.

He hugged her with all his strength, then stepped back as he felt a movement between their bodies.

There was a shining in her eyes as she said softly, "You have to be more gentle, or you might hurt your son."

He stared wide-eyed as she pulled away the blanket to reveal a tiny black face.

"His name is Adrian Augustus Sharps, Junior," she said proudly.

She held the baby out to him, and through a flood of tears, and memories good and terrible, he stood on the platform, holding his child for the first time.

Selona was standing in the cemetery when the buggy arrived at the ranch. She had wanted it that way, insisting to Hannah that she meet Adrian alone.

When she saw him emerge tentatively from the buggy her heart fell as she thought of David and Joseph and as she saw the empty sleeve pinned at the shoulder.

Then she straightened and became grateful that at least he was alive!

The sun was setting as she passed through the wrought-iron arch, then found herself running, as she saw him running toward her.

They embraced in the golden twilight of the day, saying nothing, their tears mixing as they held each other.

"Welcome home, baby," she whispered.

He said nothing; he hugged her and buried his face against her cheek and trembling shoulder, felt the softness of her buffalo fur wig and the strength of her small body.

Finally, he summoned the words: "It's good to be home, Momma."

Adrian's head rose, and he looked past her to the cemetery, where three graves had been added to those of Sergeant Major Roscoe Brassard and Sergeant Darcy Gibbs.

One would be his father, the other two for David and Joseph, whose remains now lay at the American battlefield cemetery at Mons, in the Meuse-Argonne.

At the buggy, Hannah stood holding the baby as Adrian and Selona approached.

Adrian then looked and saw Vina and Theresa approach. Benjamin and Jonathan trailed behind.

Vina and Theresa joined arms around Adrian as the boys hugged at his waist.

Nothing was said until Selona broke the silence. "You must be hungry after your trip. Let's go inside. I'll fix you a bite."

Adrian nodded, then reached for the valise. Both sabres were tied together between the handles. He took the sword that belonged to Darcy Gibbs and handed it to Vina.

Vina stared at the sword as though a missing part of her life had been returned.

Selona's hands went out automatically, palms upturned, as she said, "May I carry the Sergeant Major's sabre?"

Adrian laid the sabre in her palms and watched her fingers close around the metal scabbard.

They walked into the house, where Selona went immediately to the mantel and raised the sabre onto the wooden pegs.

She stepped down and looked at the baby in Hannah's arms, her two grandsons, then felt a chill thread along her spine as she said softly, "I pray to God that sabre will never again come down from that wall."

Then she went into the kitchen and began preparing supper.

That night Adrian and Hannah walked into the cottonwoods, where she spread a large buffalo robe that had once been shared on the same spot by Augustus and Selona.

They made love beneath stars like diamonds against the velvet night; heard an owl hoot softly in the trees, whose branches rustled slightly as the wind swirled through them. Then Adrian and Hannah slid to earth, where their faces were caressed by its coolness. He was home.

PART 1

THE BLACK EAGLE

1

✮ ✮ ✮

The rifleman perched atop a mound of huge boulders had been told that the best hunters were those with gray eyes, that gray eyes, like the color of fur on a wolf's throat, were the keenest.

At twenty-two, Samuel Sharps, the second son born to Adrian and Hannah, knew that wasn't true as he jammed the stock of his Sharps .50-caliber rifle against his shoulder. His black-diamond eyes gleamed as he eared back the hammer, sighted the target, and squeezed the trigger.

Four hundred yards away an antelope kicked upward slightly, took one step, then fell dead on the slope of Mount Graham, five miles north of Bonita, Arizona.

The tightness in his mouth loosened as he watched the blue-gray cloud of smoke clear, saw the dead antelope, and knew that what mattered most was the heart of the hunter.

Moments later, he walked to his tethered horse, slid the rifle into the carbine boot on the McClellan saddle, and stepped into the stirrup. As he climbed aboard, he suddenly felt the presence of the saddle and rifle's original owner.

Like his grandfather, Samuel loved the McClellan. Even though it was old, the open slot in the seat allowed his butt to join with the horse's spine, giving him a sense of partnership with the animal, as though both horse and rider were joined as one. The way the Sharps felt when the weapon joined his shoulder.

He resembled his grandfather—who had been killed in a riding accident shortly before Samuel's birth—he was narrow at the hip, broad across the shoulders, and heavily muscled at the chest. He was strong as a bull and had a voice that was deep, but gentle until riled.

When he reached the antelope he sat for a moment looking at the animal, pleased that the bullet cut a clean groove through the animal's heart. None of the meat would be ruined; steaks and tenderloin on the spine would be intact. Which meant more money for him when he sold the meat to the local restaurant.

Thirty minutes later, with the antelope dressed and tied to the horse's back, he rode slowly down from Mount Graham toward town.

The air that April morning was still and quiet, except for the slow, steady drum of the horse's hooves cracking against the hard ground and the distant drone of a Stearman carving its path through the clear sky as the biplane approached a vacant strip of flat land outside of Bonita. The sound was alluring, pulling him toward a dream the way metal is drawn to a magnet, a dream he had never shared with any other person, not even his mother, who was standing on the front porch of the family restaurant in Bonita as he rode up with the antelope strapped behind the saddle.

At forty-nine, Hannah Sharps was still trim and lithe, her skin the color of cinnamon, her eyes dancing with pride as she watched her son haul the antelope from the horse.

"Clean shot?" His mother always asked Samuel that, in a teasing sort of way, knowing he always shot clean.

"Clean through. Took him down at four hundred yards," Samuel said as he stepped onto the porch and carried the antelope inside, through the dining area, past the kitchen permeated with the wonderful smells of lima beans, roasting corn, and other vegetables cooking on the two huge stoves. He went out back, where he had a skinning rack, a block-and-tackle system that he used to hoist the carcass off the ground. There he stood for a moment, studying the animal, as though he were trying to recall what to do next. But that wasn't so; it was the only time he would ever allow himself to study the kill with any kind of pride. All the time spent before was in the tracking, the kill, and the transport. Now was the time to reflect— not to gloat, but to feel pride in doing the job masterfully, the way he had been taught.

Hannah followed with a sharp skinning knife, bone saw, and meat cleaver, the pride in her eyes hooded by the hand she raised to shade her face from the brightness of the sun.

"Tomorrow I'll be expecting a dozen sharp-tail grouse," she said, handing him the skinning knife.

Samuel nodded. "I'll get up early in the morning. You'll have them by the noon meal."

His mother always prepared a different delicacy for the one meal of the day, served at noon. On Saturdays, she served an additional meal in the evening.

"Use the shotgun. I don't want that old buffalo gun tearing up the meat."

"I'll take them at a hundred yards, Momma. That way I can build me a stand and not have to walk them hills all morning." Then he paused for effect. "The shots will be clean. Just the head will be missing." He glanced at her. "You don't cook the heads, do you, Momma?"

She handed him the knife, "Just your head if you bring back nothing but feathers and feet!"

He took the knife, and she watched him in silence, a slight smile on her mouth, recalling when she was a young girl during the Great War, working on a processing line in a slaughterhouse in East St. Louis, Illinois. She had taught Samuel how to process deer, antelope, cattle, any kind of creature, with swiftness and ease, never losing an ounce of prime meat. He had always been amazed that her hands, so small and delicate, could move sharpened steel with such speed and strength.

An hour later Samuel had finished the butchering, cutting steaks, roasts, and filets, using every part of the animal except the hooves and horns. He carried the meat into the rear of the kitchen and loaded the game into a meat larder, then washed his hands.

"I believe I owe you a piece of money," Hannah said.

Samuel turned to his mother. His fingers trembled as he reached for the five dollars she always paid him for providing game to her restaurant. She dropped five silver dollars into his palm. "What are you going to do with this money?"

He knew it was time to let the cat out of the bag, so he spoke without looking into her eyes. "I'm going for an airplane ride." There was caution in his voice. "That barnstormer pilot is charging five dollars for a ride in his airplane."

She looked incredulously at Samuel as though he had lost his mind. "Ride in an airplane! You got to be crazy! If God had meant for you to fly, you'd have been born with wings. And if you go off in that airplane, you'll probably get a pair. Angel wings!"

"It's important to me, Momma."

She shook her head in dismay. "You're going off to college next fall. You could use that money to buy you a new pair of boots. Or a hat. Not waste it on flying around the sky with some crazy man."

"Don't worry, Momma, it'll be all right. The pilot has lots of experience. What's more, he's a Colored pilot. He needs the business. He's working his way east by stopping in little towns and selling rides."

Hannah had met the pilot—Sparks Hamilton—the day before; when he arrived in Bonita, he had lunch at her restaurant.

"If he flies the way he eats, you'll be in the sky all day. My Lord, that man can eat like none I've never seen." She shook her head and looked into his eyes. She knew there was no arguing. "Go on then. Ride in that fool contraption, but tell him if he gets you killed, he can go somewhere else to take his meals. He won't be welcome in my place."

Samuel grinned at her, then raced through the door, mounted his horse, and rode toward the edge of town.

His dream was about to come true.

A short, wiry man, Sparks Hamilton had orange-colored skin sprinkled with red freckles, giving him the look of a persimmon. He was forty-two years old, a widower, and veteran of the Great War, where he had served with the 92nd Division in France. During the battle of the Meuse-Argonne, German shrapnel tore through his calf, nearly severing his leg. He walked with an awkward limp, wore baggy flying breeches, a worn leather coat, a white scarf around his neck, and a weathered leather flying helmet and goggles.

Samuel thought he looked like something out of a Howard Hawks war movie.

Hamilton had learned to fly after the war in his native Oklahoma City, working for free at the aerodrome in exchange for flight training.

"The only instrument we had back then was an oil gauge," he told Samuel, as they walked around the Stearman. "We flew by the seat of our pants."

"How does an airplane this big get off the ground and fly, Mr. Hamilton?" Samuel wondered aloud.

Hamilton chuckled. "Thrust over weight . . . lift over drag. You see, son, the engine—which provides the power, gives you forward thrust—overcoming the weight to give you forward speed. As thrust drives the machine forward, the shape of the wings then use the air resistance—the drag—created by the forward speed to provide lift. Take an eagle. The bird flaps its wings to build up speed, then rises into the air and holds its wings steady to float in the sky. When the eagle needs more thrust, it flaps its wings again. The difference is, with an airplane, the engine gives you constant thrust; the wings give you lift."

Samuel could figure out the obvious. "If the engine quits, you're not flying anymore."

"That's about the size of it."

"How does it climb and turn?"

"Altitude is controlled by power from the engine; airspeed is controlled by the pitch, or the attitude of the nose in relation to the horizon. Nose up, you lose airspeed, and gain altitude. You lose too much airspeed, you stall, the wings lose your lift, and the airplane quits flying. Too much pitch down, you gain airspeed, lose altitude, and fly into the ground."

"Sounds complicated."

Hamilton shook his head. "Not really. Just a matter of learning what to do . . . and what not to do."

Samuel reached into his pocket and took out the five dollars. "I want to learn to fly, Mr. Hamilton."

Hamilton took the money and pointed to the front seat of the cockpit. "Let's go punch some holes in the sky."

Minutes later the Stearman rolled along the dry, hard ground, then began to pick up speed, the ride becoming more bumpy as the front tires bounced unevenly. When Samuel felt the tail wheel break ground, the cockpit section of the fuselage suddenly lowered, bringing the Stearman parallel to the ground, giving him a clearer view.

Suddenly—Samuel felt the airplane break ground and skim along the surface a few feet in the air.

In a matter of seconds the Stearman was climbing lazily through the air, the roar from the pulsating engine near deafening. The first real fear Samuel felt was when Hamilton banked sharply to the left, giving him a panoramic view of the earth west of Bonita. To the left rear, he could see Sabre Ranch, the Sharps' family home, then it was obscured from view by the lower wing as the airplane banked again and returned to level flight.

Upward they climbed, on wings of cloth and wood. It was an exhilarating thing, this fragile machine with its heavy load, defeating gravity, soaring, swooping, climbing, banking, diving—eaglelike—on wings that held strong and steady.

The flight lasted half an hour, too short for Samuel, but he was satisfied. Hamilton landed perfectly and taxied to the small operations building and cut the engine.

They sat beneath the wing. Samuel said, "I want to be a pilot, Mr. Hamilton."

The veteran poked at the ground with a stick and was obviously in deep thought. "Have you ever thought about becoming an army aviator?"

"I didn't know there was Colored aviators in the army."

Hamilton grinned. "There will be soon. The army is going to need pilots when we get into this war. They've already started a program that trains Colored men to fly. It's at a college down South."

"Where down South?"

"In a little town called Tuskegee, in Alabama. The college is called Tuskegee Institute. In a few months the army will start building an airfield near the campus."

Samuel shuddered at the thought of going to the South. He knew how Coloreds were treated in Alabama, and knew his parents would object. "What would I have to do?"

Hamilton stood by the airplane, running his hand over the leading edge of the left wing. His face reflected a sadness, as though he had been deprived something in his life. "Apply to the college and sign up for the Reserve Officers Training Corps. That'll give you a chance to learn the military way while you're getting your education and flight training. It's a fine school, and the man who runs the Civilian Pilot Training Program is an old friend of mine. I'd be happy to write you a letter of introduction."

Samuel nodded gratefully. The two shook hands. "I'll write to the college tonight."

"I'll have your letter tomorrow," Hamilton said.

Samuel walked away thinking about the coming fury of the war; but mostly, he thought of the fury that would come from his parents.

2

Standing in the family cemetery at Sabre Ranch, Selona Sharps felt a rush of memories as the sun flooded the desert with its golden brilliance. This was where she began each day, spending a few quiet moments with the family and friends she had seen buried on her land.

Her husband, Sergeant Major Augustus Sharps, buried in 1918. Nearby lay her son David and his friend Joseph Harwood, both killed in the Great War, though the graves were empty.

But the greatest tragedy was the smaller grave of her first grandchild, Adrian Augustus Sharps, Jr., who had died of pneumonia only months after Adrian returned from France. Thank God, she thought, Hannah gave birth to Samuel, allowing a new baby to fill that terrible void.

And there were others from her past: Sergeant Darcy Gibbs, killed by Geronimo's warriors in 1885. Vina Mae Gibbs, who died in 1930. Sergeant Major Roscoe Brassard, buried in 1894.

They were all here, their tombstones silent sentinels that marked the passage of time and the history made by the Negro on the western frontier and early twentieth century.

"Lord have mercy," she whispered softly. "It seems I've always been standing in a graveyard."

She thought of others she had loved, all buried in lonesome places.

Della Liberty, her mother, buried at Fort Wallace, Kansas. First Sergeant Moss Liberty, her father, at Fort Sill, in Oklahoma. Miss Marie, her grandmother, at Fort Davis, Texas.

She said a prayer and walked slowly back to the house and into the kitchen, where she found herself caught in a whirlwind of argument between Adrian and Hannah.

Adrian, nearly standing from his chair, shook a finger at Hannah, saying, "I don't understand why you're so stubborn on that boy going off to college. There's going to be a war in Europe, and I need him here." He owned a real-estate business and was now sixty-six. Since losing his arm at the shoulder in the Meuse-Argonne, he wore his left sleeve pinned to the shoulder. He had tried one of those new artificial limbs, but it fit poorly and was always slipping, so he threw it in the closet and had not seen it since.

"War! What makes you think there's going to be a war?" Hannah snapped.

He pointed at the headlines in the newspaper lying on the table. "Hitler's occupied France, Poland, most all of Europe, and he won't stop until he owns the whole world. What the Japanese don't get, at least. There's no way to stop him unless this country gets into the ruckus. That means there'll be a need for beef. We can make a lot of money running cattle on the ranch."

Hannah's eyes flashed, then she said coldly, "We have enough money. We certainly don't need blood money, and I don't want to hear any more talk about war. That's all you men want to do . . . talk, talk, talk. You talk about war like it's some great event." She looked at his empty sleeve. "You of all people should know that war is evil. Making money off evil is evil."

"Woman, are you crazy? There's nothing shameful about selling beef to feed soldiers."

She shook her head resolutely. "There's something wrong with selling our beef when we know it'll be in the bellies of dead American soldiers in Europe."

"Hush up, you two," Selona interrupted. "I can hear you all the way from the cemetery. It's enough to wake the dead."

They fell silent as Selona sat at the table and poured a cup of coffee, then asked, "What are you two arguing about?"

"Whether Samuel should go to college or help his father raise cattle for the soldiers in the war."

"What war?" Selona asked. "I ain't heard of no war we're fighting."

"The one in Europe," Adrian said. "It's just like the Great War, when the Kaiser started that ruckus in Europe. It's come, and we're going to get involved. There's no way around that fact."

Hannah suddenly looked frightened. "Do you know what you're saying?"

The look of certainty on his face answered the question. "Samuel is old enough to be drafted if there's a war."

Hannah was startled at this. "Drafted?"

He could see the immediate fear in her eyes as she slowly rose and walked to the sink. A long silence followed. He said, "Like Pop used to say, 'When the bugle blows, young men have to answer the call.' "

Selona shook her head in disgust. "There you go with that bugle again. That bugle's gotten a lot of young men killed. Now you're talking about my grandbaby. Your son."

"He's an American, Momma. If there's a war, he'll have to serve like other young men. No one is exempt from the responsibilities we have as Americans, whether white or Colored."

A wet plate slipped from Hannah's hand, shattering on the hardwood floor. "I don't want to hear no more about war in this house! There ain't no war, and there ain't going to be a war. Samuel is going to college and be somebody. He ain't dying in a foreign land like your brother David and Joseph Harwood. I'll hear no more of it!"

She stormed out of the kitchen, leaving Selona and Adrian staring speechless at each other. Finally, after a long moment, he rose and knelt on the floor and began picking up the shattered pieces of china.

"I know it's upsetting to you and Hannah," he said. "But you of all people should understand that this country must be defended."

"Defended, yes!" she snapped. "But that doesn't mean we have to go again to the farside of the world and look for a fight."

He continued cleaning up, now in silence.

*   *   *

Later that night Samuel sat at his desk and took out pen and paper. The words came easy since he knew exactly what he wanted to say. When finished he sealed the envelope and tucked the letter beneath his pillow.

The next morning he rose early and went hunting, killed the grouse promised his mother. After dressing out the birds, he slipped across the street to the small grocery store that housed the local post office and mailed the letter.

As he rode back to the ranch, Samuel realized he had taken the first step on what he hoped would be a long journey. There was a war raging in Europe, and he knew that his country would somehow become involved. When that day came he would serve his country as his grandfather and father had served in previous wars.

But not on a charging horse; not on foot across no-man's-land in the Argonne Forest.

He would hunt his country's enemy from the sky.

3

The next morning Samuel climbed onto his horse and gently tapped the mount at the flanks. Spring roundup was now under way, and he had signed on with the BAR B, owned by the family of the late United States Senator Ernst Bruner.

He watched another rider approach and shouted, "Good morning, Teddy."

Theodore Bruner, grandson of the retired Arizona senator, was the same age as Samuel. He was short and wiry, his deep blue eyes sat within a sunburned face, framed by thick, curly blond hair nearly obscured by a large Western hat. He wore chaps, boots with rondel spurs, and the Colt pistol inherited from his father and grandfather. He wore a pained expression.

"What's wrong?" Samuel said.

"Bad tooth."

"You better go into town and have Doc Parker take care of you."

Bruner shook his head. "Too much work to do. The herd's scattered all over creation. I'll have Old Joe look at it when we're finished with the day."

"You'll never make it through the day. Not in your condition."

Bruner was a stubborn lad, Samuel knew, and not about to let a sore tooth stand in the way of meeting his responsibility. His family owned the ranch; he had to set an example.

Samuel looked around the camp and saw the other riders mounting their horses. All were in their twenties, young and hardy, except for Joe Thaxton, whom everyone called "Old Joe." He was the trail boss, veterinarian, and doctor whenever he signed on for a roundup. Nearly sixty, he could still outride and outshoot the younger cowmen. Except for Samuel and Bruner.

Old Joe approached, wiping his hands on a dirty rag. "That tooth still bothering you, Teddy?"

Bruner nodded painfully.

Old Joe eyed him cautiously. "Get down off your horse. I'll take a look."

Bruner sat on a large rock, removed his hat, and opened his mouth. Old Joe studied the tooth for a moment then reached to his gun belt and removed a cartridge. He took his knife and carefully carved through the tip of the lead bullet until he had cut off a small piece. He dropped the lead into a tin cup and walked to the cook fire. He set the cup over the fire, and, when the metal had softened, he said to Bruner, "You've got a hole in your tooth that's about forty-five caliber. I'm going to put this in the tooth. You bite down as hard as you can stand it."

Thaxton took a pair of pliers from his saddlebag, picked the hot metal from the cup, put the lead over the cavity, and nodded. Bruner bit as hard as he could, until his eyeballs appeared ready to explode from their sockets. Finally, his jaws relaxed, and he sat back, breathing hard.

"Give that a little time. It'll take the edge off until you can see the doctor." Thaxton walked to his horse. He mounted and spurred the flanks, taking the lead, with Samuel and Bruner riding at his side, the other men following.

An hour later the cowmen reached foothills covered with thick mesquite and piñons. The terrain was rugged and deadly, filled with rattlesnakes, Gila monsters, mountain lions, bears, and an occasional rustler. The land, an open range, allowed Bar B cattle to graze with cattle from other smaller ranches. After the roundup would come the sorting of calves before the branding.

Samuel took off his hat and wiped his forehead with his sleeve.

He stared at the foothills. "The Good Lord didn't do cowmen any favors when he created this country, did he, Teddy?"

Bruner wiped the sweat from his brow. "Appears to me if He was angry at the world, he took out all his spite right here where we're riding."

Samuel laughed. "Don't let my grandmother hear you talking like that. She'll skin you alive."

Bruner laughed, making the tooth hurt. Old Joe turned to the two. "If God had meant for you boys to have an easier life, you'd have been born to some banker back East."

"This is going to be a long day, Old Joe," Samuel said.

"It ain't getting shorter by sitting here. You know what needs to be done. Let's get to it."

The cowmen broke off into two-man groups, fanning out in search of stray cattle.

Samuel and Bruner rode into an arroyo and began searching for cattle, each feeling a sense of excitement and danger. Range cows could be the orneriest creatures in the world—temperamental, un-accustomed to human contact, their survival instincts honed by harsh winters and other natural threats.

The arroyo meandered lazily toward the hills, then emptied onto a dry streambed at the mouth of a canyon. Samuel rode forward, leaned over, and examined the ground. He saw the earth was scarred by heavy hoofprints. "The tracks lead into the ravine."

"Let's find them," Bruner said.

The ravine was thick with brush, providing a natural haven for the cattle to graze and find protection from the elements.

The two young men followed the trail until they reached a fork that led in two directions, separated by a tall, craggy hill.

"Time to go to work," Samuel said. Then he paused, and asked, "How's the tooth?"

Bruner nodded, smiled slightly. He was still in pain.

Samuel eased his horse to the right, Bruner to the left, then both men removed their lassos as they rode from each other's sight.

By noon Samuel had rounded up fourteen cows and ten calves. The calves were easy enough to handle, although he had to pull a few from thick mesquite. After rounding up a cow, he would ride on looking for more before driving the small herd to the mouth of the ravine.

When he neared the end of the ravine, he stiffened as he heard two distinct gunshots coming from the other side of the hill separating him from Teddy Bruner. Samuel spurred his horse and charged up a steep incline; rocks spit from beneath the horse's hooves and Samuel felt the animal skew sideways when he neared the top. He looked down.

At the bottom of an arroyo, Bruner was riding what Samuel could only consider a tornado.

The range bull had charged silently from behind thick brush, unseen until his massive horns speared the flank of Bruner's horse. Blood spilled from the wound as the animal reared, nearly throwing Brunner from the saddle, causing him to miss his first shot at the bull. The horse, reacting instinctively, tried to bolt, but the shock of the wound was too severe, draining the animal of its strength.

Bruner's second shot missed when the horse whirled violently to the right, slamming the rider's face against the animal's neck. He could no longer feel the pain in his tooth.

However, he did know he had dropped his Colt pistol!

Through glazed eyes, twirling and hanging desperately to the saddle horn, he saw the bull charge and drive his horns into the horse's chest. Rider and horse plunged to the ground, where Bruner felt the crushing weight of the animal on his leg. There was a loud snap, like dry wood cracking in a fire, then a river of pain roared through his body.

The horse tried to rise but was hit again by the bull. Bruner felt the warmth and wetness of his blood begin to fill his left boot, saw the bull prancing, snorting, kicking up dust as he prepared for another attack.

The bull charged, head down, horns aimed at Teddy, who could only stare into the dark, empty eyes coming at him. Then the dust rose from his powerful legs, shrouding the bull, painting an eerie sight on the floor of the ravine. As though it were an apparition, something from a bad dream.

When the bull came within ten feet, Bruner had accepted that the bull would rule the day. That his death was only moments away when . . .

Suddenly—the legs of the bull folded beneath his huge body. His snout plowed into the ground from the charging momentum.

Then there was the sound of the rifle and he saw the hole in the bull's forehead. The animal's tongue lolled out, and the snorting breath grew light, then ceased altogether.

Bruner struggled onto his elbow and looked up. He saw a silhouette standing on the hill, framed against the clear blue sky. Samuel.

He watched silently as his friend started down the hill, then disappeared within a grove of tall cactus.

Before the blackness overwhelmed his brain, Teddy estimated the range of Samuel's shot to be around six hundred yards.

Samuel rode up fast and jumped from the saddle, his Sharps still in hand. He dropped beside Teddy, who was drifting in and out of consciousness. Bruner's horse was twisting in agony, its huge eyes rolling. Samuel put the muzzle of the Sharps to the horse's ear and pulled the trigger. The resounding boom echoed against the hills as both horse and rider lay limp.

4

News of Teddy Bruner's injury spread throughout the county, but most of the talk was about the incredible shot by Samuel Sharps. Selona had heard the news and wasn't surprised; she knew about her grandson's marksmanship. She was thinking about him while sitting on the front porch knitting a sweater for her grandson Benjamin, who with his wife Sarah, owned a small delivery service in Phoenix. Her other grandson, Jonathan, whom she always teasingly called a scamp, lived in Tucson, where he and his wife Renae owned a restaurant. She giggled, remembering how he was always at her apron, wanting to learn to cook.

She heard a noise in the distance and lowered her knitting needles to her lap and saw a rider approaching. As he drew closer she felt a familiarity with the way the horseman handled his mount, and for an instant she felt herself tumble back in time.

The horseman sat tall in the saddle, his hat pulled low over his forehead, the butt of the Sharps rifle jutting above the saddle horn from its scabbard.

Samuel stopped at the hitching rail, then slid slowly from the saddle. That was when he heard his grandmother's laughter and knew the reason for it.

"You look like your granddaddy coming in from a long campaign," she said as she stood up from the rocker with opened arms.

Samuel had not shaved in nearly a month, and felt the hair of his mustache and beard press against his grandmother's weathered skin.

"I feel like I've been in three campaigns, Grams." Again he hugged her.

She looked proudly into his eyes, taking in the brightness that shone from a young man who had done a good job, a young man who had saved the life of a friend.

"Come inside. I'll fix you a hot bath, and you can have a shave." She started for the door, then stopped and looked at him, "Good Lord, didn't that Old Joe Thaxton feed you boys on the trail?"

Samuel was thin as a rail, gaunt in the eyes, and his jeans barely clung to his hips.

"Beef, beans, and biscuits, A cowboy's gourmet menu."

They both laughed and went arm in arm into the house. Selona said, "My menu's much better."

The Sharps family sat beneath the stand of tall cottonwoods near Theresa's house, an evening breeze rustling the branches, soothing the hot air. At the rock barbecue pit, Adrian stood turning several chickens on the grill with a long iron rod. Behind him, the women were setting out dishes and cutlery, all of them excited that this night was going to be special.

It was near dusk when the caravan arrived, three Packards filled with the Bruner family. Samuel had been home two days from the end of the roundup when young Bruner returned from the hospital in Phoenix.

Teddy got out of one Packard with Samuel's help, then settled his armpits onto the crutches he was still required to use. He laughed, then held up one crutch. "Not much of a horse, is it?"

They both laughed and embraced. Samuel looked at him, and said, "At least if it falls on you, it won't break your leg." He looked at the cast on his friend's leg. "How much longer you going to have to wear the cast?"

"Not much longer. Even if I have to take it off myself."

A voice suddenly interrupted the reunion, calling from the passenger side of another Packard. "You boys just going to stand there, or are you going to help me to a chair?"

Congressman Ernst Bruner, Jr., the son of the senator, stood leaning on a cane. "We've got two Bruners here, and can't neither one of us walk without assistance. Life sure as hell can be persnickety." He had been injured in an automobile wreck in 1935, rendering one leg useless.

Then Selona's voice was heard. "Hush up now, Ernst. I remember the night you was born. I swear, I never heard a child scream and fuss so long and loud about coming into the world as you. Nearly wore your momma and daddy clean to the bone."

Ernst extended his arm, and replied, "If you can't remember, nobody can. You're older than God."

Teasingly, Selona snapped, "Don't you blaspheme me now. Your momma and daddy wouldn't abide that kind of talk."

Ernst smiled shyly, then looked at Teddy. "Some sight, Selona. Both father and son stoved up with a bad leg." Then he sighed, adding, "At least Teddy's leg is healing good and proper. The doctors say he's going to be just fine."

Selona remembered something. "In the last years of his life, the Sergeant Major got about right well on one leg. You've done well for yourself on a crippled leg. I expect Teddy will do just fine once his leg has mended good and strong."

Then she looped her arm through his, and they walked and hobbled to the cottonwoods.

The highlight of any Sharps picnic was the telling of family stories, and this picnic would be no exception. The problem was, there were so many stories, it was difficult to choose which was the most interesting. But Samuel had one that was his favorite of all.

The sun had faded and all had gathered around a huge bonfire when Samuel said, "Grams, tell us about the day you and the Sergeant Major were married."

Selona said with a wave of her hand, "Oh, I've told that story so often over the years, I feel like I've been married a hundred times."

Theresa said, "Please, Grams. It's my favorite, too."

Selona looked to Adrian for support, but found none; he merely motioned her to begin with a wave of his pipe.

She adjusted her shawl, and said, "Well, all right. But it was my grandmother, Miss Marie's doings. I didn't want nothing to do with that big old Buffalo Soldier."

Soft laughter drifted through the group, and they knew it was the closest she had ever come to telling a lie.

"It was back in the Indian Territory, now called Oklahoma, in 1874, at Fort Sill. My daddy had been killed at the Battle of Anadarko, and it was time for his funeral. Miss Marie, who I called 'Gram,' was fit to be tied. Not knowing what we were going to do with Daddy gone. But, like always, she found the answer."

Her voice drifted softly over the fire, as a page of family history unfolded for the gathering. . . .

The moment the bugler completed Taps, Miss Marie grabbed the hand of Selona Liberty and led the girl toward Sergeant Major Brassard, where Augustus stood beside Brassard, watching the two approach. Selona now wore her wig with distinction and dignity, and in her own way, had become legendary in the eyes of the 10th Cavalry.

Marie came directly to the point. "What we going to do now that Moss' dead? How's this child going to survive?"

Selona stood behind her grandmother, peering past the edges of a floppy bonnet that was betrayed at the edges by curls from the buffalo wig. Her eyes were on Augustus, watchful and obedient.

Brassard put his hands out as though to defend himself. "Hold on, now, Miss Marie. You know we're all sad about Moss. But I don't know what you mean."

"What I mean is, what's me and this child going to do now that her daddy's dead? The money coming in off the laundry ain't enough for a bird to live on. Now that Moss' dead and we ain't got his army pay, we can't make a living."

"The regiment's going to take up a collection. You'll get a nice piece of money." Brassard was starting to sweat in the hot sun. Or, wondered Augustus, was it the hot wrath of this woman.

"That ain't good enough. Last trooper to go down, his wife got eighteen dollars. Eighteen dollars! And I heard talk the army's going to start using different laundresses."

"There's some talk about that, Miss Marie."

"Say they going to have to be married to soldiers."

"I believe that will come, Miss Marie."

Marie grabbed Brassard by the sleeve. "Come on, I want to talk with you."

Brassard followed, leaving Augustus standing with Selona.

"I'm sorry about your father. He was a good man." Augustus remembered the promise. "If there's anything you need, I'm at your service. I promised your father I would look after you."

"Did you now? And how you going to look after me?"

Augustus flushed. He was schooled as a soldier, but not in the ways of handling a woman, even if she was a girl of seventeen. "Like I said, if you need anything, you just have to ask."

A grin curved her mouth. "Would you take supper with us tonight, Augustus?"

Augustus was quick to answer. Word had it she was the best cook on the fort. "I'd be delighted."

She giggled. "You're so polite." She walked off toward her grandmother, who was talking a storm to Brassard.

Brassard came back to Augustus. "Come on, boy." His voice was serious.

"What's wrong?"

"Never you mind. I'll tell you."

They went to the Evan and Fisher trading post and found a table near the bar. Brassard poured a drink for both of them and lifted the glass, saying, "To the regiment."

"To the regiment." Augustus had only drunk whiskey a few times in his life, and found the taste too bitter for his liking. He had stayed away from the whiskey and hog ranches near the forts, where a dollar could buy a bottle of mean whiskey and an hour with an even meaner prostitute.

Brassard poured another glass for himself and one for Augustus. "What do you know about women?"

Augustus looked at him. "Women? Why do I need to know about women?"

Brassard downed the whiskey and poured another. "You best

learn something about women right now. When they come after you, there ain't but two things you can do: step or fetch."

Augustus laughed. "What does that mean?"

"That, young soldier, means you better step quickly out of sight or fetch up the broom."

"The broom?"

"You were a slave. Get ready to jump the broom."

Augustus understood. It was the way slaves wed in the South because they were forbidden legal marriage. The bride and groom would hold hands and jump over a broom. That was the wedding ceremony.

Augustus grew flustered. "What are you talking about, Sergeant Major?" He gulped down the drink in front of him.

"I mean Miss Marie's got plans. Matrimonial plans that include you and her granddaughter. And, unless I don't know Miss Marie, those plans include her as well." Brassard took a deep breath. "Boy, you only got two choices: You going to get married . . . or you want a transfer to another post?"

Brassard poured Augustus another drink. Augustus stared at it and sat there, wondering.

The Sergeant Major had personally helped Augustus dress for dinner that night, to the hoots and jeers of his comrades in the barracks. The word had spread quickly, as news generally traveled on an army post.

Augustus made the long walk to the tent where Selona and Marie lived wearing his ceremonial dress uniform, pistol belt, sabre, and highly polished parade helmet with plume. He carried a fistful of flowers Brassard handed him as he shuffled through the door of the barracks to the raucous laughter of his comrades.

Augustus was in a terrible sweat by the time he reached the tent. He knocked lightly at the flap and waited until Marie appeared. She was smoking her corncob pipe and was holding a freshly beheaded chicken in her hand.

Private Augustus Sharps stepped inside the tent, where he felt his head begin to spin, and he would never know if it was the whiskey, the tight collar, the smell of Marie's tobacco, the pressure of the moment, or all those factors combined.

The moment he saw Selona he fainted dead away to the floor.

Augustus and Selona were wed the following week by the regimental chaplain.

The bride and groom didn't jump the broom; they recited the marital vows from the *Book of Common Prayer* and walked from the church beneath an arc of poised cavalry sabres. Sergeant Major Brassard gave away the bride, and that night there was a party in honor of the new couple.

They began their life on the prairie together in the tent where Selona and Marie lived. That first night, they slept alone in the tent, but the next night they shared the tent with Marie, who laughed at the giggles coming from behind the blanket that divided the tent into two rooms.

Marie was awakened later in the night as the two newlyweds slipped from the tent, Augustus carrying a heavy buffalo robe.

She lit her pipe in the darkness of the tent, and rose, watching over the two as they settled into the soft earth of Indian Territory, becoming lost beneath the heavy robe, oblivious to the stars above, the dangers not far in the distance.

When the picnic ended, everyone said good night and drifted their private ways, including Selona. She didn't go inside, not yet; there was something she did every night before going to bed, weather permitting.

Some years before, she had asked Adrian to build her a bench to place inside the cemetery, where she could sit in the evenings with her loved ones and friends. She called it her "Remembering Bench." It was white, and sturdy. She seated herself beneath the stars and stared at the various graves, listening to their voices.

She sat there for an hour, then walked back to the house, pausing only once to glance over shoulder for one last look before disappearing inside.

5

* * *

The daughter of a Negro father and Cherokee mother, Shania LeBaron had dark eyes that glowed with delight within her honey-colored face, a face that appeared more sculptured than natural, with high cheekbones and a mouth that was full and sensual.

Her reverie was only interrupted by the voice of Charles A. Anderson crackling over the radio. "You all right back there, little missy?"

The wind whipped steadily at her long, dark hair, giving her the look of a thoroughbred racehorse in full flight. She was in flight, she thought, but not on the ground; rather, she was two thousand feet above the earth in the cockpit of an airplane.

"I'm fine, Chief. This is the most wonderful thing I've ever experienced."

Anderson, known as "Chief," added power, banked hard right, and smoothly eased back on the control stick, putting the Stearman into a climbing turn.

At nineteen, Shania was taking her first airplane ride with the country's most famous Negro pilot.

Over the thundering prop blast she called into her microphone. "Can we fly upside down?"

Anderson smiled, then rolled the Stearman over. Shania looked and saw the earth upside down, the way she had while swinging in her backyard as a child, her head thrown back to see the ground. But now, there was so much of the ground to see! She giggled, then reached down, trying to run her fingers through the trees that seemed just beyond her grasp. Then she felt the airplane return to normal flight and heard the Chief warn, "Don't want to stay inverted too long. The blood will run to your brain and knock you unconscious. You remember that every time you fly inverted."

She would remember that, she thought, then shuddered, thinking what her father would say when learning of her latest adventure.

Again she felt the airplane bank, felt the power throttle back, and begin a slow descent toward the small airport north of Tuskegee, Alabama.

Patrice LeBaron was a small man with a thick mane of long, dark hair, framing delicate features and dark eyes that were presently gleaming like banked coals as he watched the Stearman turn on final approach and land on the runway at Moton Field. His hands twitched slightly as the aircraft taxied to the small operations shack and came to a stop.

When he saw his daughter Shania climb down from the front seat his temper neared the boiling point. But, as always, he kept his composure, saying nothing until she was standing before him.

"Young lady, you have disappointed me with this escapade."

She smiled meekly, then said, "I just wanted to see what it was like to fly, Poppa."

He forced back a smile, not wanting her charm to overpower his ire. "Well, you've flown. I expect that will be the end of this matter."

Her long hair danced around her shoulders as she shook her head. "It was wonderful. I never thought anything could be so wonderful."

Chief Anderson approached, carrying a book in his hand. "This is your flight manual. Learn it from cover to cover. Everything you need to know is in here." He handed her the book to the surprised look of her father.

"What is the meaning of this, Shania?" LeBaron asked.

"I'm going to take flying lessons, Poppa. The Chief is going to instruct me."

There was a long pause as LeBaron stared first at Shania, then at Anderson. "This is absurd. Flying airplanes is not a fashionable pastime for a lady."

Shania said, "Oh? Bessy Coleman flew airplanes. She even started the Chicago School of Aviation."

"You'll recall she was killed while flying."

"Actually, she was killed when she rolled her airplane and fell out of the cockpit. That was a freak accident."

"Dead is dead, young lady." He looked at Anderson, and snapped, "Charles, you should have discussed this insanity with me before you took my daughter up in your airplane."

Anderson stood his ground. "She's a natural, LeBaron. She's as smooth on the controls as any man I've had for a student."

LeBaron wasn't convinced. "How are you going to pay for the lessons?"

"I have my job at the college cafeteria, and my cleaning work for Mrs. Doster. Some of her friends have asked her if I could work in their homes a few days a week. I will use that money for flight instruction."

Mrs. Althea Doster was an elderly local white woman who hired Shania for housework one day a week. While the money was helpful, he thought her wages should be used for other purposes. "That money is supposed to be used for tuition."

"The dean has already assured me there will be tutorial opportunities once school starts. I can pay for most of my tuition by tutoring."

LeBaron knew she had him, as she generally could find a way to slip through any web standing in the way of what she wanted. He looked at Anderson. "Her schoolwork and employment is more important. However, if you want to teach her, I know you're a capable instructor."

Without another word, LeBaron walked to his old Ford and started the engine.

Shania's face was radiant as she hugged Anderson and raced to the car, her flight manual clutched in her arms.

He watched with a big grin as they drove away, remembering Bessy Coleman, and how she pioneered aviation for the Negro in the United States. He gave little thought to his own pioneering accomplishments, though there were many. He was to become the first Negro pilot to fly from the United States to the Bahamas and was now the chief instructor for the new Civilian Pilot Training Program established by Congress to train Negro aviators.

He watched Shania and her father drive away and hoped the young men who arrived for the next class had half of Shania's potential.

Shania and LeBaron rode in silence until they reached the main street of Tuskegee, where he parked in front of the Mercantile Bank. The street was lined with old trucks and cars, most of them belonging to farmers. He glanced to the courthouse, where a group of elderly white men sat playing checkers beneath the statue of a Confederate soldier. As in all Southern towns, the statue stood facing south.

They went into the bank and sat quietly on a wooden bench until he was summoned by a rotund white man sitting at a large oak desk.

Ron Munson was fifty, nearly bald, with a freckled red face. His suit appeared too tight, as were his shirt and tie, causing his neck to bulge over his collar. "Afternoon, LeBaron." He nodded at Shania. "Shania. How y'all doing this afternoon?"

LeBaron nodded politely, not looking the man directly in the eye. Another tradition of the white South. "Just fine, Mr. Munson." The banker looked quickly at Shania, who met his gaze. "Just fine, Mr. Munson. I just went for my first airplane ride with Chief Anderson."

Munson's eyes widened, then he laughed. "Now, girl, why would you waste your money on flying?"

LeBaron said suddenly, "My exact question, sir."

Munson shook his head in dismay. "What can I do for you, LeBaron?"

LeBaron sat upright and explained an idea he had had for several months. "I understand you hold the title on the old Jessup place."

He nodded. "Jessup had that family of nigras sharecropping his land, then they picked up and moved up North. To Chicago, I believe. Damn Northerners. They're luring our young nigra to the

North with promises of streets paved with gold." He blew his nose hard, then added, "Without his nigras he couldn't make his payments. I foreclosed on him last month. Why does that particular piece of property interest you?"

LeBaron made his pitch carefully and forthrightly. "With this new CPT program at the Institute, there's going to be a need for more housing. You know how difficult it is for Colored students to find a decent place to live." He glanced quickly at Shania, who bristled at the use of the word "Colored" when talking about the Negro.

The banker steepled his fingers on his chest. "Go on, LeBaron. Say what you've got to say."

LeBaron leaned forward. "I would like to buy the home and turn it into a boardinghouse for the students. There's four bedrooms, and with two in a room, I know the rent would pay the mortgage, and then some." LeBaron sat back and straightened himself, watching the banker's blue eyes, now appearing contemplative.

"What about the land? You're no farmer. You're a college teacher."

LeBaron said proudly. "A professor of agriculture, Mr. Munson. I may not farm, but I know farming. There's acres of good land. Just right for what I have planned."

"What do you have planned."

"To plant vegetables. It'll be what is called a truck farm."

"Truck farm! This is cotton country."

"Yes, sir. All the farmers have their land planted except the Jessup place. There's plenty of time to plant all the vegetables the army will need."

The banker leaned forward onto his elbows. He looked interested. "What about the army?"

LeBaron handed an envelope to Munson, who read the enclosed letter intently. "How did you get this?"

"I made an appointment with the Quartermaster officer at the new army airfield that's been constructed. I believe you know the construction contractor is McKissack and McKissack, of Nashville."

Munson reddened. He had tried every political maneuver in the book to land that contract. The government surprised Munson—

and the state of Alabama—by awarding the contract to a Tennessee company. A Negro-owned company.

"The two nigras from Nashville."

LeBaron nodded. "I spoke with one of the McKissacks about my idea. He told me the government was required to give some of the commissary business to Coloreds who could produce. I have been given one of those contracts."

The banker blew his nose again, then mumbled, "Vegetables. Huh. I never thought of that crop." He paused. "What's your proposal?"

"You're asking five hundred dollars for the house and land. I'd like a two-year mortgage. I'll keep the profits on the boardinghouse to pay the mortgage, and you and I split the profits and expenses on the forty acres of vegetables."

"What if you can't make the mortgage?"

"I'll make the mortgage."

"But what if you can't?"

"You keep the house and land."

He thought for a moment. "I'll agree, with some changes."

LeBaron nodded, and Shania watched and waited for the banker's terms.

"Two years on the mortgage is fine with me. But I want the vegetable deal for two years." He leaned forward. "I need to see some profit as well."

LeBaron stood and extended his hand. "You have a bargain."

The banker shook his hand, saying, "I'll have the papers drawn up. They'll be ready by tomorrow at noon."

LeBaron and Shania left. Munson walked to the window and watched the two get into their car. He chuckled, saying softly, "Dumb nigger. I'd have agreed to one year on the vegetables."

In the car, LeBaron said to Shania, "The dumb cracker. I'd have agreed to three years on the vegetable deal."

Shania laughed as they drove away in the shadow of the Confederate soldier.

Two days passed before LeBaron was able to begin making the necessary repairs on the Jessup farm. He brought tools, paint, and Shania, who stared in utter amazement at the house. Most of windows were broken, the front porch needed to be replanked; the interior was worse—the smell of dust filled the air and the kitchen sink would have to be replaced. An old icebox sat in the corner, inside it a raccoon's nest. She took a broom and chased the critters through a broken window and heard her father laugh.

"You should consider zoology instead of mathematics, Shania. You have a way with wildlife."

Shania's eyes glowed with disgust. "This house is a disaster, Poppa. We'll never get things in order for the start of the semester."

"That's not for another two months."

"Two years is more realistic."

LeBaron smiled proudly. "We'll have this house looking like a king's palace by the time our boarders arrive."

"Boarders? This place looks like a pigpen. No self respecting Negro college man would live here. They're mostly city men. They won't like country living."

LeBaron lit his pipe and walked onto the back porch, where he stood for a long while, studying the fields, now overgrown with weeds. He sighed heavily and prayed she was wrong.

That afternoon LeBaron was relieved to see Johnson and his team of mules approaching, the dust dancing lightly as the old farmer urged them along by skipping the reins off their rumps. Johnson was nearly seventy, but still worked every opportunity that came along, whether clearing a field of rocks and trees, or plowing fresh fields for planting. He stopped his wagon in front of the house and slowly climbed down, then went directly to the rear of the wagon and unloaded his plowing equipment.

Shania watched Johnson, who refused LeBaron's help. His hands were old and twisted, like grapevines, but he moved with a certain youthfulness she found intriguing. It was generally known through-out the county he would work from sunrise to sunset to finish a field. Another fact was that he was one of the wealthiest Coloreds in the county. He lived in an old shack and wore the same overalls for years, never spending a dime on himself except for food. Rumor also had it that he had his money buried somewhere on his small farm.

Johnson sharpened the plow blade with a heavy file, then harnessed the mules to the plow and began his task. For hours he followed behind the mules, cutting straight furrows into the earth. LeBaron and Shania followed, stacking the weeds in large piles to be burned, the last chore before planting.

Johnson would stop occasionally to sip from a flask LeBaron knew contained muscadine wine, made from a purple grape that grew wild in Alabama. Most of the locals called it "scuppernong." Johnson offered the flask to LeBaron, asking, "Join me, Professor, suh?"

LeBaron sipped from the flask while Johnson never missed a beat with the plowing. By early evening the field was plowed and cleared, and the glow of the burning stacks of weeds etched the dark night with a soft glow.

When the work was finished, Shania joined her father and Johnson on the front porch with a picnic basket, spread a cloth on the rotten planking, and passed around fried chicken.

"It's a beautiful night," LeBaron said proudly. He was pleased at how well the day's work had gone.

Johnson ate voraciously, like a man who had known deep hunger and wouldn't fail to take advantage of the feast. LeBaron ate slowly, as visions of his vegetable crop danced in his brain.

Johnson said teasingly, "Lots of folks think you're crazy for not planting cotton. They say vegetables ain't much of a cash crop. Not in Alabama."

LeBaron smiled thoughtfully. "There will be hundreds of soldiers posted at the airfield. Mr. McKissack assures me the airfield will be here for several years."

Johnson stared at the burning piles of weeds. "You think Mr. Roosevelt's going to get us caught up in that war over in Europe?"

LeBaron sighed heavily. "I don't see how we can stay out of it."

"I understand some of these young Colored pilots over at the Institute are trying to get into the army as fliers."

LeBaron reflected on the futility of the project, now being called the "Tuskegee Experiment." He wiped his hands on a napkin and leaned back on his elbows, gazing at the stars, trying to imagine what lay in the future. "The Great War brought about a lot of changes for the Coloreds in this country. I expect the next one will bring even more."

Johnson shook his head. "It would be sad to die on the other side of the world. So far from home and family." He stood and stretched. "I reckon I best be going. I got another piece of property to plow tomorrow morning." He stepped down from the porch and took the two five-dollar bills owed him by LeBaron. He nodded and walked away.

Shania and LeBaron watched in silence as the man climbed into his wagon and skipped the reins off the mules. They stood watching until he was gone from sight, with only the creak of his wheels to mark his passing, along with a freshly plowed field with furrows as straight as arrows.

6

＊　＊　＊

For Samuel, growing up in Bonita gave him a special way of viewing the world. The racism of the South seemed too distant to be important; his family was affluent and respected.

The incident with the range bull, and saving Teddy's life, had now earned him his individual respect in the community.

He was sitting in his mother's restaurant watching dust devils spiral down the main street when something peculiar caught his eye. A gray automobile suddenly appeared, followed by a large machine moving on what appeared to be wide tractor treads. Then another appeared, and another, until he counted eight of the machines as the column came to a halt in the center of the street.

The doors of the automobile opened, then the hatches of the tanks popped up, and from one turret a head appeared wearing a heavy helmet. Within minutes the soldiers had climbed from the tanks and stood by their machines stretching their muscles, lighting cigarettes, and drinking water from canteens

A tall officer walked into the mayor's office, then reappeared minutes later with Mayor Ben Woolford. The mayor pointed to the north of the street, and the officer shook his hand and climbed back into his automobile. The soldiers returned to their tanks and within seconds the column ground its way toward the north, leaving a storm of dust in its wake.

"What in the world is all that commotion?" Hannah called from the kitchen.

"They're tanks, Momma."

She came out of the kitchen wiping her hands on an apron and stood at the window watching for a moment. "I don't understand why tanks are in Bonita."

Samuel didn't know either, but he was going to find out.

He walked to the mayor's office and found the man sitting at his desk. Woolford, a short stocky man in his fifties, was the mayor, but his primary business was running the land office. Being mayor of Bonita didn't require much time; therefore, the position was more figurehead than necessary. "Did you see those tanks?" Woolford looked over his glasses.

"What are tanks doing in Bonita, Mr. Woolford?"

"The army is going to conduct maneuvers near Mount Graham for the next ten days." He shook his head in amazement. "They sure make a hellacious noise."

"Tanks?" Selona said. "What are tanks doing in Bonita?"

Samuel was sitting on the steps of the porch with Selona, who sat in her rocker, a shawl around her shoulders. She was smoking a pipe, a habit she had taken up a few years back.

"There might be some opportunity in this for you, Samuel."

"What kind of opportunity?"

"If the army rations haven't changed much over the years, I'll bet you a dollar to a dime them men are eating out of tin cans."

"They're called K-rations, Grams."

"Meat out of a can is worse than hardtack. And dangerous, too. Why, back in the war with Spain we lost more boys to poisoned food than Spanish bullets."

Samuel looked at her curiously. She was leading up to something. "What does that have to do with these soldiers?"

"Fresh game. That's what. Them soldiers might pay a young hunter a piece of money to supply them with fresh game."

*   *   *

The next morning Samuel saddled his horse and rode north, then east until he discovered the first signs of the tank column. Deep furrows were cut into the earth, as though some great plow had swept over the ground. He followed the tracks for two miles until he found their bivouac near a meandering stream.

Tents sat in two neat rows, overshadowed by the huge tanks parked in military formation. Soldiers could be seen walking around the bivouac area, all moving toward one particular tent—the one his grandmother had told him to look for. The tent with smoke rising into the air would be the cook tent, she said.

He rode slowly to the rear of the tent and dismounted amid the clatter of cooking utensils, the clanging of mess kits, and the chatter of the soldiers. Then he smelled the morning chow and let his nose lead him to the man his grandmother had instructed him to find. The moment he stepped from behind the tent to where the soldiers stood in line, the chatter stopped, and there was only stone silence.

The soldiers stared at him as though he were some alien form of life. Samuel removed his hat, and asked, "Can you tell me which one of you men is the mess sergeant?"

The soldiers continued to stare. Finally one soldier pointed to a man wearing a white apron.

"What you want, boy?" Sergeant Clifton James was a heavyset man with thick, bushy eyebrows and a heavy walrus mustache. Dark, searching eyes peered from his sunburned face. He was standing behind a table where several large pots sat, ladles jutting over the edges.

"My momma owns a restaurant in Bonita. I hunt for her, supplying fresh game."

James's eyes narrowed. "What kind of game?"

"Antelope. Venison. Partridge. Prairie chickens. I can even supply beef from our ranch."

The sergeant continued to eye Samuel as he came from behind the table. At the rear of the tent James noticed Samuel's horse.

"Fine-looking animal, boy." He saw the rifle in the boot and nodded at the weapon. "Is that yours?"

"It belonged to my grandfather. He was in the Tenth Cavalry for thirty years."

A look of sadness flashed across James's face. "I started with the cavalry back when I was your age. Too bad there's no need for horses in this modern army."

Samuel stepped to the horse and untied a heavy bundle strapped to the saddle. "My momma said I should give you this meat, whether we make a deal or not."

James unwrapped the cloth, revealing a hindquarter of meat. He sniffed it and smiled. "This smells like antelope."

"You've got a good nose, Sergeant."

James wiped at the sweat on his forehead. "After smelling army chow for twenty years I ought to have. Come on, boy. Let's me and you go see the captain."

An hour later Samuel rode off with a letter designating him as the official supplier of fresh game for the soldiers.

"You're some entrepreneur, son. Just like your momma and grand-mother," Adrian said.

It was evening, and the family was gathered for supper at the pic-nic tables in the cottonwoods. Selona watched as her grandson swelled with his newfound success. "I knew that mess sergeant would make you a deal," she said.

7

Samuel chose to make a camp near the bivouac rather than have to make the ride to and from the ranch each day. The first order of business was building a skinning rack. He cut three long poles and joined them at one end to form an apex, connected a block and tackle, and was ready to begin the first day's hunt by midday.

He rode out of the camp to the roar of the tanks playing war games in the hills east of Mount Graham. A packhorse followed in his trail, saddled with a wooden frame to secure the game.

He traveled west, knowing the commotion of the tanks would clear all the game from the area to the east, scattering them in his direction. An hour later he reached one of his favorite hunting spots, a rocky outcropping that gave him a commanding view of a small valley where a stream ran lazily below. He then unlimbered the Sharps, stacked several rocks to use as support for the barrel, lay on his stomach, spread five cartridges near his side, and began the worst part of the hunt: the wait.

The sun was boiling hot, but he couldn't wear his hat for fear it might give away his position with each movement of his head. So he lay there, practicing the patience taught him by his father, as he had been taught by his father.

Nearly two hours later he heard a sharp cracking from the rocks below, near the stream. He had chosen this spot knowing that any game flushed from the east by the tanks would be heated and thirsty from their panicky run. Which meant they would be less cautious, more vulnerable.

Samuel eased up and scanned the stream, his eyes moving slowly across the terrain, his heart pounding. His greatest fear was that he would return empty-handed and fail before he had really begun. When he returned to camp he wanted to bring back a prize. His grandmother had taught him the importance of first impressions.

Then he saw the first doe, then the second, then a third. They walked carefully to the water, alert noses in the air, but Samuel had the wind to his face. He carefully eared back the hammer, waited, lying still for what seemed an eternity, sighting a large doe.

Then he saw the prize. He knew that a buck was the least chivalrous of all creatures, that bucks would lie behind, sending the does ahead, using them to test for possible danger.

He watched as the buck stepped from the shadow of a large boulder, sniffed the air, then walked carefully toward the stream.

Samuel took aim and squeezed the trigger. The Sharps boomed, he reloaded and sighted on the large doe, her tail pointed skyward as she fled for her life. He squeezed the trigger and saw the doe pitch forward only a few feet from the safety of the boulder.

Then there was silence, except for the cracking hooves of the fleeing does.

Samuel approached the bivouac at an easy pace, trying desperately to mask his feelings. The two deer were tied on the packhorse, ready for skinning.

He stopped at his camp, slid from the saddle and untied the doe, allowing the soldiers—who were now gathering—to have a look at his day's work.

Half an hour later the doe was skinned and ready for uttering when Samuel saw James approach.

"Mighty fine piece of work," Sergeant James said loudly. "Ought to be more than enough for a fine stew for the men."

"Thank you, Sergeant. I hit her through the heart. None of the meat was damaged."

Samuel realized the sergeant had not called him "boy."

"What you going to do with the buck?"

"I'll be taking him to my momma's restaurant in town."

James thought about that for a moment. "Reckon you could get four next time? I believe the men would like barbecued venison."

"I can do that, Sergeant."

James motioned to two privates, who quickly shouldered the carcass and marched toward the mess tent. James stepped forward, his hand extended to Samuel. In his palm lay five one-dollar bills.

When the buck was skinned, Samuel cleaned up at the stream, washed his tools, and put on a clean shirt. When he rode out of the bivouac, he smelled the aroma of venison stew from the mess tent.

8

✳ ✳ ✳

He reached the back of the restaurant at nightfall, unlocked the door, and carried the buck inside. He turned on the light, started to open the door of the walk-in freezer when he heard a displeased voice.

"Good evening, son."

His mother stood in the doorframe; behind her stood Adrian and Selona.

"Good evening, Momma. Pop. Grams. What are you doing here? I thought you'd be at the ranch."

Adrian walked to the freezer and looked inside. "Mighty fine piece of work, son." His voice dropped to a whisper. "Your momma is madder than a two-legged dog."

Hannah walked to a small table and laid an envelope on the top. "This came for you today, son."

Selona stood eyeing the situation with suspicion, but said nothing. She knew this was between Samuel and his mother and father.

Samuel was dumbfounded as he picked up the envelope. His eyebrows knitted together in anger when he noticed the envelope had been opened.

"Did you open my letter, Momma?"

Hannah didn't respond.

His father said calmly, "It's a family characteristic, son."

Selona merely grumped and watched Samuel pull the letter from the envelope and read:

"Dear Mr. Sharps,

"It is with great pleasure that I inform you of your acceptance into Tuskegee Institute for the fall term, beginning September 1, 1941. If you have any questions do not hesitate to contact my office . . ."

"Do you want to explain this to me?" Hannah interrupted his reading with a demanding voice.

Samuel finished reading the letter and put it back into the envelope.

"Let's go sit out front. It's more comfortable," Adrian suggested. "Probably the only comfort we'll have for the rest of the night."

They sat silent for several minutes, until Hannah finally spoke. "We thought you were applying to the University of Southern California."

Samuel jutted his chin, and said, "I want to go to Tuskegee."

Selona looked dumbfounded. "What's Tuskegee?"

"Tuskegee Institute, Grams. It's a fine college for Negroes."

Selona shrugged her shoulders. "Sounds good to me. What's all the fuss, Hannah?"

Hannah looked hard at Samuel, then said in a low voice, "Tell Grams where Tuskegee Institute is located, son."

He sighed. "It's in Alabama."

"Alabama!" Selona exploded to her feet, her eyes wide in disbelief. "What do you mean 'Alabama.' " Boy, have you lost your mind. Coloreds don't *go to* Alabama, they *run away* from Alabama!"

Samuel saw that his mother wore a satisfied look in having his grandmother's support. Nor did Adrian look particularly pleased with the notion.

He put his hands out, as though fending off a rattlesnake. "Now settle down, all of you. I'll explain."

"You better explain," Hannah said.

Selona muttered in the background, *"Alabama?"*

Adrian absently ran his hand over the top of the table. "Why do you want to go to Tuskegee?"

"Tuskegee has been approved for the new Civilian Pilot Training Program—called the CPT—a civilian pilot program designed to give young college men basic flight training."

Adrian asked cautiously, "Tuskegee wouldn't happen to have a Reserved Officers Training Corps, would it?"

"Yes, sir. I plan to become an army aviator. Tuskegee is the only college where a Colored can become a pilot and an officer."

"Son, there is no such thing as Colored army aviators," Adrian said. "The army is segregated, and only the white boys are fliers. There's no Colored aviation squadrons in the Army Air Corps."

Samuel began to argue his point of view. "I'm sorry, Pop, but you're wrong. There's one squadron—the Ninety-Ninth. That barnstormer I flew with—Sparks Hamilton—said that'll just be the first. The rest of the world is at war, and the Germans and Japanese are building large air forces. When we get into the ruckus the army will need all the pilots it can find. White and Colored."

Selona sat in disbelief, recalling when she and the Sergeant Major had the same discussion in 1917, at the same table, when Adrian and David had received letters of acceptance to the 17th Provisional Training Regiment, the first Negro Officers Training Corps at Fort Des Moines, Iowa.

She had not only intercepted and read those letters of acceptance, but, much to the ire of the Sergeant Major, she had hidden them from her sons for weeks.

"But Alabama?" Hannah moaned. "Samuel, I was born and raised in Florida. You have no idea how they treat Coloreds down South. Worse than they treat dogs."

"Those Kluxers in Tennessee shot the Sergeant Major like he was a dog. Shot his leg nearly clean off," Selona said.

Samuel knew the story of how the Sergeant Major tried to stop a group of Klansmen from lynching a young Colored man who had escaped from a cruel chain gang.

"Ain't nothing good down South for us Coloreds," Selona snapped. "Them crackers are mean and evil. Oh, yes, they're good to their own, but not to Coloreds. Alabama is a place you want to avoid, not pay train fare to get there."

Samuel held his ground. "I'm going, and that's final. I want to fly airplanes. I want to be a fighter pilot. If we go to war with Germany—and I believe we will—I want to serve my country."

Selona's voice was acid. "Why would a Colored man want to serve a country when he can't be served a decent meal in half the restaurants in this country? It don't make sense. It just don't make sense. Dying for the liberties of white folks on the other side of the world when you don't have those liberties right here in this country? Dying for this country when it won't even let you live?"

"Look what happened to your Uncle David," Hannah said. "Not to mention your father. One dead, another crippled for life. For what? You tell me, boy? You tell me why you want to fight for this country?"

He thought for a moment. "Because it's the only country I have. If it's going to be better, the Coloreds have to stand shoulder to shoulder with the white man. Fight and die if necessary, for liberties we won't ever have if we don't do our share."

His grandmother stiffened, recalling the Sergeant Major saying the same thing at Fort Davis, Texas, in 1882.

Hannah looked frightened, remembering the sadness in her mother-in-law when she learned her son had been killed in the Meuse-Argonne.

Adrian, too, remembered the agony of holding his dead brother's body.

Hannah sounded defeated. "There's no changing your mind?"

The look on his face gave her the answer.

"Then I guess there's nothing more to say. We best by getting back to the ranch," she said.

Samuel went through the kitchen and into the back alley and locked the rear door. He mounted his horse and rode out to the bivouac.

9

* * *

Captain Forrest Terrell was a leader, an administrator, meticulous and disciplined, in the tradition of the military. He was a Southerner, and believed in racial segregation in society and the military. His father had commanded Colored soldiers in the Great War and spoke highly of them on his return from Europe, but despite that believed the Colored soldier inferior to the white.

Terrell had watched the young man for the past ten days, never speaking to him directly, thanking him through Sergeant James for the fine game provided his troops. But they never spoke a word.

His men were getting bored; the training filled their days, leaving little time for recreation, except the baseball games in the evening. Bonita was off-limits, except to buy supplies, and he knew the men needed something to stir their morale.

The idea he had conceived several days before brought him to his first meeting with Samuel.

"Good afternoon, Mr. Sharps," Terrell said as he approached the camp.

Samuel stopped skinning the antelope and wiped his hands on a rag. "Good afternoon, Captain."

Terrell walked to Samuel's horse, ran his hand along the mane. "Fine animal."

"Thank you. I raised him from a colt."

There was a suggestive look on Terrill's face. "Too bad the army doesn't use horses any longer. It was a glorious part of the history."

Augusts nodded. "My grandfather was a horse soldier. My father rode with the Rough Riders, and he still talks about how wonderful it was to make a cavalry charge." He pointed to one of the mechanized units in the distance. "I guess things have to change."

Terrell nodded. "I've watched you ride. You're an excellent horseman. Which gave me an idea."

"What's that?"

"A race."

Samuel's eyes brightened. "A horse race?"

Terrell smiled. "Of sorts. But not between horses. Between horse and machine, over rough terrain. I think the men would find that entertaining."

Samuel gave that a momentary thought. "You want me to race one of those?" Samuel pointed to a Sherman tank.

"I think it would be challenging for both horse and machine," Terrell said.

"How long of a course?"

"Five miles."

"Where will you lay it out?"

Terrell spread a map on the ground. A red line traversed a course that put the race in the most rugged terrain in the area. "It's mostly mountainous. That'll make it more even. I doubt your horse could outrun a tank in open country."

"Doubtful." Samuel replied, studying the route of the race. He thought for a moment, then asked slyly, "Will there be betting?"

Terrell grinned. "I imagine there'll be a wager or two."

Samuel went back to the skinning. "You've got yourself a race, Captain."

Hannah was not a woman to hide her displeasure, nor her piety. "That's blasphemous. Racing for money on a Sunday is a sin."

Adrian viewed the situation differently, seeing an opportunity for the entire town to become involved. "We can make it a picnic. It'll give the folks here in town something different, a chance to meet the soldiers and show our appreciation for the fine job they're doing. A race that might put a few dollars in a few pockets. I don't think God will be too angry."

Hannah continued to show her disapproval. "Probably be whiskey and card playing as well. Not to mention loose women. You'll turn our town into a bordello."

Adrian roared with laughter. "Hannah, why must you always find something evil when men want to have a little entertainment?"

"Call it what you like. I'll call it what I believe it will be—a drunken fiesta." She tore off her apron and walked out of the restaurant, slamming the door behind her.

Adrian rose. "You plan on riding your horse in the race?"

"Of course. Why wouldn't I ride my horse?"

"You'll be beaten before you start."

Samuel was perplexed. "What makes you say that? My horse is one of the fastest around these parts."

"That's rugged terrain, son. Your horse can't run in those hills and beat that tank. Your horse can't climb those steep inclines and ravines. Not in a race. Moving slow and easy, the way you do when hunting is one thing. A flat-out race is another."

Samuel thought about that for a moment, recalling how he had never run his horse over the rough terrain of the mountains. His father had always warned him to be cautious, especially since he was hunting alone. A fall could mean death in the mountains.

"What do you suggest, Pop?"

"Come with me. I think I have a solution to the problem."

They went outside and climbed into Adrian's car.

Thirty minutes later Samuel stood in a stable on a ranch eight miles south of Bonita. "Pop, you must be out of your mind if you think I'm going to ride that animal."

Tall and lanky, Jasper Bodine, the owner of the ranch, stood by the animal and gently stroked its mane. "Your pop is right, Samuel. Can't no horse run a race against a tank, but the mule here, he can turn those hills into flat ground."

Samuel stared into the creature's wide, brown eyes, looked at the long ears, and stammered, "But a mule! I'll look ridiculous in front of everybody."

The mule was a Missouri mule, tan in color with a dark mane and tail. He slowly chomped on hay being fed to him by Bodine, oblivious to what was going on around him.

Adrian shook his head. "Not as ridiculous as you'll look if you lose that race. The mule here can beat that tank. Mules are born for bitter ground. Their legs and gait are perfect for the rough country you'll be traveling over. They're more durable in the long run. Granted, he's not as fast as a horse on flat ground, but the course is all through hills and gullies."

Samuel looked at the mule, who continued to chew. As they left the stable, the mule broke wind.

He could only shake his head in bewilderment and pray he wouldn't be the laughingstock of Arizona.

"A mule? Hah! My baby's gonna race a tank on a mule! Lord, Lord, I wish the Sergeant Major was here to see this race!" Selona was bent over with laughter. Even Hannah found the notion amusing, figuring it served the boy right. Blaspheming on the Sabbath cut deep into her grain. A little humility might be in order, she thought. "What are you going to use for reins . . . plow lines?"

The kitchen at the ranch exploded with laughter. Even Adrian was laughing, and it was his idea.

Samuel fumed. His hat was crushed down nearly to his eyes, as though he were trying to hide.

"We had mules in the Great War," Adrian recalled. "They are the most ornery, cantankerous, downright meanest critters on God's good earth. I saw one kick an artillery caisson completely to splinters. But Jasper is right. A mule is the best animal with sure footing for mountains. Even old Buffalo Bill Cody used to ride one during his buffalo-hunting days. He told me he once had a race with Colonel Custer out in Kansas. Said he beat Custer by a mile or more. A mule can travel like a rabbit over rough ground."

Samuel didn't feel any better by these words, but he knew his father wouldn't betray him. If he thought a mule was the answer, then a mule it would be.

He only hoped *he* didn't wind up looking like the jackass!

10

On the following Sunday, the army welcomed the citizens of the area to their bivouac. They came by automobile, horseback, in buggies and buckboards, and a few rode bicycles.

Only one arrived towing a mule.

Samuel had studied the map into the early hours of the morning. While he knew the terrain better than most older men in the region, he had never ridden a direct course through the mountains. He recognized each gully, arroyo, and crackback ridgeline. He figured the tank would stay in the open as much as possible, but there were areas of steep inclines and loose rock and arroyos the tank driver might find too deep and lose time finding a suitable crossing.

By two o'clock the crowd, which had eaten on picnic tables—food supplied by both army and locals—cleaned up the mess and gathered for the race.

The greatest excitement came when the Sherman fired its engine and put on a demonstration for the crowd: running in tight circles, then wide loops, churning up the ground with frightening ease.

When Samuel appeared walking the mule, the crowd quieted—until the mule broke wind—then erupted in laughter.

At first Hannah had refused to go to the race, but Selona and Adrian convinced her it wasn't sinful for folks to come together on a Sunday afternoon and at least enjoy the company.

Now she watched with a satisfying smile as Samuel walked to the starting line, where he was joined by her husband.

"Now you remember what Jasper told you," his father said.

Samuel nodded, staring straight ahead, his face burning with embarrassment. Then the tank rolled to the starting line and Samuel saw Captain Terrell appear.

Adrian knew it was time for him to leave. He whispered to Samuel, "Remember now, keep the shortest line and stay out of the open as much as possible." He walked off, then turned as his son mounted. He chuckled. "Boy, you sure are a sight on that mule!"

Sixty seconds later Captain Terrell fired his Colt .45 pistol, and the race was on, to the excited shouts of soldiers and civilians.

Samuel was suddenly riding a tempest. The sound of the Colt, the roar of the tank, and the screams from the crowd had a dramatic impact on the mule. The mule broke wind, brayed like thunder, then went into a wild, bucking frenzy.

The tank roared away as Samuel twirled through the air, holding on to the reins as though they were his only salvation. The crowd then saw the danger as the mule kicked and bucked in their direction. Men dropped beer bottles. Women grabbed up children. The soldiers ran like hell, with the mule kicking over tables, chairs, finally working his way into the bivouac area.

Sergeant James stood at the front of the mess hall, cigar clamped tightly in his mouth, watching the beast charge directly for him. James missed being trampled by inches as the mule exploded into the mess tent, sending pots, pans, and cutlery flying.

Diving for cover, James caught the terrified look on Samuel's face, and shouted, "Hang on, Samuel!"

Samuel's heart was pounding as he held to the reins. Then, when it seemed he could hold on no longer, the mule suddenly settled into an easy gait and began plodding toward the rooster tail of dust thrown up by the tank.

One mile later, the flat ground ended at the mouth of a twisting, crackback ridge, slowing the tank, which had to traverse the steep terrain. First thirty degrees to the right, thirty degrees to the left, allowing the monster machine to climb without capsizing.

Samuel spotted the tank and saw his chance to gain time and distance. He took a deep breath, remembered what Jasper had told him, and kneed the mule up the rocky ridge.

The mule plodded steadily, its large hooves finding purchase with each upward step. Rock spilled, cascading down the ridge, but the mule proved steady and dependable. Nearby, the Sherman turned wildly as the treads crunched slowly through the loose rock.

Reaching the crest of the ridge, Samuel saw the tank nearing the rise.

"Come on mule—down we go." Samuel prodded the mule's flanks, then felt the downward plunge on the back side of the ridge.

Down the rider and mule rode to the sound of spraying rocks, the labored breathing of man and beast. Samuel held the reins taut, shifting his weight to the rear, compensating for the pull of gravity drawing them dangerously toward the bottom. Moments later the animal's hooves cracked off the ground at the base of the ridge, where Samuel looked to his left and saw a stake bearing a red flag. He spurred the mule as the tank slammed furiously onto the bottom, nearly pitching over from the impact.

Samuel swung the mule to the left of the stake and he raced toward the next flag. He saw the turret of the tank pop open; the helmeted sergeant, Reuben Bell, appeared, a broad grin beneath his goggles. Bell shouted something, but the words were drowned by the roar of the tank's engine, while Samuel watched helplessly as the Sherman pulled easily away and sped toward the next flag.

The laughter of the crowd rang in his brain; dust covered his face, and the acrid taste of the Sherman's diesel fumes stung his nostrils as he leaned into the mules' thick neck. "Go, mule. You can do it. Go, big boy. Go!"

As though understanding the urgency of the moment, the mule suddenly burst forward with such energy that the reins nearly pulled from Samuel's grip.

A smile crossed his face as he saw the tank approach the next obstacle, a high ridge with an almost impossible incline.

But there was something Samuel knew from having hunted this country, an important thing the tankers could not use to their advantage even if they knew of its existence.

A small stand of trees stood at the base of the ridge, just inside the red flag. He eased the animal to the left and headed straight for the trees. When he reached the stand, he reined in and jumped from the saddle, and had his shirt stripped from his back before the mule could come to a complete stop. He took the shirt and wrapped it over the mule's eyes, then grabbed the bit and charged toward the trees.

Samuel and the mule disappeared into the trees, where he could see the narrow channel leading through the ridge. The thick thorns and branches cut at his skin as he urged the hooded mule through the biting tangle, his eyes protected by the shirt until Samuel pulled and urged the creature along the channel to the other side of the ridge.

Looking quickly to the top of the ridge, Samuel saw that the Sherman was nowhere in sight, though the grind of its motor cut the stillness of the air. He quickly pulled away the shirt, climbed into the saddle, and charged toward the next flag, lying at the base of another ridge.

Two miles to go, he told himself as he spurred the mule, and felt the animal bolt across the quarter mile expanse with the heart of a thoroughbred, his long tail flagging, his hooves tearing huge chunks from the hard ground.

Samuel reached the base of the ravine as the tank slammed onto the surface at the base and raced across the open terrain.

Rider and the mule were halfway to the crest of the ridge when the tank charged upward, its treads leaving deep grooves in its wake. The grinding of gears and the incessant noise from the Sherman's engines told him the tank was drawing closer as he reached the summit and kneed the mule over the edge. They reached the bottom as the Sherman roared over the crest of the ridge and plunged down wildly, sliding and swerving as the treads found the loose shale of the ridge.

Samuel spurred the mule as he saw the bivouac in the distance, where soldiers and civilians could be seen cheering.

Now on open ground, where the tank's speed gave the trailing Sherman an advantage, Samuel could feel the Sherman closing, until it had the distance to fifty yards. Then thirty yards. Then ten yards. Samuel could see the large cannon, appearing like a spear closing on his back.

That's when he saw the tank start to pass him. He pulled the reins to the right, maneuvering the mule into the path of the Sherman. Samuel could feel the machine pulsating, but he held his position until the tank tried swerving left. Samuel anticipated the move and did likewise, staying in front of the Sherman.

The creek and the finish line were in sight, with the crowd all around.

Again the tank tried to pass, and Samuel pulled in front of the tank, slowing the Sherman again and allowing him to maintain the lead.

The two contestants reached the stream with Samuel in front. When the mule hit the water Samuel swung from the saddle and ran for the far banks, leading the mule by the reins as the tank slammed into the water, spewing a geyser of water.

Samuel pulled with all his might. The mule charged furiously, as though realizing the stakes.

His father was standing on the far shore, watching incredulously as the Sherman closed on rider and mule. He was almost too afraid to hope for victory, but the tank suddenly swerved right as though out of control. Samuel didn't look back as he heard the sudden racing of the Sherman's engine.

Adrian laughed!

He knew the treads had burrowed into the soft mud bed in the middle of the stream.

That one spot in the stream was a waiting tank trap the soldiers had not discovered before the race began.

Samuel had recalled Captain Terrell warning the tank commanders not to traverse the stream since it was their source of drinking water and he did not want the water or stream damaged during maneuvers.

Samuel reached the victory side of the bank five yards in front of the tank, pulling and clawing his way past the blue flag marking the finish of the race.

The crowd exploded with cheering and clapping as Samuel collapsed on the ground beside the flag.

That night, tired and scarred from the thorns, he arrived at Sabre Ranch, a broad smile beaming from his tired face. The family was gathered at the cottonwoods, recounting the race when Samuel approached. Hannah kissed him lightly on the cheek, saying nothing, but obviously proud.

His father eyed him warily, asking, "You won the race. But did you win any money? A lot of folks lost money betting on the tank. Especially the soldiers."

Samuel reached into his pocket and pulled out a wad of rolled bills. "Sergeant James and a few soldiers covered the bets, mine included."

Hannah's eyes bulged. "How much money did you win?"

Samuel said calmly, "Four hundred and fifty dollars"

"Good Lord," said Selona. "That's enough money to pay for your college, and then some."

Samuel grew serious, asking his grandmother, "What do you think the Sergeant Major would say now?"

She shook her head. "I don't know what he'd say . . . but I know he's proud."

That—and the money—was enough for Samuel.

Tuskegee

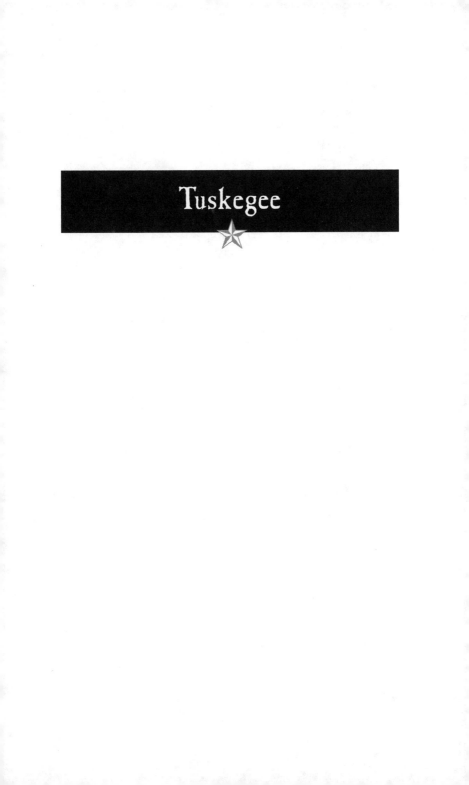

11

The summer drew to an end. Samuel enjoyed the time, visiting with friends who had come home from college, listening to their experiences while conjuring thoughts of his future. As the day of his departure for Alabama neared he grew quiet, even withdrawn, but he felt both exhilaration and tentativeness, having listened for hours to his mother's and grandmother's woeful tales of the Negro in the South. Especially in Alabama. Despite the foreboding, the thought of flying airplanes and becoming an officer in the Army Air Corps overcame the horror stories.

Even though there was an official policy of segregation in the Air Corps, he knew the day would come when Negroes would fly in combat for the United States. He knew that Adolph Hitler and Emperor Hirohito would see to that historical change.

On a bright morning in late August he saddled his horse and rode west, the sun against his back. He rode slowly and deliberately, taking in every sight and sound, memorizing what he would need when the pain of homesickness set in, as he knew it would. Homesickness was a good thing, his grandmother used to say: "It reminds you that you have a home."

He had more than a home. He had family, community, tradition, and a stake in this country. He knew that his father and grandfather had to fight for the right to serve; he would do the same if necessary. His father's tales of Negro soldiers being used in the Great War as stevedores and road-construction workers was puzzling, though the men of the 93rd ultimately found their way into the great battles in France. Why, he wondered, would a nation train hundreds of thousands of Negro troops to be infantrymen, then relegate them to unloading ships and repairing roads?

Was the nation that frightened of the rise of the Negro as a legitimate part of the culture in America?

So many questions with only one answer: The Negro had earned his right to fight for his country . . . even in the air.

The *Pittsburgh Courier* had reported that the Civilian Pilot Training Program had been expanded to include young Negroes through Public Law 18, a law supported by a senator from Missouri named Harry S. Truman, who had served in the Great War.

He returned from his ride and pulled the Sharps from the boot and unsaddled his horse. He curried and combed the stallion with affection, recalling with each stroke the hours he had spent aboard his mount. He had just finished when he heard the sound of an automobile driving up, then another, and figured the company was arriving for that afternoon's picnic and farewell.

He would be leaving for Alabama the next morning.

As he stepped from the stable, he was stunned to see his father and Ernst Bruner standing by a shiny new DeSoto. The vehicle was black, its tires dusty but new; the finish gleamed beneath a coat of wax. Adrian opened the driver side door and motioned his son forward.

"I figured the first of the Sharps family to go off to college ought to have a comfortable means of transportation." He handed the young man the keys.

Samuel slid behind the steering wheel and studied the fine interior with wide-eyed astonishment. He tried to speak, but the words would not come. Finally, he heard his father say, "Start it up. Take it for a spin."

Samuel started the engine and sat listening to the soft purr, then he pressed on the clutch and shifted into gear. He eased away from the yard, then shifted into second gear and pressed harder on the accelerator. By the time he reached third gear he was traveling forty miles an hour, the ranch obscured in the rearview mirror by a cloud of trailing dust.

He drove for nearly an hour before returning, to find the ranch filled with the friends who had come to wish him farewell.

When the sun began fading the throng thinned out, with all shaking Samuel's hand and wishing him well. The last to leave was Teddy Bruner, who limped slightly on a mended leg.

The two stood by the DeSoto watching the sun, saying nothing; neither able to find the proper words. Finally, Teddy, turned and extended his hand, saying, "You take care of yourself down South. Some of those folks can be mighty ornery."

They shook hands and embraced. Teddy pulled himself away suddenly and walked silently to his car, where his father waited. The Senator tipped his hat, and smiled. "The Sergeant Major would be proud." Then he slipped into the car and the vehicle sped away, leaving the Sharps family to their last evening together as a whole family at Sabre Ranch.

That night there was a full moon surrounded by what Samuel thought were all the stars in the universe. Sparks crackled from the fire in the cottonwoods, rising into the night and disappearing. There was silence, even from Selona and Hannah. Adrian sat on a chair stoking the burning logs with a long stick, staring deeply into the fire as though recalling when he left home the first time. That was in 1898, when he rode to Scottsdale to join Colonel Roosevelt's First Volunteer Cavalry. He didn't return home until after the War with Spain ended that summer. Then came the Great War. He left for France from this same place, carrying his father's curved cavalry sword.

So many years ago, he thought, staring at the glowing tip of the stick. Now he was sending his only son off to college, knowing that there surely was another war around the corner. The world had a way of doing that: starting wars that would kill the innocent while their loved ones endured the terrible agony waiting.

He had known the going; now he prayed he wouldn't have to eventually suffer the wait.

Selona looked at her grandson and suddenly felt her thoughts tumble back into time to another tall man, named Augustus Sharps. She recalled the first time they met in the muddy streets of Fort Wallace, Kansas, when she was a young girl. She chuckled as she recalled how filthy he was; two years' worth of buffalo blood and dirt covered him from head to toe. But beneath that she saw the young man she hoped to marry one day.

Hannah's face was etched with that special mask of pain only a mother can know when she sees her child go alone into the world. Who would wash his clothes? Cook his meals? Darn his socks? Hold him when he was frightened?

She shook her head, trying to rid her brain of such thoughts, knowing her life—and the families—had reached a new plateau with Samuel's leaving.

As though on some silent cue, the four rose and started toward the house, with Selona trailing off toward the cemetery. She was carrying a lantern, and called to Samuel, "Would you join me for a bit of a talk?"

He followed her beneath the two hanging sabres.

Adrian stopped at the side of the house and watched for a moment, out of sound of their voices. He watched Selona put her hand on Samuel's shoulder, and she appeared to be asking something of him.

He saw Samuel nod, then the two knelt by the Sergeant Major's grave. She had apparently placed a small bucket there earlier, and with her hands, dug at the soil, carefully placing several handfuls into the container. When finished she smoothed over the grave and handed the bucket to Samuel, who walked to the trunk of his car. He placed the bucket inside and closed the boot, then stepped onto the porch, where he walked silently past his father and into the house.

Adrian turned quickly away, not wanting his son to know he had seen the tears streaming down his son's face.

The next morning, Samuel rose and fed his horse. He gave the animal an extra helping of oats while thinking aloud to himself at times. "I never thought I'd miss the smell of this old stable. Or the sound of you champing on your oats, but I guess I will." He looked around, trying to remember how many times the stable had been re-built since the Sergeant Major first erected it in 1886.

The stable smelled of time, of history, a history most Americans didn't know and would probably never know. He shoveled out the manure, hung the tack neatly in the proper place, and started to leave. He turned one last time, took in the smell deeply, then turned and walked into the rising sun of the morning.

He had not slept well, awakened by the memories that sur-rounded him. Surrounded his life. As he stepped onto the front porch he saw his father coming through the door. He obviously had not slept well either. Inside there was silence, except for the clanging of dishes and skillets, and the sizzling of bacon and eggs on the stove. Hannah was bushing herself, while Selona sipped coffee at the kitchen table.

They ate without saying a word, then it was time; Hannah cleared the table while the others went to the family room. Two heavy suitcases sat near the front door, which Samuel loaded into the trunk of the car.

The family came onto the porch, with Adrian carrying his son's Western hat. He handed the Stetson to Samuel. They shook hands, neither seeming to want to let go.

Adrian hugged his son. "I'll miss you, boy. You drive careful and write every week. You call if you need anything." He started to turn, then paused, "I wish I was going with you, but a man has to start his journey in life alone. It's the way things are meant to be."

Samuel nodded. Selona embraced him long and hard, then put him at arm's length. "Don't you go getting yourself in trouble. Re-member what I told you. This is your home when you're ready to come back." She then hurried into the house and returned carrying the Sharps, sheathed in a leather pouch, and the cartridge belt. "You best take this with you in case of Kluxers."

"The Kluxers aren't going to bother me, Grams."

She shoved the rifle into his hands. "There ain't no law that says a Colored man can't own a hunting rifle. Not even in Alabama." She pointed at the trunk of the DeSoto. "Don't forget your promises."

"I won't." His voice broke for a moment. He looked at his

mother. She had tears in her eyes and fumbled nervously with her apron. She kissed him on the cheek and hurried into the house.

Samuel walked slowly to the trunk, laid the rifle and cartridge belt next to the bucket. He drove away slowly, not wanting to look back, but he had to have one last glimpse. He stopped, got out, and gazed back at Sabre Ranch. A long, consuming look, wanting to remember.

12

* * *

The first two days of Samuel's journey to Alabama had gone smoothly, the Arizona country seeming endless, as was New Mexico. He had spent the first night as he had the second, pulling off the highway, making a small camp, eating the food prepared by his mother, and sleeping beneath the stars on a buffalo robe given him by his father. The robe was old, but in good condition, making him comfortable on the ground. Like the Sharps, which he kept close at hand in case of varmints.

The third day he passed through El Paso, traveled east, then turned south, off his original course, but a necessary detour nonetheless. He had made a promise to his grandmother, a promise as important to her as his trip was to him.

He reached Alpine, Texas, some 150 miles from El Paso, a small town in the Big Bend country of west Texas. He stopped at a filling station and found an old man sitting in front. Samuel was quite amazed, for the man was a Negro, though not ebony, more reddish brown. He was old, with a weathered face, and stooped at the waist. As he started filling the gas tank he studied Samuel with a curious eye. The man wore a red-calico shirt with a green sash tied around his waist, Apache-style. Indian jewelry hung around his neck; and his hatband was made from rattlesnake skin. He looked more Indian than Negro.

The man saw Samuel's curiosity. "You ain't from around here, are you, boy?"

"No, sir. I'm from Arizona."

"Arizona, huh. I heard there was Coloreds living in Arizona." He thought for a moment, then asked, "Was any of your kinfolk a cavalry soldier?"

Samuel beamed. "My grandfather spent thirty years in the Tenth Cavalry. He retired a Sergeant Major."

"Your grandpap, you say?" The old man hawked and spit. "My pap was in the Tenth Cavalry. Course, I never got to know him. He was killed by Texas Rangers when I was just a papoose."

This caught Samuel's attention. "What was his name?"

"Private Winston Jackson. H Troop, Tenth Cavalry. Killed right near Fort Davis, back in eighteen-and-eighty-two. Buried there at the fort, along with a whole lot of Coloreds. Mostly soldiers, but a few wives and children."

Samuel felt as though he had been swept back in time. He knew the man!

Not by acquaintance, but by the stories told around the fire in the cottonwoods. The stories told by Selona and Adrian, who had become the family historian, recounted the years the Sharps family served on the western frontier. From Fort Wallace to Fort Sill, Fort Davis to Fort Grant. Not a page in their family history left unaccounted for.

And there was one he always especially enjoyed: The story involved murder, revenge, and flight to another country. But what made it most intriguing was a name so unique it stuck in his memory.

He took a deep breath. "Might you be kinfolk to a man named Chihocopee? Chihocopee Jackson? The son of Juanita Calderon Jackson? I know he used to live in these parts. And your name is Jackson."

"There's lots of Jacksons in these parts. Especially over in Brackettsville. There's a whole town of Coloreds over there."

Samuel had heard of Brackettsville, where descendants of the Buffalo Soldiers had chosen to build their own town. But he sensed something deeper. Perhaps the place, the name, or the way he dressed. "Are you related to Chihocopee Jackson?"

The old man stopped pumping, and stared at him, a long, pene-trating perusal that made Samuel uncomfortable. "How would you know my name, boy?"

He felt a wave of exhilaration. "When I was a youngster, my grandmother used to tell about when she was with my grandfather at Fort Davis. She had a friend named Juanita Calderon who married a soldier named Jackson. They had a son named Chihocopee."

Jackson laughed. "That's a Seminole Indian name, given to me by one of my great-uncles. His name was John Horse. He was an escaped slave from Georgia who lived with the Seminoles in Florida, then moved to the Indian Territory in the 1850s when the federal government put them and four other tribes on reservations. The Seminoles and their Colored friends came to Mexico after slavers started capturing and selling them to plantations in Arkansas and Louisiana. They made a deal with the Mexican government to patrol the Rio Grande and protect settlers from Indians. In return, the government gave them sanctuary. After the Civil War, many of them crossed back into Texas and served as army scouts. They was called—"

"Seminole Negro Scouts!" Samuel said.

Chihocopee laughed. "You know your history, I'll say that for you, boy." He pulled the pump from the gas tank. "What did you say your name was?"

"Adrian Samuel Sharps. Folks call me Samuel. My grandfather served with your father in the Tenth. My grandmother is Selona Sharps. She and your mother were friends."

Like the past meeting the present, their hands were drawn to each other by a mutual history.

"Lord, have mercy," Chihocopee said. "I'd have never thought it possible. My momma used to talk about your grandpap and grandmam like they was saints."

"Not saints. But good folks. My grandfather died just before I was born. While my father was fighting in France during the Great War." He paused, then asked, "Whatever became of your mother?"

He smiled proudly. "After the *incident,* she took me to Piedras Negras, across the Rio Grande from Del Rio. I grew up there with the other Coloreds. When I was thirty-four I went into the army. I fought in France, myself. With the Ninety-Second Division."

"My father fought with the Ninety-Third."

"It is a small world, Samuel Sharps. A small world, indeed."

Then Samuel remembered the "incident." "Your father was murdered by Texas Rangers. Your mother killed the one she thought was responsible, scalped him, then stole an army horse and rode off with you strapped to her back. Word was she took you back to Mexico to live with her family. I don't remember the Ranger's name, but I know he had once done harm to my family."

Jackson chuckled. "Captain John Armitage." He pointed to the northeast. "He's buried up yonder, along with the Coloreds." He cackled. "I'll bet he's still rolling in his grave. Sleeping alongside all them Coloreds."

Samuel chuckled at the irony. "I would imagine."

There was a sadness on Jackson's face. "My momma is buried there with my pap."

"Alongside him?"

He shook his head slowly, as though remembering something important. "There wasn't room to bury her alongside him. I dug her grave on top of his. She's buried in the same plot. You want to go there?"

"To the cemetery at Fort Davis? That's why I've come here. To keep a promise to my grandmother."

"Let me lock up. We can be there in a few minutes in your car."

He locked the front door of his filling station and climbed into the DeSoto. Moments later Samuel was driving toward the cemetery . . . to keep a promise.

The fort had been abandoned for decades; the parade ground was overgrown with tumbleweeds. In the distance Samuel could see the dilapidated barracks buildings appearing like gray skeletons against the alkaline terrain.

They stopped where the road ended, at what was once the fort trading post. Samuel remembered the stories of his grandmother starting her first cooking venture with Frank Conniger, who was the sutler.

He took his Kodak camera and opened the trunk, where he removed the bucket. "Where's the cemetery?"

The old man pointed, and they walked through the scrub brush, past ghostly houses once called Officers' Row, then to Suds Row, where the laundresses lived with their enlisted husbands. The adobe huts were now nothing more than small mounds surrounded by weeds, silent markers of the past, eroded by time and wind.

When they reached the cemetery at the base of Sleeping Lion Mountain, Samuel stopped suddenly. "I don't believe this."

Jackson smiled proudly. "I did it all myself."

The cemetery was well kept; flowers were on many of the graves, the markers were painted, and the ground cleared of weeds. A white picket fence framed the place.

The two made a slow progress along the rows of graves. Some bore names while others were nameless, their markers the only evidence they once existed. Jackson stopped at the grave Samuel figured was Jackson and Juanita's. There were bones of various animals spread on the top; flowers framed the grave, and there was a coyote skull nailed to the wooden marker.

"My mother made me promise to mark her grave in Seminole tradition," said Jackson.

Samuel looked around, noting one grave that stood out from the others. It was grown over, in terrible need of attention, like a weed in a flower garden. "Whose grave is that?"

The old soldier laughed. "Captain John Armitage. He don't get much respect around here. But I didn't dig him up. That would have been spiteful."

Samuel began strolling again until he found what he had been instructed to find, two wagon wheels embedded into the ground, painted white. He knelt and took the bucket and poured the red dirt of Arizona onto the alkaline dirt of the two graves.

"Do you know them?" asked Jackson, noting the name on the two wheels. "All I know is their name is Talbot."

Samuel nodded slowly. "I didn't know them. I only knew of them. They are my grandfather's parents. Their slave name was Talbot. My grandmother asked me to sprinkle some of the dirt from my grandfather's grave onto their graves. She thought it might bring their spirits closer together. They spent so little time together while alive."

Jackson said nothing. He understood. His parents shared a similar fate.

Samuel handed him the camera. "Would you take our picture?"

Jackson took the camera and snapped several photographs of the younger man kneeling between the two tiny graves. Samuel rose and started looking again until he found another grave. The name was barely readable, but he could still make out the name of "Miss Marie."

"Did your family know her?" Jackson asked.

Samuel smiled. "She was my great-great-grandmother on my mother's side of the family. She died not long after my grandfather was posted to Fort Davis."

"Sometimes I sleep here at night. It's peaceful, and no harm will come from these folks," Jackson said.

"I doubt there's ghosts here that we have to fear."

Jackson grinned and pointed at Armitage's grave. "Only him, and he ain't said a word or roamed this ground since he was planted."

They laughed and walked together toward the DeSoto to get his gear.

That night they slept beneath the west Texas stars where their kin had slept six decades before, not knowing if they would see the sun rise should Indians, bandits, or Mexican revolutionaries attack the soldiers and their families.

Samuel slept on the buffalo robe between his grandparents, while Jackson slept atop the grave of his parents. Coyotes barked in the hills and mountains, and the sound of sidewinders twisting through the brush etched the still night, but they slept soundly, knowing that should there be a threat, they would be guarded by the ghosts of the Buffalo Soldiers.

13

⁎ ⁎ ⁎

He drove the entire day without a break, except to stop for gaso line in Odessa, reaching the outskirts of Fort Worth by midnight. He camped along the side of the road and fell asleep quickly, ignoring the rumbling trucks on the nearby highway.

The next morning he washed by a small stream, then started driving east, passing through Dallas and stopping again for the night near Longview. He noticed how the terrain had changed from Fort Worth toward the east. Gone was the hard desert and dry hills; now there were huge grain fields and forests of trees on what he considered the flattest ground he had ever seen. But the most astonishing was the vastness of Texas. He had driven for three days and was still in the Lone Star State.

The humidity of Louisiana was uncomfortable, but he was soon to learn there are greater discomforts than muggy weather.

East of Shreveport he pulled into a gas station, got out, and stretched the stiffness from his back. Four white men sat playing cards at a small table. One of the men looked up, and said, "Pay for the gas before you start pumpin'." Then he went back to his cards, pausing to sip corn liquor from a fruit jar. Samuel ignored the insult, gave the man four dollars, and filled the tank. Then he felt nature's call, and asked the man, "Where's your toilet?"

The cards stopped as though lightning had struck the table. The man looked at him spitefully, then rose slowly, laying his cards face-down. "What did you say, boy?"

Samuel shrugged. "I asked, 'Where's your toilet?' "

As if on cue, the laughter exploded from the men, all guffawing and slapping their legs. The one man walked to the rear of Samuel's car and looked at the license plate. "Arizona, huh? Tell me, boy, do they let niggers piss in a white man's toilet in Arizona." His face suddenly turned hard; his eyes narrowed to beads.

Samuel nodded slowly. He felt his fists ball, and felt the hatred in the beady eyes watching his hands. He slowly uncurled his fist and relaxed.

"You're in Louisiana, now, boy. Niggers don't use a white man's toilet." He nodded over his shoulder, saying, "You got to go in the trees."

Samuel looked past the man to a stand of trees nearby. A sign was nailed to the tree, saying: FOR COLOREDS.

Samuel said nothing; he merely tipped his hat and climbed into the DeSoto and drove away to the laughter of the rednecks.

He didn't hear the laughter; he only felt the anger burning in his gut as he sped down the road lined with drooping magnolias. Several miles from the station he stopped and relieved himself in a stand of trees, then continued his journey.

Throughout the day he was overwhelmed by one particular aggravation: It was the first time he had ever been called a "nigger"!

Samuel realized his education was beginning to take a turn in a new direction. Wherever he stopped for gasoline he was eyed with suspicion. Near Jackson, Mississippi, he glanced in the rearview mirror to see the flashing lights of a patrol car. Easing off the highway, he reached to the glove compartment for the vehicle registration. That was when he heard the harsh, Southern drawl, and felt the cold steel against his ear.

"Get out of this car, boy!" A voice boomed in his ear, and looking over his shoulder, Samuel saw a tall, lanky white man holding a pistol. On his shirt was a badge; a Western hat nearly covered his eyes. And for the first time in his life, he understood terror.

"Yes, sir. Right away, sir." Samuel had the registration in his hand as he slid out of the DeSoto.

There was a chuckle in the background, then another voice said, "He's got good manners, ain't he, Bubba?"

The man called Bubba said, "Sure do, Horace. Sure do." He waved the pistol at Samuel, motioning him to the rear of the automobile. "Where'd you steal this car, boy?"

Samuel said shakily, "I didn't steal this car, Deputy. It belongs to me. A gift from my father."

"Gift! That's rich. How come a nigger's got a fancy car like this?" He looked at the Arizona plates. "Do all niggers from Arizona ride around in fancy cars?"

Samuel replied slowly, "They do where I live."

That was when he felt the crash of the barrel against his skull; a storm of lights burst through his brain as his legs gave way and he crashed to the ground.

"Hit him again, Bubba. He's a smart one."

Bubba raised the pistol and slammed the butt across the back of Samuel's neck. Pain shot through his body, and he was taunted by the warnings of Selona, then everything turned into darkness.

The stench of urine and excrement was the first signal that he was still alive; a burning miasma permeated the jail cell that was no more than a cage. He opened his eyes slowly, then saw what could only be described as a scene from Dante's *Inferno*. The cell was eight feet wide, approximately ten feet long. And he wasn't alone. Five Negro men lay like sardines beside him, pressing his body into the corner. Near the door was a lard bucket, where one Negro man was relieving himself.

"Where am I?" Samuel asked weakly.

"Where? In jail, boy. You in the county jail." The man relieving himself spoke while completing his business. When finished, he sat by the door, ignoring the stench from the bucket. He was short, with rusty-looking knuckles; a mean scar ran along his left cheek. He was young, like Samuel, but his eyes appeared to be ancient with yellowish splotches surrounding the pupils.

Samuel rubbed his neck; the pain shot through his head. He looked at the man and asked, "Who are you?"

The man said acidly, "What you want to know my name for, boy?"

"Just curious." Samuel tried to rise, but the pain forced him back to the floor.

" 'Curious'? You sound like an educated nigger." The man shifted uncomfortably.

Samuel shook his head, like a man who doesn't understand what is happening. "Why did they arrest me?"

"Say you stole a car."

"I didn't steal a car. That car belongs to me. It's bought and paid for. I have the title and registration." He rubbed softly at his neck, trying to soothe the injured muscles.

The man laughed. "You in Mississippi now, boy. If the Man say you stole a car—you a car thief. That'll get you ten years on the chain gang."

Before he could respond, the deputy named Bubba appeared, hitting the bars with a nightstick. "Get up, boys. Time to see the judge." He opened the door, and the others began stirring from sleep. Samuel watched them rise and walk single file through the door.

Bubba looked at Samuel, who was still sitting on the floor. "Get your ass moving, boy. The judge ain't got all morning."

He pulled himself to his feet and walked through the door, where he was prodded in the back by the nightstick.

Court was held in the sheriff's office, where an elderly white man sat waving a bamboo fan. Judge Phineus Taylor was in his sixties, frail-looking, with tobacco juice staining his filthy white suit. He motioned to the prisoners, who formed a line in front of his desk. He looked at the men, seeming to recognize them all; but he stared at Samuel. "You must be the car thief. I know these other boys. They're just drunks."

Samuel shook his head. "No, Your Honor. I'm not a car thief."

Again the nightstick slammed into his back. Bubba leaned, and said spitefully, "Don't talk unless the judge gives you permission, boy. You understand?"

Samuel nodded painfully. "Yes, sir."

"That's better," Bubba said.

Judge Taylor went down the line, saying to each prisoner, "Five dollars or thirty days on the chain gang." Then he reached Samuel, and leaned back in his chair. The air was thick as gunsmoke as the judge examined the papers showing title, registration, and Samuel's driver's license. Taylor looked at Bubba, and asked, "Have you checked out this boy's papers, Bubba?"

Resignedly, Bubba said, "Yes, Judge. I called the sheriff out in Bonita, Arizona, and he said the boy is who he says he is, and the car belongs to him."

Samuel glanced to Bubba, but the words meant nothing compared to what he saw on a table in the corner. His Sharps, camera, and buffalo robe lay with his suitcases, which had been opened and ransacked. His heart fell, thinking these rednecks had touched his grandfather's rifle.

The judge thought for a moment, then slammed his gavel. "I find you innocent of car thief charges. But I charge you twenty dollars for the phone call to Arizona and the aggravation you've caused this county."

Samuel nodded slowly, then mumbled, "Thank you, Your Honor." He looked at the man beside him, noting that the yellows in his eyes seemed darker. Then the other prisoners were led away to a hell that Samuel could only imagine in his worst nightmare.

He paid his fine, then packed his suitcase. He was picking up the rifle to sleeve the weapon in the scabbard when Bubba stepped beside him, asking, "What kind of old gun is that, boy?"

"It's a Sharps buffalo gun, sir." Samuel felt Bubba rip the rifle from his hands. He examined the rifle, shouldered the stock and swung the barrel around the room, settling the sights on Samuel's chest. He stood there, a dominant force, as though trying to send a message to the young Arizonan. "You in Mississippi now, boy. There ain't no buffalo here. The closest thing is niggers. You gonna shoot niggers, boy?"

Samuel shook his head. "No, sir."

Bubba kept the rifle trained on him, saying, "Too bad. We got plenty of niggers. I'd like to see them all shot and skinned. Especially the uppity bastards running around causing trouble. Are you a trouble-makin' nigger, boy?"

"No, sir. I'm just trying to get to college in Alabama."

Bubba grinned. "They gonna love you in Alabama. 'Bout as much as we love you in Mississippi." He handed the rifle to Samuel. "Damn rifle looks like it'd blow up if it was fired." He looked at Horace, saying, "It ain't worth keepin'."

Horace laughed and spit tobacco into a tin can.

Samuel felt a flood of relief as he sleeved the rifle in the scabbard and picked up his belongings. He started for the door, but was stopped by Bubba's threat, which warned, "Don't let the sun set on your black ass in Mississippi. You got my meanin', nigger?"

He nodded politely, then said, "I'll be moving along."

He loaded his gear into the trunk under the watchful eyes of Bubba and Horace. He drove away slowly, following the highway that would lead him out of Mississippi.

14

✯　✯　✯

Samuel arrived in Macon County, Alabama, on a hot afternoon to the sound of thunder. The sky was cloudless. A flash of sunlight streaked across the horizon; a moment later an airplane appeared overhead. He pulled off the road as the plane suddenly flipped onto its back, then rolled back to straight and level flight then disappeared over a tree line. He checked his map. He was north of Tuskegee; he must be close to Tuskegee Army Air Field.

He drove for twenty minutes until he came to what looked like a sentry booth. A Negro military policeman stepped out and saluted smartly.

"Can I help you, sir."

"Is this the airfield?" Samuel stammered.

The MP smiled. "Yes, sir. This is Tuskegee Army Air Field."

"I'd like permission to come onto the field."

The MP straightened. "No, sir. Unless you have official business the field is off-limits to civilian personnel. Anything else I can do for you, sir?"

Samuel shook his head, backed up, and drove toward Tuskegee. He still couldn't get the roar of the airplane out of his mind.

The campus was smaller than he had imagined: Buildings stood in neat rows, their redbrick structures gleaming in the sun. He parked his car and strolled along the campus, stopping at the statue memorializing Booker T. Washington, who had founded the Institute in 1881. He stared at the figure on the pedestal, trying to imagine the strength and courage of the man who defied all the obstacles that stood before him.

In the administration building he found the admissions office, and in the tiny cubicle bulging with stuffed bookshelves, he saw a man, small, with wire-framed glasses perched on his nose, at a desk.

"Can I help you?" There was an amused smile on the man's face.

Samuel removed his Western hat. "My name is Samuel Sharps. I've been accepted into the fall semester."

The man rose and extended his hand. "I am Professor LeBaron. I assist with admissions this time of year, but my primary position is professor of agriculture." He scanned a ledger in front of him. "I see you're majoring in agriculture. No doubt you'll take one of my classes."

Samuel nodded nervously and fumbled with his hat, not knowing what to say.

LeBaron knew what was going through his mind. "We need to get you enrolled and figure out class schedule." He looked again at the ledger. "There is one problem." LeBaron tapped the ledger softly. "In your application you didn't request dormitory facilities."

"Why is that a problem, sir?"

"Limited facilities, Mr. Sharps. Now that the army has begun training young Colored men to become fighter pilots, our dormitories are overflowing."

Samuel looked dejected. He looked around feeling foolish. "I guess I can find a place in town."

LeBaron laughed. "This is Alabama, Mr. Sharps, not Arizona. A young Colored man can't just go and 'find a place in town.'"

Samuel was beside himself. He had come so far to fulfill a dream and now it might be ruined because he had overlooked an important detail. "I suppose I could sleep in my car."

LeBaron looked at him strangely, then burst into laughter. "I don't think that would be a healthy way for a student to attend college." He paused, then added, "May I make a suggestion?"

Samuel nodded. "I'd be grateful."

"I have a place outside of town that I'm preparing for young men in your situation. There's four rooms, two beds to a room. It's clean and away from folks in town. I have one more vacancy. If you don't mind living in the country."

Samuel beamed. "Not at all. I grew up on a ranch in Arizona. I know all about living in the country."

"That's good. I think you'll like the accommodations. You'll receive breakfast and supper seven days a week as part of your rent. My daughter will do the cooking, but you'll have to share household chores with your roommates."

"That sounds fine with me, Professor."

LeBaron sat back down and took out a form. "Now, let's get started with enrolling you in your classes."

They worked together determining what classes he would need: biology, English, mathematics, and others until Samuel said, "I'd like to take ROTC."

LeBaron looked at him with surprise. "You want to become an army officer?"

"No, sir. I want to become an army aviator. That's why I chose Tuskegee Institute. I can do both while going to college."

LeBaron sat back and studied him closely. "Do you have a pilot's license?"

"Not yet. But I intend to take primary flight instruction from a man named Charles Anderson." He handed LeBaron the letter he had received from Sparks Hamilton.

"I set aside enough money for the training."

LeBaron shook his head. "There's thousands of young Colored men trying to get into the flight program. Most have been rejected for one reason or other. Most all are college graduates and have pilots' licenses."

"I think that will change when we get into the war, Professor. I want to be ready to do my part."

"You think there will be a war, Samuel?"

"Yes. Our country can't stay out of the ruckus much longer."

LeBaron filled in the last blank with the words "Reserved Officer Training Corps," and handed him the form. "Classes start on

Monday." He wrote out the directions to his home, and watched Samuel walk out. The professor had filled his boardinghouse with eight tenants in the last two days, each one an agriculture student; all were strong and had worked on farms, and now this one was a rancher.

Only two were pursuing the ridiculous notion of becoming army aviators.

Samuel followed the directions to the house that was only a few miles from the Institute. He parked in front beside two other automobiles with out-of-state license plates. He took his suitcases and started up the steps when he heard the sound of voices near the side of the house. Two men in their early twenties appeared wearing work clothes.

"Good afternoon," said one of the men. He was tall and lanky and had a thick mustache. The other nodded, a heavyset man with a shaved head.

"I'm Willis Reeves," the tall man said, offering his hand. "Are you a new tenant?"

"Yes. My name is Samuel Sharps." He extended his hand. "Professor LeBaron sent me here. I'll be bunking with you fellows."

"Daniel Cook," the heavyset man said as he shook hands. "Looks like you and I'll be sharing a room." He took one of Samuel's suitcases and went into the house.

The smell of fresh paint and fried chicken greeted him in the front room of the boardinghouse. Samuel looked around, pleased with what he saw. There was a parlor, then a hall leading to the bedrooms. He put his suitcases beside an empty bed and looked around. He looked through the window and saw a woman walking through the backyard. She carried a chicken, freshly beheaded and plucked.

"Does she live here?" Samuel asked.

Reeves laughed. "You'd think she owns the place. Her father is Professor LeBaron. Her name is Shania."

Samuel said her name softly. She was the most beautiful woman he had seen in his life.

"We better get back to work," said Cook.

Samuel turned to them. "Do you need some help?"

Both laughed. "We're digging a hole for the outhouse. You sure you want to help?"

Samuel grinned. "I've dug plenty of outhouse holes in my time."

The two left while Samuel put on his work jeans and boots. He went through the kitchen and saw the young woman standing at the sink. She looked up from the chicken she was preparing. "I hope you like chicken. Papa called and said we had a new tenant for supper. He said you was a big man and I should fix another chicken. You look like you could eat a whole frier by yourself."

"I could eat a horse."

Shania laughed. "I hope chicken will do."

He took off his hat. "I'm Samuel Sharps."

She wiped off her hands on a wet cloth and shook his hand. "I'm Shania LeBaron. Supper is at six."

He clamped his hat on his head. "I better go help the fellows with the digging."

Samuel walked to the back, where he found Reeves and Cook digging a trench; a small wooden house stood nearby, the white paint still drying in the heat. A zinc-lined vat lay on the ground. That would serve as the septic tank, preventing contamination of the ground.

The three worked together. Cook dug with a pick, while Reeves shoveled the dirt into a wheelbarrow, and Samuel hauled the dirt to a nearby mound. After two hours of digging and shaping, the three hefted the zinc liner into the trench. Finally, the small outhouse was placed over the hole and the three stood looking at the structure.

Cook said, "I've never used outdoor facilities before. We had indoor toilets on our farm back in Virginia."

Reeves laughed. "I grew up on a tobacco farm in Kentucky. All we had was outhouses. You'll get used to the smell. It's the winter cold that makes you miserable."

"I wouldn't mind the cold right now," Samuel said, wiping the sweat pouring from his body. "Is the humidity always this bad?"

"It can get even worse," Reeves said, "but in the winter it'll sink into your bones and freeze you half to death."

So much to learn, Samuel thought. A voice called from the back porch. "You boys done a good job."

Samuel looked up to see a young man wearing an army uniform. His hat was cocked to the side and he stepped off the porch with a swagger. A patch on his left shoulder was that worn by ROTC. He had light skin, a thin mustache, and stood as tall as Samuel. "Afternoon, gents. I'm Thomas Guillard, your new roommate." He shook hands with the three and looked around the place. "Reminds me of home back in South Dakota."

"South Dakota?" Reeves asked. "I didn't know there were Negroes in South Dakota."

"Lot of Coloreds have lived up there over the last seventy years," Guillard said. "My granddaddy served there in the army."

Samuel looked at him curiously. "Was your grandfather in the cavalry?"

"The Ninth Cavalry. Fought at Milk River along with the Seventh. That was the last big battle of the Indian campaigns. There wasn't threats from Indians after that, so when he retired he married a Sioux woman, bought a piece of land near Belle Fourche, and started farming."

Samuel felt a bond with this young man. "My grandfather retired a Sergeant Major with the Tenth. Our family lives in Arizona and raises cattle." He looked at Guillard's uniform admiringly. "You're in ROTC."

"Just picked up my uniform this afternoon." He straightened in military fashion. "How do I look?"

"You look great. You look like the grandson of a soldier," Samuel said.

Shania's voice interrupted through the kitchen window. "Better wash up, fellows. Supper will be ready in thirty minutes."

The diggers washed while the soldier inspected the outhouse. He seemed familiar with the structure and its purpose.

The other roommates arrived just before supper was served. During the meal LeBaron suggested, "Why don't you gentlemen tell us a little about yourselves." He looked at one of the new arrivals.

"I'm Delbert Hughes, from Pennsylvania. I'm an agriculture major."

They listened as the others introduced themselves. Austin Braxton from Tennessee, Fillmore Hall from Indiana, and Terrence Spann from Illinois. All raised on the farm.

LeBaron looked at Guillard. "What about you, Mr. Guillard?"

Guillard shrugged. "I grew up on a wheat farm in South Dakota. My grandfather was Colored, my grandmother a half-breed Sioux. Her father was a white man." He could see they wanted to know more. "My mother is a white woman."

The forks stopped in midair.

"Your mother is white?" asked Reeves.

Guillard nodded. "White as winter."

Cook shook his head. "Down here a white woman would be jailed."

"Or lynched," Braxton snapped.

Samuel wondered aloud, "Wasn't it tough growing up with a white mother and Colored father?"

Guillard shook his head. "Folks in South Dakota aren't prejudiced against Colored. Just Indians. They hate them so much they don't have any spare hate or time to use it on Coloreds. We get along just fine."

"What did she look like?" Shania asked.

"She had blond hair, blue—"

Shania interrupted. "Not your mother. Your grandmother?"

"She looked like you," Guillard said.

Samuel thought of Chihocopee Jackson, and how he and Shania were similar in skin color.

LeBaron coughed and turned toward Samuel. "What about your family? Are they still living?"

"Yes, sir. At least my mother, father, and grandmother. She's getting old, but she's still spry." He told them about his family and the part the Sharps family played in settling the western frontier. The scalping. Buffalo Bill Cody. The Rough Riders. His father and uncle in the Great War. He even told them about him beating a tank on a mule.

"Sounds like you gentlemen have already had interesting lives," Patrice said.

"Wait until classes begin," Shania grumped. "Life will become very boring."

                                *   *   *

That night Samuel sat on the front porch oiling his Sharps. He sat looking at the moon as he rubbed the stock and barrel, and summarizing the days events in his mind. He later wrote a letter to his family, telling them about the trip from Arizona. The best part was the last half of the letter telling them about his first day in Tuskegee: He had seen an army airplane, enrolled at the Institute, signed up for ROTC, helped his new roommates dig a hole for an outhouse, made new friends, and eaten dinner with a cultured man and his beautiful daughter.

At the end he added . . . "Except for the digging and the humidity, I consider my first day at Tuskegee as being perfect."

He left out the incident in Mississippi, not wanting to alarm his family with the details.

15

*   *   *

Shania had been right, thought Samuel. He was sitting in biology class, listening to the professor outline the course for the semester. The nauseating smell of formaldehyde permeated the room, glass jars filled with animal specimens lined the bookshelves on the wall, insects were pinned to boards. The students were all young, the women wore dresses, and the men suits and tie. Except Samuel, who wore jeans, boots, and a Western shirt with a string tie. He looked as out of place as if he were a horse. But he could deal with that; he had always seemed out of place in school. In Bonita, he was the only Colored student at the school—the only Colored in town, for that matter. He had learned how to adjust to the surroundings and make the best of the situation.

He knew nothing mattered, except why he was here: to become an army aviator. If he earned a degree along the way, that would be fine. But the prize on this hunt was going to be more important than a ten-point buck. And more elusive.

At noon, he joined Guillard in the cafeteria, where they discussed the morning classes. Guillard wasn't wearing his uniform; he, too, was dressed like a Westerner. Students sitting nearby eyed them curiously, like they were something out of the past. Samuel felt their eyes and was beginning to feel uncomfortable when every eye in the cafeteria suddenly shifted to the doorway.

The man standing there wore an army uniform with captain's bars on his shoulders and on his lapel the insignia of an army aviation cadet. The officer was tall, thin, light-skinned. The captain walked to the serving line and took a tray, selected his food, and found an unoccupied table.

Guillard whispered, "That's Captain Benjamin O. Davis, Junior. He's a graduate of West Point. His father is a full colonel, the highest ranking Colored in the military."

"West Point?"

Guillard nodded. "Spent four years getting the silent treatment. Ate his meals alone and without a civil word from his classmates. Even his instructors ignored him in the classroom."

"What's he doing here? Is he an ROTC instructor?"

" 'Was.' He was an instructor here for several years. Now he's a trainee in the first aviation class at the army airfield. On paper it's called the Ninety-Ninth Pursuit Squadron. Except there's only trainees and no commissioned pilots, or fighter planes. Colonel Davis is in the first class. They started with thirteen. Now there's only six left."

Samuel remembered Sparks Hamilton talking about the all-Colored fighter squadron.

"He's part of what they're calling the 'Tuskegee Experiment.' To see if Coloreds can fly airplanes."

Samuel looked at Guillard with a stunned expression. "Of course Coloreds can fly airplanes. I know one with a commercial pilot's license. He gave me my first flight lesson."

Guillard explained how he had come to Tuskegee the year before. "I put in my application for the program, but I haven't heard anything in six months. I thought ROTC might be a boost, but it's no guarantee. I have a friend with a degree in aeronautical engineering, and he was sent to mechanics' school. He should have been an officer, but there's no openings in the Air Corps."

"There will be," Samuel said. "When the war starts there'll be plenty of room for Colored pilots. That's why I came here. Just like you—to fly in combat."

Guillard pointed to a man who had come into the cafeteria and sat with Davis. Like Davis, the man was in a uniform but wore no insignia of rank.

"That's Charles Alfred Anderson. They call him 'Chief.' He's the chief flight instructor for the primary flight school at Moton Field."

Samuel felt the letter from Hamilton burning in the pocket of his coat, and before he realized what he was doing, he was standing in front of Anderson. "Good afternoon, Chief Anderson. My name is Samuel Sharps." He pulled the letter from his pocket. "This is from Sparks Hamilton. I believe you know him?"

Anderson smiled as he took the letter, and asked, "How is that old barnstormer?"

"I saw him in April, and he was fine. It was Sparks who told me about Tuskegee. That you might teach me to fly airplanes."

Anderson read and replaced the letter and handed it back. "Sparks suggests you get into the CPT program. But our program is filled, and there are thousands of applicants. Most of them are college graduates."

Samuel's disappointment couldn't be concealed. "Then I've come all this way for nothing."

He heard Davis say, "I find it hard to believe a young Negro man would think a college education is wasted. It's going to be more important to you in the long run than flying airplanes."

Samuel face flushed. "Yes, sir. I know an education is important. But my father and grandfather both served in the military and fought in all the wars since the Indian campaigns."

Anderson and Davis waited for Samuel to continue.

"My grandfather served for thirty years in the Tenth Cavalry. My father served with Colonel Roosevelt's Rough Riders in Cuba. Twenty years later, he lost his left arm in the Meuse-Argonne serving with the Ninety-Third Division. They were the first Coloreds to serve during those periods. I feel a need to do the same. It's family tradition, and I want to be one of the first Coloreds to become an army aviator."

Davis found this interesting. His own father was a colonel, and commanding officer of the 4th Brigade at Fort Riley, Kansas.

Samuel had turned to leave when Anderson said, "Maybe you can earn a private pilot's license. With that and your ROTC, you might have a better chance to get into the program."

A slight smile crept across Davis's mouth. Anderson continued, "Come out to Moton Field Saturday around three o'clock. We'll talk about your flight instructions. But lessons don't come free."

"I've got the money. I'll be there," Samuel said.

He could barely eat supper, he was so excited. This prompted Shania to ask, "Are you sick, or does the food taste that bad?"

Samuel looked at the ham, potatoes, and lima beans. "The food is wonderful. I'm just not hungry tonight."

"Something bothering you?" asked LeBaron.

Guillard answered all their questions. "He spoke with Chief Anderson today about flying lessons."

This brought an immediate response from Shania, one that made her father cringe. "The Chief is a wonderful instructor. I've started taking flying lessons from him."

All the boarders stopped eating at once, staring at her in disbelief. She speared a piece of sliced ham with her fork. "Men aren't the only ones who can fly."

LeBaron ate in silence, as did the others. Samuel and Shania talked about flying.

"I liked the loops the best," she said.

Samuel remembered Sparks flying one particularly thrilling maneuver. "The chandelle is the most difficult. It requires a pilot to use precision airspeed and climb while executing a one-hundred-eighty-degree turn."

They talked as though they were sitting alone in a restaurant. Long after the table had been cleared they continued to talk, until LeBaron interrupted. "Time to go home, Shania."

Samuel stood at the door and watched the walk to the professor's car. As they drove away he heard Guillard's raucous laughter coming from the kitchen. He walked past them and went to his room, where he sat at his desk and opened one of his books. The words ran together as he could only think of one thing: Shania.

16

John Parks first arrived in Tucson in 1918, coughing and choking on a cot anchored to the floor of a hospital train transporting wounded soldiers to various hospitals throughout the country. Government hospitals were overflowing with the wounded from the Great War, and Parks was sent to Tucson for a particular reason: The dry climate would help his respiratory condition, caused by a mustard gas attack at Verdun.

Twenty-four years later he stepped down from the Pullman passenger car onto the same platform, but nothing looked the same. The platform was nearly empty; now there was laughter from children and the hustle and bustle of passengers arriving and departing.

He was a thin man, bent and frail, his voice no more than a rasping sound, his black forehead gleaming with perspiration. The most captivating feature of the man was the glass monocle he wore on his right eye.

"Can I help you with your valise, Mr. Parks?" a voice called from the step of the Pullman.

Parks turned to see a Colored porter step onto the platform and approach, his hand extended. The man took his valise and the two began walking toward the baggage area of the station.

The porter, a member of the Brotherhood of Sleeping Car

Porters, had been helpful to Parks since the older man boarded the train in El Paso the previous morning. "You're going to burn up wearing that dark suit here in Tucson, Mr. Parks."

Parks shook his head. "No, young man. The heat feels good on these old bones. Not like the cold of Colorado."

The porter stayed with him until his baggage was loaded into a taxicab. He gave the young man a tip, and they shook hands. From his wallet he removed two pieces of paper. One was old and frayed, the writing barely readable. The other, which he handed the driver was clear, the writing only two weeks old. "Take me to this address, please."

Fifteen minutes later, the taxi stopped at a large home on the east side of town. In front was a sign that read BOARDINGHOUSE. A smaller sign attached beneath read VACANCY.

Parks's mind seemed to drift back in time, as though recalling how the house looked different. Where there once had been dirt for a yard, there was a thick carpet of grass. Flowers lined the sidewalk and edge of the house. A large swing was suspended from the ceiling of the front porch. The taxi driver carried his trunk to the porch, where Parks paid the fare, then left. He walked inside the house and was greeted by a woman sitting in the parlor.

"Good morning. Can I help you?" she asked. The woman appeared to be in her thirties, trim, with cinnamon-colored skin. She held a baby in one arm, a basket of laundry in the other.

"I am the Reverend John Parks. I believe you're expecting me." He handed her a letter he had received two weeks before.

The woman read quickly, then said, "I'm Abigail Withrow, Reverend. Your room is waiting."

He started to pick up the trunk. "Leave it, Reverend. My husband will carry it to your room."

He nodded his appreciation and, with valise in hand, followed her to a room in the back of the house. "I was surprised when your letter requested this particular room. I'm glad it was vacant."

Parks nodded politely and looked around amid a flood of memories. "So am I, Mrs. Withrow. Are you related to Mattie Withrow?"

"She was my mother-in-law."

"*Was* your mother-in-law?"

"She died five years ago. Her son and I took over the boardinghouse. He drives a truck for a shipping company here in Tucson, and I run this place."

"Sounds like you have a good life."

She held up the baby. "This is Jason, our first child."

"He's a fine-looking child."

She could see he was tired. "Why don't you take a nap. I'll call when it's suppertime."

He sat on the bed, removed his coat and necktie, and lay back. He recollected the times he had lain staring at this very ceiling in 1919, not certain if he would wake up to see another day. He took the faded paper from his wallet, and though the writing was barely legible, he knew the name and town by heart. He had read the name many times over the past twenty-four years since it was given to him by an extraordinary Colored woman after he was brought to Tucson—to this very house—to recuperate from his wounds.

At last he drifted off to sleep, the face of the woman as clear in his mind as if it were yesterday: a good woman with the most un-usual hairpiece he had ever seen.

A hairpiece made from the fur of a buffalo robe.

Hannah had just finished washing the dishes when the telephone rang. She hurried to the wall, hoping to hear Samuel's voice, and was momentarily disappointed to hear a raspy ancient-sounding voice. She walked into Selona's room, where she was reading her Bible.

"Grams, there's a long-distance call for you."

"Is it Samuel?"

"No. It's a man with a very strange-sounding voice."

"What kind of voice?"

"Sounds like a creaky old wagon wheel that needs greasing."

"Did he give a name?"

"Reverend John Parks. He said he met you and Vina Gibbs dur-ing the Great War. It was after the Sergeant Major died. He said he was sent to Mattie Withrow's boardinghouse for recuperation."

Selona searched her memory but couldn't recall the name. She picked up the receiver. "This is Selona Sharps. How may I help you, Reverend Parks?"

She talked for nearly half an hour, then hung up the receiver. She rose from her bed and went to the parlor where she found Adrian and Hannah talking in low, conspirational voices. She said nothing, but wore a mysterious smile as she walked to the kitchen and poured a cup of coffee. She waited what for she figured was long enough to have them both sitting on the edge of their chairs with curiosity.

Adrian sat staring at her, perplexed by her attitude. "Well?"

"Well what?"

He shifted in his chair. "I understand you had a gentleman caller."

Selona sipped her coffee, her eyes wide as she looked over the cup at Adrian. "A very fine gentleman."

"Who is he, Grams?" Hannah asked.

Selona placed her cup on a small table. "A young soldier I met in Tucson, back in nineteen-nineteen."

"What did he want?" Hannah said.

Selona picked up the cup and sipped. "He wants to take me to dinner."

Adrian and Hannah stared at each other incredulously. There was only the sound of Selona sipping her coffee.

And the mysterious twinkle in her eyes peering over the rim of the cup.

As if on cue, Adrian offered to drive her to Tucson. "I have some business I'd like to tend to in Nogales. It'll only take a day."

Hannah looked at him suspiciously. "What kind of business do you have in Nogales?"

Adrian stood and left the room under the skeptical eyes of his mother. He said nothing as he went to his desk where he sat late at his desk, poring over figures he had compiled for a business venture he had planned for nearly a year. He knew it would cause problems with Hannah, and perhaps his mother, once she knew the name of the man he would approach with his proposal. But there was opportunity on the horizon, and he would not sit back and watch others capitalize while he let the chance slip through his fingers.

Even if it meant he had to deal with a notorious bandit.

17

Selona had promised her grandson Jonathan she would visit his family in Tucson before the summer ended, and with the telephone call from John Parks, she found a perfect reason for the journey. She had spent the next day packing her trunk, making certain she had a different hat for each of the five days she would be gone. She loved hats, loved traveling, although she had done little in the past few years. Her arthritis gnawed at her back and hips; at her age, a jouncing car was worse than riding a covered wagon in 1885 from Fort Davis to Fort Grant.

Adrian had decided to take her in the Packard, combining business with a brief visit with his nephew. He had an idea that would require traveling to Mexico for a few days. Then he could pick up his mother and bring her home. Hannah decided to stay home, but Theresa wanted to see her son and grandchildren and spent the day before packing.

The midmorning was already hot as the three drove away from Sabre Ranch. Clouds were forming to the south, prompting Selona to give Adrian a warning. "You might run into bad weather down in Nogales. You know them Mexican roads ain't nothing but narrow ruts in the dirt and get mighty treacherous. Reminds me of some old wagon trail."

"I'll drive careful, Momma." He glanced at Theresa, sitting in the backseat. "You look a little peaked, Theresa."

She looked out of the window. "I didn't sleep well last night. I guess the excitement of the trip's got me all on edge."

"Not me," said Selona. "It's got me all excited." She looked quickly at Adrian.

"Momma's got a beau," Adrian said. "I reckon she is a little excited."

Selona looked at him sternly. "I only had one beau in my life. That was your papa. Reverend Parks is just a nice young man wounded in the war." She shook her head, and said with amazement, "Imagine, after all these years he still remembered my name and where I live." She looked at Adrian. "I wish Hannah had come along. She could've gone with you to Mexico. Keep you out of trouble."

"I won't get into any trouble."

"You ain't carrying money to Mexico, are you?"

"No. I have a bank draft."

"Good. You might get robbed by Mexican bandits."

Adrian laughed out loud. "Mexican bandits! There hasn't been trouble with Mexican bandits since Pancho Villa."

Selona grumped and folded her arms. "The army never even saw him, much less caught him."

"Those days are gone. There's peace on both sides of the border. Even the cattle thieves have been chased out of business."

"Not all of them." She looked at him warily; he squirmed uncomfortably.

"What's that supposed to mean?"

"I know you're going to see that old thief Joaquin Samorran."

"What makes you think that, Momma?"

"There ain't nobody else in Nogales that's got money or power for a Colored man to do business with."

Adrian laughed. "Nothing slips past you, Momma."

"They should have hanged that man back in the thirties. Now he's a rich banker. Probably got the money for his bank by robbing other banks."

Adrian just shook his head in amazement. "I don't believe you trust anyone."

"I trust folks. But not Mexican cattle thieves. Especially a Mexican cattle thief who owns a bank."

"Joaquin's an honest man. Despite what you think, he isn't a thief."

Selona said nothing more on the subject. If he was fool enough to deal with a thief, there was nothing she could do. But she still had to give him warning. After all, she always figured meddling in the affairs of their children was a mother's privilege and duty.

They rode mostly in silence after discussing Samorran. Theresa slept quietly in the rear seat. Adrian drove, seemingly in deep thought, his fingers tapping a steering knob attached to the wheel.

Selona thought about John Parks. She remembered the young man over all the others she and Vina Gibbs had visited in Tucson. Both their mothers had been born slaves; both their fathers had been killed by the Indians while serving in the Buffalo Soldiers.

Several hours later, Adrian pulled off the road between Wilcox and Tucson and stretched a blanket between two tall cactus, giving them shade. Theresa spread a blanket, and food was supplied from a large wicker basket. They ate fried chicken and potato salad, sipped cool iced tea, then napped in the shade for an hour. When it was time to leave they cleaned up the area and repacked the automobile and continued the journey.

They arrived in Tucson at sunset.

Jonathan Sharps strolled casually through his restaurant to the vibrating sound of a mariachi band playing from a small stage. The dining area smelled of frijoles and fried meat and barbecue sauce.

Selona giggled as she saw Jonathan approach. How much he looked like his father! He was now thirty, slightly balding, with a thick, drooping mustache.

"Grams." Jonathan hugged Selona, then Theresa, and shook hands with Adrian. "Come on, folks. Let's go to the back and sit."

Like his grandmother and Aunt Hannah, he kept a special table in the kitchen for relatives and special guests to sit and talk away from the restaurant noise and clatter.

"What brings you to Tucson?" Jonathan said.

"To see you"—Selona looked at Adrian—"and give your uncle a chance to do some business in Nogales."

Adrian butted in, "Your grams has an old beau she's going to meet with tonight."

Jonathan looked puzzled and turned to Adrian. "What business do you have in Nogales?"

"Joaquin Samorran," Selona snapped.

Jonathan's eyebrows rose. "Samorran? Why do you want to deal with that old horse thief?"

Adrian gave both an angry glance and picked up a menu. "What's the special of the day?"

"Lobster. I have a fresh shipment in from Guaymas." He tightened his tie, suggesting something important was forthcoming. "I'm doing a little business in Mexico, myself, Uncle Adrian."

"What kind of business? Lobster?" Adrian asked.

"Among other things. Seafood. Lobster. Shrimp. Fish. Even clams. I'm going to start an import business."

"Seafood!" Selona said. "Folks around here don't know much about seafood. Fish and such never went well in a restaurant."

"That was before refrigeration. Now seafood can be delivered fresh and kept chilled until it's served."

"Seems like a lot of trouble just to add a few items to your menu." Selona said.

"Not just my menu, Grams."

"Whose menu are you talking about?"

"Menus in Phoenix, El Paso, Denver, even Kansas City."

"How does your plan work?" Adrian asked.

"I've got a man down in Nogales who will supply the trucks and drivers. He buys from the fishermen in Guaymas and sells to me. I've contacted several restaurants in the cities I mentioned. They're interested in having me supply them with fresh seafood."

Adrian suddenly looked very interested. "Who's your partner?"

A broad smile filled Jonathan's face. "Joaquin Samorran."

"Lord have mercy," Selona said. "You just called him a horse thief, and you want to go into business with him? You're crazier than Samuel. All he wants to do is fly like a bird. You're looking at crawling with snakes!"

"It's perfectly legal. We both have licenses from the American and Mexican governments."

Adrian saw a great potential in the plan. "You'll need a warehouse to store the merchandise before it's shipped to your customers. A warehouse that's near the railroad."

"I know of such a warehouse; I was going to contact the owner this week." Jonathan said.

Adrian smiled widely. "Is that right?"

"What's so funny?" asked Selona.

"You know that piece of property I own in Wilcox?" Adrian asked.

"You mean that piece of land with that run-down old barn outside of town?" Selona said.

"Yes, Momma. That barn could be turned into a warehouse with just a little effort. It would be perfect. We could run east and west on the Southern Pacific. They have refrigerated boxcars and reasonable freight prices. We could have everything set up and ready to go by the time the war starts."

Selona said, "There you go again, Adrian, making plans on something that ain't even happened."

Jonathan didn't agree. "Uncle Adrian's right, Grams. There is a war coming, and this country is going to change. There's going to be a lot of opportunity for new business. Forts and training centers will have to built in the central part of the country, not just on coastal areas. Just like during the Great War. My plan includes having agents acquiring orders from restaurants, hotels, even Officers' Clubs at the military installations. Officers can afford lobster and other seafood delicacies, especially at the prices we'll be giving the customers. We can undercut the West Coast outfits since we're dealing with fishermen in Mexico. Those poor folks will be glad to sell their seafood at a higher profit. Makes a better life for both sides."

Maybe he was onto something, Selona was telling herself. But she didn't like the idea of profiting off the horror of war. Then again, she knew if there was a war, someone always profited. Why not her family? Selona looked at Adrian. "You still want to turn that warehouse into a shipping point? I thought you wanted to go into the cattle-processing business?"

Adrian sipped some coffee. "We could do both. The company could ship seafood and processed beef from the same warehouse. The agents could sell both products."

Selona shook her head. "That'll cost you more money than you can afford. We are still in a bad way all over the country as far as the economy."

"We could do it if we had one more partner with a piece of money to invest," Adrian said.

"Did you two have this planned?"

Before they could answer a voice came from the door leading to the dining room. "Why, Mrs. Sharps. I thought that was you."

Selona studied the man.

He bowed politely. "I'm John Parks. You used to visit me at Mattie Withrow's boardinghouse back during the Great War."

She stood and extended her hand. "John Parks. I swear, it's been ages. It was so wonderful of you to remember me after all these years. Where in the world have you been?"

"Denver, Colorado. I returned to Tucson for my health. I liked Colorado, but the winters were more than I could bear."

Selona said to Adrian, "Mr. Parks was wounded by mustard gas at Verdun. He served in the Ninety-Third Division, just like you and David. His father served with the Ninth Cavalry during the Indian campaigns."

Adrian said to Parks, "My brother and I served as infantry officers in France with the Three-Seventy-Second Regiment."

Parks shook his head. "I served with the Three-Seventy-First Regiment."

"The draftee regiment," Adrian said reflectively.

"That was the only Colored regiment composed of draftees. The other regiments were volunteers and National Guard units. We trained at Camp Jackson, South Carolina, then shipped out to France. I suffered from mustard-gas poisoning and was sent to Tucson for hospital care, where the climate was more suitable to my condition. The problem we faced was that Tucson didn't have a large hospital system, so the government recruited dozens of homeowners to take in soldiers recuperating from the deadly gas. Doctors would visit the homes on a daily basis, seeing to the needs of the wounded."

"That's how we met," said Selona. "He was placed in Mattie Withrow's boardinghouse. Vina Gibbs and I used to visit the Colored soldiers sent to Tucson." She shook her head in amazement. "What have you been doing all these years?"

Parks shrugged. "When I was released in 1919, I returned to Kentucky, and graduated from the seminary at Knoxville College. My health continued to deteriorate, and on doctor's orders, I returned to the dry air of the West. My wife and I moved to Denver, where we built a church and I ministered until her death in 1935. Then I moved to Colorado Springs."

"It's good to have you back," said Selona. "I expect you'll be preaching again before long."

Parks shook his head sadly. "My voice can't reach beyond the pulpit, much less shake the pews and rafters. I'm afraid my days of preaching are over, Mrs. Sharps. I haven't preached a sermon in five years."

Selona reached over and affectionately patted his hand. "There's more to being a preacher than shouting the Victory, Reverend Parks. I'm sure a man of your education has a lot of usefulness."

"Not much usefulness for a wore-out old Colored preacher, Mrs. Sharps."

"What were you doing in Colorado Springs, these past years?" Jonathan asked.

"My brother owned a bank there, so I worked for him as a teller."

"You were a bank teller?"

"I was head teller and chief accountant for the bank. It's a small bank, so the work wasn't too demanding. The customers were mostly Coloreds and Mexicans living in the area, so the accounts were small compared to the white banks."

There was a sudden gleam in Adrian's eyes. He knew how to spot opportunity, and judging from the look on the faces of his mother and nephew, as they studied John Parks, he sensed they shared the same thoughts.

Jonathan's home was small, but cozy, large enough for his wife Renae and their three-year-old daughter Martha. Theresa doted on

Martha, always showering her granddaughter with gifts whenever she visited. The child was a juggernaut, constantly in demand of Renee's attention. Renae was short, with a large frame, reminding Selona of her friend Vina Gibbs.

They arrived late and it was obvious to Selona that Theresa was bone-tired.

"Theresa, you get ready for bed. I'll fix a pallet for Adrian. You and me can sleep together in the back room." She walked out but paused at the door. Theresa appeared to collapse on the bed.

In the front room she found the others already preparing a pallet for Adrian. Jonathan saw the worried look on his grandmother's face.

"Something wrong, Grams?"

Selona began helping, layering quilts onto the wooden floor until a thick pad had been formed. "Your momma's been feeling poorly. I think she needs to see a doctor while we're visiting."

Renae fluffed a feather pillow, then asked, "What's wrong with her?"

Selona shook her head. "I'm no doctor, but I think she needs to see a real doctor. Not that old sawbones in Bonita."

There was a worried look on Jonathan's face as he glanced at Adrian, who nodded solemnly.

"We can take her tomorrow, Grams, while the men are in Nogales," Renae said.

They finished making the pallet, then retired for the night. But Jonathan had trouble getting to sleep; his thoughts were pained by concern for his mother.

18

S amuel could not sleep, so, rather than sit and wait for the hour
to come he climbed into his car and drove to Moton Field. As
he neared the airport he heard the distinct sound of an airplane approach for landing.

In 1940, Eleanor Roosevelt and the members of the board of the
Rosenwald Fund of Chicago held its annual meeting at Tuskegee.
During her visit, the First Lady toured the campus and took an airplane ride with Chief Anderson. Mrs. Roosevelt had flown with
Amelia Earhart and had incurred the ire of her husband. At
Tuskegee, she again ignored the pleas of the Secret Service agents
and did as she pleased. Following the ride, the Rosenwald Fund
loaned Tuskegee Institute $175,000 to build an airport for CPTP
training. The field was named after Robert Russa Moton, an advocate of Negro aviation and the man who succeeded Booker T. Washington as president of the Institute. The airport had two parallel
grass runways, operations facilities, and hangar space for eight airplanes.

Samuel sat in his car watching the Piper Cub approach the
airstrip. He noticed that the plane was too high on the glide slope
when the pilot began slipping the aircraft to lose altitude and avoid
a stall. The wheels touched down with a crunch, then rose, por-
poising some ten feet in the air before settling to a slow roll. The

Piper taxied to a tie-down point, where a young Negro pilot shut down the engine, climbed from the backseat, and chocked the wheels. He wore a look of satisfaction on his face. Chief Anderson climbed from the front seat wearing a broad smile.

Samuel got out of his car and walked toward Anderson, who was angling toward the flight-center building.

"Good morning, Mr. Anderson."

"Most folks around here call me 'Chief.' "

Samuel followed him inside to a room with maps on the walls and stacks of training aids for flight instruction everywhere. Anderson motioned to a chair. "Samuel, what are you doing here?"

He was caught off guard by the question. "To learn how to fly, Chief."

Anderson shook his head. "Why did you come to Tuskegee? You could have gone to other schools and joined the program. Why Alabama? Don't you know how Coloreds are treated in the South?"

"My mother and grandmother asked the same questions. My grandmother was born a slave and my mother grew up in Florida. They wanted me to go to Southern Cal, but I wanted Tuskegee because I knew there was going to be an army airfield here for Negro flight training."

"Negro pilots aren't made very welcome in these parts. You should know that right off." Anderson pointed at the map, noting one special section. "The white man who owns this piece of property occasionally shoots at our airplanes, so we stay away from this area."

From the map, Samuel could see the property was near LeBaron's land.

"The man who owns the place—Creed Shilton—has put a few holes in the wings, but no one's been injured. Do you understand what I'm saying?"

"I might see combat before I get into the army?"

Anderson slapped his knees. "Let's get started."

"What's the first step?"

"Ground school. We have to get you ready to take your private pilot's test. That'll get you ready to take the test you'll need to get into the Air Corps."

"Will I get to fly?"

"You'll take flight instructions as you progress through ground school. But remember, the flight training means nothing if you don't pass the written exam. You can fail the exam, then take it again, but you won't get into the CPT program. You'll only get one chance . . . if you get that." He handed Samuel a book. "This is the private pilot handbook. Learn it by heart."

Samuel thumbed through the pages and understood Anderson's meaning: There was no room for error if he was to succeed.

Anderson put on his flying jacket, and said, "Are you ready to go for an airplane ride?"

Samuel was out of the door before Anderson could zip up his jacket.

LeBaron was in his fields with several of the boarders when he saw a long, black Cadillac approach. He knew the owner was Ron Munson, that bastard banker! The car came to a stop in the front and Munson got out. In his hand he carried a weathered briefcase.

The banker came to the side of the house and, in a pleased voice, said, "LeBaron, I believe you could grow crops in the desert. I hope you don't mind my dropping by without warning on a Saturday. I'm on my way to Montgomery and thought I would check on my investment. I'll be out of the bank for a week, so I thought I'd take care of our account on the way out of town."

The fields were lush and green, nearly ready for harvesting. "No bother at all." LeBaron looked proudly at the fields. "It took hard work, sir. But I do believe we're going to have a fine harvest."

Munson's fingers began tapping the briefcase, a signal to all his customers it was time to take care of business. LeBaron motioned to the house and they went into the parlor where he counted out his monthly installment and handed it to the banker.

"Here's your receipt," Munson said. LeBaron took the paper and put it in his desk.

"I better be on my way," the banker said, starting for the door. "I'm visiting my sister, and she worries when I'm late."

Munson left, and LeBaron returned to the fields, where he became lost as he walked into the tall corn.

*   *   *

Samuel stared in awe at the patchwork of multicolored fields surrounding Tuskegee. The flight had been as wonderful as the one
with Sparks Hamilton, only the Piper handled quicker, giving him
a feeling of what it must be like to fly a fighter plane. He shut his
eyes, trying to imagine closing on an enemy aircraft, his hands going
to the stick serving as his firing mechanism.

"Are you all right back there?" Chief Anderson asked over the
radio.

Samuel tapped him on the shoulder. "This is great!"

Anderson pointed to the ground below. "That's the area I warned
you about. Don't fly too close. The farmer that lives there hates Coloreds. The law won't do anything about it, so we just avoid the
area."

Samuel saw that the farm bordered on LeBaron's land, but the
fields were in great need of tending. "He's not much of a farmer.
Not according to his fields."

The Chief shook his head. "He's much better with a rifle."

Samuel looked again at the farm, and saw a long black automobile pull into the front of the farm. Then he felt the Piper bank hard
to the right and fly toward the east.

Creed Shilton sat drunk on the front porch of his rundown farm, a
.22 rifle cradled in his lap as he sipped corn whiskey from a Mason
jar. He didn't take his eyes off the sky, even while drinking, hoping
he might see what he called "silver crows." That was his way of re-
ferring to the airplanes flown by the Negro pilots from Moton Field.

Shilton, at forty-two, wore a black patch over his right eye, a reminder of Château-Thierry in France, where he was wounded in
1918. He had been married, with one child, when his wife ran off
with a traveling shoe salesman from Atlanta. That had been in
1930, and he had no idea where the child—a boy—was living, and
didn't really care. Overall, he considered his life a complete failure,
especially as he stared through his bloodshot eye at the forty acres
of corn he raised for his illegal whiskey. The crop was now rotting
in the field, dark and dry, and appeared equally miserable as
Shilton, who tried to rise and fell back cussing.

He started to right himself when he saw a long, black automobile stop in front of his house. He hawked and spit, and felt his stomach burn as he drowned another swig of corn whiskey.

Ron Munson stopped at the front gate, which hung from one hinge, and stared for a long moment at the shabbiness of the property on which he owned the mortgage.

"Afternoon, Mr. Munson. How y'all doin' today?" Shilton smiled broadly, rifle in one hand, whiskey jar in the other. His face was beet red, and Munson could smell his breath from where he stood.

"I'm saddened, Creed. I am truly saddened."

"Sorry to hear that, sir. You got illness in your family?"

The banker stared at the rifle, looking uncertain of his next words. "Not in my family."

"Then what?"

Munson pointed a chubby finger at the bootlegger. "The sadness is in my business. In you. I have not received a mortgage payment from you in three months. I thought I could trust you to keep your word, and I find you drunk and my property run completely into the ground." He looked around disgusted. "My better judgment should have prevailed. I should have known a piece of white trash like you couldn't manage his affairs."

Hatred burned in Shilton's eyes. His finger inched to the trigger. He watched Munson wiped the sweat from his face with a handkerchief.

"You ought not talk to me like that. I've just been down on my luck the past few months."

"More like down in the bottom of a Mason jar," the banker shouted. "I'll be leaving today with my money or I'll come back with the sheriff."

Shilton's voice broke. "You can't do that. This place is all I've got to my name."

"That's your problem."

"I don't have your money. I lost my crop, and I can't buy mash for my liquor business."

Munson knew Shilton was a bootlegger; a good one, but without corn he was just another unlucky farmer. "I'll send for the sheriff, Shilton. You leave me no choice." He started for his car when he caught a motion from the porch from the corner of his eye. He froze with fear as the burly Shilton stumbled toward him with his rifle raised.

Shilton fired a single shot, striking the banker in the left ear. Munson slumped over the edge of the door, then slid to the dusty road. A thin trickle of blood flowed from his ear into his dead eyes.

For a long moment, Shilton stood trembling, staring wild-eyed at the dead man. He looked around, saw no one coming along the road. He opened the trunk, dragged Munson to the trunk, hoisted him inside, and slammed the lid. He was sobering fast, as he climbed behind the wheel and drove the automobile to the rear of his house.

Shilton eased the car into the barn and covered it with a heavy tarpaulin, then raced to the house, clutching the banker's briefcase. He sat in the kitchen, his hands trembling, as he counted the money.

"Two thousand dollars," Shilton whispered to himself. He started to take another drink, then set the jar on the table. He stared long and hard at the whiskey as an idea formed in his liquored brain. He drained the last of the moonshine and stared at the barn. "You were wrong, Mr. Munson. I ain't white trash." He held up the money, as though the dead man could see and hear from within the barn. "I'm a moneyed man."

It was midnight before he went back to the barn, wanting to be certain the countryside had settled into a deep sleep. He took his lantern and walked to the automobile which he had parked in front of a row of baled hay. He wrestled the bale to the side, revealing a metal ring in the dirt. He gripped the ring and pulled. He felt the large trapdoor begin to rise.

Dust swirled when he started down the ramp that led to a large cavern beneath the dirt floor of the barn. Heavy wooden struts supported the sides of the room, thick beams supported the ceiling. In a corner sat large metal vats over black coals that had lain cold since he cooked his last batch of moonshine.

Shilton spent the next few hours sweating the alcohol from his system, bathed in the light of the lantern. He removed the dirt from the boards covering the ceiling of his still, then removed the planking. A long and wide opening yawned in the barn floor. After moving the vats to the far end, he was ready.

He put the car's transmission in neutral and pushed from the bumper until he felt the wheels move slightly, slowly inching toward the edge of the hole. When the front tires went over the lip the automobile lurched upward in the rear and pitched forward with an earsplitting crash. A storm of dust billowed from the hole, then began to settle.

Shilton took the time to replace the planking, making certain to smooth the dirt over it and pack it with his shovel. He spread hay on the dirt and wiped away the tire prints, leaving no trace of the automobile.

It was dawn when he staggered toward his house. He turned one last time to look at the barn. The banker would spend eternity in a vault that no other person knew existed.

Near noon, Shilton pulled himself from a deep sleep and stumbled into the kitchen. He hurriedly packed an old suitcase with his few belongings and went to his truck. He drove away from the farm slowly and carefully, not wanting to appear in a hurry.

He slowed only once as he saw another truck approach on the road. He recognized the driver and cursed the man beneath his breath.

LeBaron pulled to the side of the road, allowing Shilton's truck to pass easily. He didn't like the man, not because he was a racist. That was common among white farmers in Alabama. What he didn't like was Shilton's poor farming methods. His experience told him Shilton would lose his farm and acreage to the bank.

Further extending LeBaron's opportunity, who had plans for the forty acres once it was repossessed by the bank.

19

✫ ✫ ✫

It was Sunday afternoon when Adrian and Jonathan crossed the border to visit Joaquin Samorran. The tolling of church bells filled the dry air of Nogales, a dusty town seventy miles south of Tucson in Hermosillo province, a stone's throw across the border from its sister city of Nogales, Arizona. The immediate impact of poor sewage control was always expected, as the smell of urine and excrement stung their nostrils. The streets were crowded with villagers returning from mass, wearing brightly colored clothes that reflected centuries of the blending of Mexican and Indian cultures.

The terrain west of Nogales was rugged and barren, and, except for an occasional jackrabbit running through the cactus, there was no sign of life. The road consisted of two narrow ruts carved by automobile tires. Gone was the memory of wagon wheels and pullcarts, erased by the elements and progress.

Thirty minutes after leaving Nogales, Adrian spotted a building in the distance. "There it is."

The hacienda de la Samorran rose from the loamy earth like a castle totally out of place in the desert wilderness. A high wall surrounded the main house, and armed guards could be seen walking between the parapets at each corner. Adrian eased to a stop in front of the huge wooden gate at the entrance and honked his horn. The gate swung open, and a guard motioned them to enter.

They parked beside a Cadillac. "Looks like business is good for the old bandit," Jonathan said.

"You better watch your tongue, or Samorran will have it for supper," Adrian replied.

At the front door they were led into a huge library, where Joaquin Samorran sat at a large ormolu desk. He gave Adrian the impression of a king waiting to hold court.

"Come in, my friends." Samorran rose and motioned to two chairs as he came around the desk, his hand extended. He wore dark clothes; his thick beard and mustache were trimmed neatly, framing dark eyes that darted from Adrian to Jonathan as they shook hands.

Adrian looked around the room, impressed by the polished hardwood floors and the paintings adorning the walls. A large fan turned slowly overhead, giving a light and comfortable breeze to the library.

Samorran snapped his fingers, and a servant appeared carrying a tray with a decanter, three glasses, a small jigger of salt, and a bowl of sliced limes.

"Mescal?" Adrian and Jonathan nodded politely as the *patron* poured the thick liquor.

They drank Mexican-style, a drink of mescal, a pinch of salt, followed by the lime to cut the bitterness of the liquor.

Samorran sat in his large leather chair and leaned back, lacing his fingers as he studied the two men across the desk. "Have you discussed our business venture with your uncle?" he asked Jonathan.

Jonathan sipped at the mescal. "I have, and he's interested in becoming a partner."

He nodded approvingly at Adrian. "Your letter of last month said you are interested in cattle. Is that still an interest?"

"Yes," Adrian said. "I see an opportunity here to combine resources and form a larger and more profitable alliance."

" 'Alliance'? I like that word. It gives a sense of solidarity to the arrangement. Like two countries looking after each other's mutual interests."

"In a sense we will be like two countries. You and your associates on this side of the border. We and our associates on the other side. One cannot succeed without the other."

"You have a warehouse?"

Jonathan said, "My uncle has a warehouse near the railroad in Wilcox. It's large enough for both beef processing and seafood storage and distribution."

"What about a quarantine area for the cattle?" asked Samorran. He knew cattle brought from Mexico had to spend a period of time in quarantine to prevent disease from crossing the border.

Adrian assured him. "We'll build pens on the land behind the warehouse. Once the quarantine period is over, the cattle will be inspected and the processing will begin."

Samorran rose, and said, *"Esta bien."*

"We'll have our accountant contact yours. They can work out the financial arrangements," Jonathan said.

"Your accountant? Can he be trusted?"

"He can be trusted. He's a retired minister. What you would call a priest."

"A priest? I trust a priest with my soul, but not with my money."

"This priest is also a former banker. Your investment will be safe on the United States side of the border," Adrian said.

Samorran's eyes narrowed, chilling Jonathan.

Adrian didn't show any sign of intimidation as he asked, "I know you have the cattle in the province, so there shouldn't be a problem getting the beef we need. Can you show us your plan of operation for the seafood?"

Samorran spread a map of the Gulf of California on the desk and tapped his finger on a small village two hundred miles to the southwest of the gulf. "The seafood will be processed in Guaymas, then trucked to Nogales, where your agents will take possession upon payment to my agent." He looked at Jonathan. "You do have transport for the seafood to be shipped across the border?"

"I have contracted a trucking firm in Tucson. They will transport the seafood and the cattle to our warehouse in Willcox."

This pleased Samorran, and an hour later the details had been worked out to the satisfaction of all parties.

The Sharpses left as the sun was setting, both excited that the new venture was beginning to take shape.

20

Samuel was still flying the Piper in his mind while sitting in Professor LeBaron's agriculture class, when the door opened and three armed white men entered led by Frederick Patterson, the president of Tuskegee. Patterson was the third president of the Institute, a square-shouldered man with round, wire spectacles on a square face. LeBaron put down his chalk and walked slowly to them, a look of concern on his face. He stopped in front of Patterson, who spoke to him in a low voice, then followed the men into the hallway.

The professor returned a few minutes later, nervous and obviously distressed, to the front of the class and closed the folder containing his lecture notes. "That will be all for the day. Please read the next chapter for Wednesday." Without another word, he left the classroom, giving his daughter a worried glance on his way out.

The classroom slowly emptied, with only Samuel and Shania remaining behind. Samuel had come to understand the threat to a Colored man confronted by the Southern law. He had learned that in Mississippi, and knew there could only be trouble.

Shania was trembling as Samuel sat in the chair beside her. "My God, Samuel, what would the sheriff want with my father?"

Samuel knew LeBaron was a good and decent man; to be summoned from his classroom by the law was not to be taken lightly. Not in Alabama. "I'm sure there's nothing wrong. President Patterson is with him, so it must be a matter that concerns the Institute."

She knew he was trying to spare her torment, but she had lived in the South long enough to understand the undercurrents of such things as they had just witnessed. "If that's the case, why didn't they wait until the class was over?" she said.

Samuel had no answer. He, too, was becoming concerned. Racial tensions in Tuskegee were increasing as more Colored soldiers were arriving as part of the 99th Pursuit Squadron's support element. Segregation was being practiced at the army airfield along the same traditional lines followed by the civilians of Tuskegee and surrounding Macon County.

He eased her from the chair. "Come on," he said, "let's go over to the president's office. I'm sure they've got it all sorted out by now."

He took her arm and led her from the classroom, feeling her body quiver as he guided her through the door.

In Dr. Patterson's office a tall, lanky man in a dark suit took a small notepad from his shirt pocket. LeBaron recognized Paul Henderson, the county attorney, who studied his notes for a moment, then asked, "When was the last time you saw Ron Munson?"

"Mr. Munson?"

Henderson asked again, this time with impatience. "Yes, the banker. I understand he was out at your place on Saturday." He glanced again at his notes. "His secretary said he was going to stop there before going to Montgomery."

"He came by in the afternoon, collected the mortgage payment, then left. He said he was going to visit his sister in Montgomery."

There was a long pause. "He never made it to his sister's," Henderson said.

"I don't understand."

Henderson's voice grew angry. "His sister contacted the sheriff yesterday morning. Munson has been missing for four days, and you're the last person to see him." He glanced again at his notes. "According to his secretary, you were the only one he was to see before going to Montgomery."

LeBaron began to perspire as he shook his head in confusion.

"He was fine when he left. I paid him his money and he gave me a receipt."

"Where's the receipt?"

His mind tried to sort through the hundreds of thoughts colliding in his brain. "In my desk at the house I'm buying from Mr. Munson."

Henderson folded his notepad and put it in his pocket. "Let's go get it." He nodded at the door. The gesture was not a request; it was a command.

In the hallway, Samuel and Shania saw the group come out of Patterson's office.

She ran to her father and put her arms around him. "Papa, what's this all about?"

Before he could answer, a deputy stepped forward and pulled them apart, flinging Shania against the wall. "Stay out of this, girl. This is a legal matter."

Samuel stepped forward, his eyes boring into the deputy's. He had learned it was prudent to remain silent when dealing with the law, but there were lines that he would allow no one to cross. He gripped the deputy's wrist. "You don't have to be rough. She's just concerned about her father."

The lawman had a cold, lifeless stare, as though looking through Samuel to something down the hall. "Don't interfere, boy. This is none of your concern." His fingers tapped lightly on the butt of his pistol.

"Who are you?" Henderson asked.

"I'm one of Professor Lebaron's students, and one of his boarders."

Henderson couldn't help but notice the western accent. "You're not from around here, are you, boy?"

"No, sir. I'm from Arizona."

Henderson chuckled slightly. "Don't they teach nigras in Arizona not to interfere with the law?"

LeBaron now intervened, taking his student by the elbow. He whispered, "We'll get this sorted out in a short while." He looked desperately at his daughter. "Why don't you and Samuel go on to the library now."

Shania took Samuel by the arm and guided him down the hall.

"Don't they teach you anything out there in Indian country!" She seethed through gritted teeth. "This is Alabama! Not Arizona! You can't question a white man. Law or no law. Do you understand?"

Looking back, they saw the white men leading LeBaron down the hall in the opposite direction.

What Samuel didn't see was the mysterious smile on Shania's face. It was the first time in her life a man had stood up for her. More importantly, a Negro man standing up against a white man.

She walked with Samuel toward the library, feeling proud . . . and terrified!

The two stayed at the library as her father instructed, but neither could concentrate on their work. When the bell rang for the next class session to begin Samuel stood quickly and stuffed his books into his valise. "Come on," he said to Shania.

She grabbed up her books and followed as he walked furiously from the building and did not catch him until he reached his car in the student parking lot.

They sped from the campus and roared along the streets, both oblivious to the speed. Reaching the dirt road he was about to say something when Shania shouted, "Look out!"

An old Ford truck pulled out from the run-down farm that bordered on LeBaron's land. Samuel veered, nearly running off the road, and didn't see the drunk Creed Shilton shaking his fists and ranting like a lunatic from his truck, which was now in a ditch in front of his house.

Shania looked back, then covered her face with her hands, laughing so hard tears came to her eyes. "First you talk back to the county attorney and put your hands on a deputy sheriff; now you just forced the craziest racist in Macon County to run into a ditch in front of his own house. I swear, Samuel Sharps, you are the most unpredictable man I have ever known."

He shrugged. She went on, "You didn't know any better, that's all. Just like grabbing that deputy's wrist. You're lucky he didn't take out his gun and shoot you dead on the spot."

Samuel remembered Mississippi. "There were too many witnesses."

She shook her head in amazement. "You have a lot to learn."

"Like what?"

"First, you never look a white person in the eye. They don't like that from Negroes. Second, you step out of their way if they're walking in your direction. Third, you let them go first if you're standing in a line."

He shook his head. "I don't know if I can do that, Shania."

Her eyes widened. "But the most—*the most*—important thing: you never put your hands on a white man. Especially if he's the law."

"Is there anything else?"

"More than you can imagine. But those principles are enough to get you started at being a good, subservient Colored."

Before Samuel could say anything more they reached the boardinghouse. LeBaron was standing at the front gate with Henderson and the deputies.

LeBaron looked calm as he hurried to them. "It's all right. Mr. Henderson has seen the receipt from Mr. Munson." He held up the paper for them to see.

Henderson walked over to them. He looked suspiciously at the DeSoto, then at Samuel. "That car belong to you, boy?"

"Yes, sir. I have title and registration."

"Get the papers and show them to the deputy."

Samuel did as he was told, and for the second time he wished he had taken a train—or ridden his horse—to Alabama.

When the documents were checked to Henderson's satisfaction, he asked Samuel, "Did you see Mr. Munson leave here on Saturday?"

"I don't know Mr. Munson," Samuel said.

"Hell, boy, you can't miss him. He drives a big, fancy black Cadillac."

Samuel suddenly recalled the flight with Chief Anderson Saturday afternoon. He had seen a long, black car pull into the front of the neighboring farm. A farm owned by a white man.

Henderson could see that Samuel wanted to say something. "Well, come on, boy. Did you see a black Cadillac?"

"I was flying with Chief Anderson in his Piper on Saturday. We flew over this section of the county. He wanted to warn me about flying over a farm near here. He said the farmer shoots his rifle at the airplanes."

Henderson looked at LeBaron. "That's Creed Shilton. We've warned him about shooting at the airplanes, but we can't do anything until we catch him in the act." He said to Samuel, "Did you see anything that looked like a Cadillac?"

"I don't know if it was a Cadillac, but a black car stopped in front of the farm. I didn't see the driver, but I saw the car stop."

Henderson fell into momentary deep thought, and when he spoke, it was as though he was speaking aloud to himself. "Shilton's farm is between here and the highway to Montgomery." He turned to the deputy. "Let's get over to Shilton's place."

The lawmen started to leave. Henderson paused at the gate and pointed at Samuel. "You better not be wrong about this, boy."

Samuel stood frozen, fighting the need to glare, but felt Shania's fingernails digging into his wrist.

He had hunted the mountains of Arizona with white men and been treated with respect, had supplied game to American soldiers and beat one of their tanks fairly on a mule in a race and was treated like a man. Now he was called "boy" and "nigger," and was forced to chose between being called "Colored," or "Negro," to choose between pride or shame. But Shania's fingernails reminded him it was a time to be prudent.

He and Shania went inside. LeBaron followed, wearing a broad grin on his face. He was looking at Samuel's arm draped around Shania's shoulder. Her arm wrapped around his waist.

They heard Henderson's car racing toward Creed Shilton's farm.

Clouds of War

21

✫ ✫ ✫

Thanksgiving at Sabre Ranch was normally a joyous occasion for the Sharps family, but on this particular holiday Hannah felt a sadness at not having Samuel home for the festivities. The rest of the family had arrived the day before, a caravan from Tucson bringing Jonathan, Benjamin, his wife Francine, and their five year-old son Joshua. She was delighted the Reverend John Parks had joined the troupe. That would give Selona company and keep her out of the kitchen.

Adrian sat at the small table reading the latest letter from his son. Like the father he was, he didn't take for granted what Samuel had written. What concerned him most was what was missing.

"All that boy does is talk about flying and that young woman. He doesn't say anything about his schooling," he said.

Hannah's head tilted slightly as she recalled the day she had met Adrian. He was an officer candidate at Fort Des Moines, and she had just arrived in town and was staying at Selona's boardinghouse. She had been illiterate, but had she known how to write, she would have written about him and not the tedium of work.

Adrian shook the letter as though he was angry at the paper. "He better start concentrating on his schoolwork."

Hannah's voice carried a certain sadness. "Samuel has never had a girlfriend in his whole life. Now that he has one, you make it sound like it's unimportant. Well, it is important. A strapping young man like him is bound to find more interest in flying airplanes and pretty girls than stuffy old books."

"You mean you approve of him taking flying lessons?"

"I didn't say that, Adrian. I said he's starting to find out what's important to him as a man. All he's done in his life is hunt and ride horses. There were no Colored girls at his high school, and while he was the most popular boy at school, when it came to the local girls he was always reminded that there was that certain line that couldn't be crossed."

Adrian folded the letter and returned it to the envelope. "I suppose you're right. I imagine she's quite a fine young lady. She sounds beautiful, intelligent, and she loves flying."

Selona came into the kitchen. Her face was ashen, and she moved without her usual spryness.

Hannah said, "You feeling poorly, Grams?"

Selona didn't answer as she poured a cup of coffee and sat at the table. She sipped her coffee, staring at the envelope over the rim of the cup. "I wish he was here for Thanksgiving."

Hannah went to the icebox and took out a large turkey. She spread the legs and began stuffing it with her dressing. She was quiet for a moment, wishing for the same thing, but she knew it wasn't going to happen. She might as well get on with the business of what she had, not what she didn't have. "He'll be home for Christmas. I know he will."

Adrian found John Parks in the sitting room, staring at the long, curved sabre mounted above the fireplace mantel.

"That sabre belonged to my father when he served in the Tenth Cavalry," Adrian said.

"It's magnificent." He studied the sword for a long moment, as though listening to the weapon tell its glorious tale. "He must have been quite a man."

"The best I've ever known. He was more than a father. He was a friend and a teacher."

A sadness hooded Parks's eyes. "You're fortunate. I barely knew my father. We lived in Tennessee most of the time he was in the army. He was killed in the Spanish-American War."

"In what battle?"

"Las Guasimas."

Adrian remembered the battle. "I was at Las Guasimas. So was my brother and father."

"The Rough Riders?"

Adrian nodded. "All rough and no riding. At least, once we got to Cuba. Colonel Teddy was the only man on a horse. Most of our mounts drowned getting off the ships at Daiquiri. Didn't matter, though; the jungles were too thick for mounted cavalry, and the fastest way to move was on foot."

Parks watched as Adrian stepped to the mantel and brought down the sword. "My father gave me this when I left for the Great War. My brother David carried his father-in-law's sabre. His name was Sergeant Darcy Gibbs, and he was killed by one of Geronimo's Apaches."

"I recall seeing Sergeant Gibbs's grave in the cemetery. They must have been close friends."

Adrian held out the sabre, scanning the burnished metal scabbard.

"Did you carry the sabre throughout the war?"

Adrian nodded, then remembered something about the sabre he had never told a soul. Not even Hannah. "There was only one time I let it out of my sight during the entire war."

Parks didn't want to pry. He knew a man's thoughts about war were private. If to be shared, the memories must be offered, not requested.

Adrian looked at Parks, and said softly, "It was in the final push of the Meuse-Argonne offensive."

Parks sat in a chair and listened as Adrian's thoughts flashed back in time.

The tedium of the wait wears at a soldier more than facing the enemy. Adrian Sharps and his platoon had grown irritable and even sloppy in the previous two months waiting for the "big push," as the anticipated offensive along the Hindenburg Line was called.

The 372nd had been moved so many times from the frontline trenches to the rear for further training the men no longer believed there would be a big push.

September 23, 1918, found the 372nd at Dommartin-sur-Yvre, ten miles east of Sainte-Menehould, where the anticipation of the big push ran high.

That afternoon, Adrian and his platoon were bivouacked in the woods outside the village, cleaning their equipment in preparation for another move, this time toward the German lines.

He walked among his men and began chatting with Sergeant Hatch, one of his squad leaders, when First Sergeant O'Doul appeared. O'Doul, the white first sergeant of the company, was carrying a Chugach gun, a French automatic weapon that was drum-fed and heavier than sin. O'Doul motioned for Adrian.

He stood with the Chugach perched on his hip. "Lieutenant Sharps, the company is moving forward at zero-two-hundred. Your platoon will take the point." He walked away with a grin.

Adrian walked back to Hatch. "Get the men to ready their gear. We're moving out at zero-two-hundred." He looked around. "I've got something I need to take care of. I'll be back shortly."

Adrian picked up his rifle and removed his sabre from the back of his field pack. He made the short walk to where the Second Platoon was positioned, some two hundred yards away, and found David.

"I guess this is going to be the big push," David said.

"I think you're right. O'Doul has my platoon on point. He wouldn't do that unless we were going into a ruckus."

"I think you're right. God, that man hates you, Adrian."

"Not as much as I hate him." He paused, then held out his sabre. "I think we need to do something before we get moving."

"What do you have in mind?"

"Grab your blanket and come with me. I know someone who might help."

The two brothers walked a short distance to the village, where headquarters was located. The buildings were in typical frontline condition—mostly blown to hell—but served as a reference point for the companies.

Since their arrival in France, the 372nd had been trained by a company from the French Foreign Legion. The legionnaire company had been assigned to stay with the battalion command post and were easy to find. The building they occupied had no roof and only two walls.

Adrian found Captain Girard, the company commander, and Sergeant Watts, with their men, making final preparations for the move north toward the front. Watts was a Colored American expatriate who had joined the Legion to find a home. He had escaped from the New York police after killing a cop who was trying to beat Watts to death. They had become friends, and Adrian knew Watts could be trusted.

"Good evening, gentlemen. I hope you are prepared for the evening's activities."

Adrian shook hands with Girard. "We are, Captain. We sure as hell are."

"*Bon, très bon*. It will be, as you say, 'a real ruckus.' "

"A hellacious Harlem street brawl," Watts added.

Adrian said, "Sergeant Watts, I would like to ask you a favor. We're going to be at the point, and I'm sure you know what that means."

Watts nodded.

Adrian held out his sabre. "My brother and I want these to get back to our family in Arizona, should something happen to us."

"What do you suggest?"

Adrian knelt and spread the blanket on the ground. "Do you have a spade?"

He and David folded the blanket around their sabres, wrapping them tightly, then took a piece of heavy twine and bound the bundle.

Watts returned with a spade. Adrian walked to the corner and began digging where a large chunk of the flooring had been blown away.

When finished, he placed the bundle in the hole and covered it, then tamped down the dirt. He took a folded piece of paper from his pocket, and said, "Send them to this address."

Watts nodded, "I will, if I'm able."

Girard turned to the legionnaires and spoke in French while pointing at the corner. When finished, the men shouted in unison, "*Oui, mon capitaine!*"

Adrian looked confused. Watts said, "At least one of us here should survive. Your precious sabres will be returned to your family. You have the promise of La Légion Étrangère."

Adrian shook hands with Watts, and said, "When this war is over, you could possibly return to America. Perhaps under another name."

"No, my friend. The Legion is my home—my country. In France I am treated with respect. My race does not matter."

John Parks had listened attentively. He asked, "How did you recover the sabres? Did you go to the village after the Armistice?"

The question broke the reverie, pulling Adrian back to the present. He didn't want his mother to know they had been separated from the sabres; she thought they were some protective armor for him and his brother. They had survived months of combat unscathed, and the one battle in which they did not carry the sabres was the most disastrous of their lives.

"No," Adrian said. "I never wanted to see that hellhole again."

"Then how?"

He felt a sudden chill as he recalled the darkest day of his life; of the loss of a brother, friends, a part of his body, and his self-respect as a man and a soldier.

Adrian's arm was gone at the shoulder, and waking up he tried to move, but a bolt of lightninglike pain shot through his shoulder, then his body, driving him back onto the bed.

Through a haze he saw a white apparition approach and thought it might be an angel, and that he had "gone west," the American soldiers' term for killed in action.

"Lieutenant Sharps, I'm your nurse. You've been severely injured and you must remain quiet."

"How long—"

"You have been here four days. But you spent three days at a field hospital at the front before you could be transported to this hospital."

"A week?"

He then felt the cool, damp cloth wiping the perspiration from his face and the dryness in his mouth when he tried to speak. "Where am I?" he said in a hoarse whisper.

"In Paris. You're at the army hospital at Casernes de Vincennes. Now please, don't talk. You've lost a lot of blood."

He couldn't talk but he could think and he remembered David, Kenny, and Hatch, and the agony was far worse than any bullet could cause.

Four days later he still lay amid the stench of gangrenous flesh and the pitiful agony of the maimed and wounded filling the hospital ward. Hour after hour, more men were brought into the ward until many were sleeping fitfully or rolling in pain on pallets strewn about the floor.

He had come to realize that there was no glory in war.

The nurse's voice pulled him from deep thoughts. "I think it's time you got on your feet and moved about the ward, Lieutenant Sharps."

He shook his head, and a lightning bolt shot through the arm that was no longer there.

"I don't want to do anything except lie here," he said.

She perused his chart quickly. "You're not eating. You refuse to get out of bed. What do you want, Lieutenant Sharps? Do you want to die?"

He stared at her through hollow eyes. "You have others to take care of."

Her eyes sparked. She turned and walked away, only to return minutes later.

Her stern gaze softened, then she sat on the edge of his bed. "You have seen so much death. You've nearly been killed. How can you walk away from life so easily without a fight?"

"I don't have any fight left in me."

She waved her hand around the crowded ward. "A few hours ago I held a young boy who begged God to let him see the sun just one more time. Don't you want to see the sun? If not for yourself, then perhaps for him? He was one of your comrades. All he has now is the emptiness of death. You're alive, Lieutenant. You're alive! Don't let the war do to you in this hospital what it couldn't do to you on the battlefield!"

He wanted to say something; then she suddenly bolted upright from the bed. "There's something I have forgotten. Wait one moment."

She returned a few minutes later, saying, "This arrived for you this morning. A doctor coming from the front brought it to me. It's addressed to you."

In her hands she held a long parcel wrapped in a cloth, bound by twine.

She loosened the twine and carefully removed the cloth.

Two dented sabres, both blackened by time, each scratch on the hilt and scabbard a proud battle scar, lay on the bed.

"They do belong to you?"

His eyes glistened. "Yes. This one belonged to my father. The other to his best friend, my brother's father-in-law."

"Which one is yours?"

He pointed to the one she now held in her left hand.

With his only remaining hand, he gripped the metal scabbard, felt the weight of it.

He remembered the words of his father, telling him the sabre would remind him of who he was, where he came from, and the sacrifice made by his family in defending his nation.

He pressed the scabbard against his face, tears running onto the dented metal.

The nurse held an envelope. "There is a letter for you as well."

"Would you open it?"

She nodded and opened the envelope and unfolded the letter. "It is in French. Do you read French?"

He shook his head and suddenly felt a deep sadness.

"I will read it for you," she said as she unfolded the letter.

" 'Dear Lieutenant Sharps,

'As promised, here are your beloved sabres. I wish you a speedy recovery and safe journey to America. Sergeant Watts would have sent them, but he was killed at Monthois. France has lost a great soldier. We have lost a great friend. *Au revoir, mon ami.*

François Girard, La Légion Étrangère' "

Adrian wiped at his eyes, then stood shakily as the nurse placed her arm around his waist, and Adrian walked to the door, stepped onto a balcony, and stared into the sunlit sky.

Adrian released a long breath, then returned the sabre to the pegs over the mantel. He had shared this personal episode of his life with a man he hardly knew, but Adrian trusted Parks. They, too, were brothers.

Adrian stared again at the sabre and thought: There's much to be thankful for. He had not enjoyed a large piece of the American dream, but he had a slice.

Though small, a slice is better than none at all.

22

Were it not for Shania, Thanksgiving would have been the worst day of Samuel's life. All the boarders were taking the holiday meal with other families, and he would have eaten alone had he not been invited to dinner at the LeBarons'.

This was an interesting day for him. Since arriving in Tuskegee his days had been filled with school, flight training, and returning to the boardinghouse to study and sleep. He knew little of the town except that Tuskegee was a Muskhogean Indian word for "warrior," and that the Coloreds lived in their own section, a dreary part of town. The only affluence in the Negro community appeared among those employed by the Institute, or by the Veterans Administration hospital.

When he drove up in his shiny DeSoto the children gathered at Professor LeBaron's driveway and stood gawking as though they had never seen a young Colored man driving such a fine car. It made him feel good, and sad, knowing he truly had something to be thankful for on this day.

"Happy Thanksgiving, Samuel." LeBaron stepped onto the front porch of his frame house, puffing his pipe. He wore a shawl over his shoulders, and he seemed to Samuel to appear frail.

They went inside, and it was as though Samuel was swept back in time. The smell of turkey roasting, corn boiling, sweet potato pie cooling on the counter all brought back thoughts of home.

Shania giggled at him standing there in his Western clothes, fumbling nervously with his big cowboy hat. But the glint in her eye gave her true thoughts away.

After dinner, after the dishes were washed and dried, they sat in the front room and exchanged family remembrances. LeBaron told stories of his boyhood, growing up in the Smoky Mountains of North Carolina, where his father was a farmer and his mother a teacher at an Indian school.

"The most memorable Thanksgiving was when we gathered at my Aunt Peach's house in 1914," he said. "She was a wonderful cook, and could bake a turkey that was out of this world." He settled back, eyes narrowed, as though trying to see more clearly through a rain-streaked windowpane. "She had a whole passel of dogs. Bluetick coonhounds. They're a great breed of hunting dog, with their blue-black and tan patches of color on their fur, big floppy ears, and long tails. They were always on the move, always running through Aunt Peach's house. Well, just as it was getting to be sitting-down-to-dinner time, we heard this terrible scream from the kitchen. We all went running and found Aunt Peach standing by the stove, holding the remnants of a twenty-pound turkey. She had put the bird on the table to cool, and the dogs had got hold of it and devoured it while she was in the front room visiting with all of us."

Shania giggled. "At least the dogs had something to be thankful for."

"I guess that ruined the dinner," Samuel said, nearly laughing.

"Not quite," LeBaron said. "She ran outside to the woodshed and returned directly carrying a skinned possum. My uncle was a trapper and sold the meat. That's how he supported his family. Trapped and hunted for meat in the fall and winter. Fished the rivers in the spring and summer with big hoop nets and trotlines. Aunt Peach cut up the possum, putting each piece in flour and into a skillet. It wasn't more than thirty minutes before we were all sitting at the table saying grace." He lifted one eyebrow. "Of course, the dogs had to stay outside."

The conversation moved from North Carolina to Arizona, and Samuel shared his memories of Thanksgiving. He discovered that he was no longer homesick. He was with family.

LeBaron retired for his afternoon nap. Samuel wasn't sure if he should leave or stay when Shania said, "Let's go for a drive."

They drove north toward the airfield, windows down, the cool breeze whipping through Shania's hair. He could barely keep his eyes off her, and realized it was the first time he had ever been alone with a woman his age. Like being on a date, but not really. He knew he had never been on a date; even at his high-school graduation, he had to go alone to the dance.

She had been quiet, her gaze straight ahead, when Samuel slowed and pulled off the highway. In the distance he could see the airfield, the buildings gleaming from the fresh coat of white paint. He hoped he might see an airplane, but knew since it was a holiday there wouldn't likely be any flight activity.

He got out and leaned against the hood. Shania followed, wrapping a shawl around her shoulders. "Classes will be over for Christmas holidays in a few weeks. Have you thought about what you're going to do?"

"I think I'll go back to Arizona. My mother wants to buy me a train ticket." He laughed. "She doesn't like the idea of me driving through redneck country."

"I can't blame her. We're going to North Carolina to spend some time with my father's family. I think he misses them more now than before Momma's death."

"How did your mother die?"

"From pneumonia. I was ten years old, and loved her dearly. I remember that night. Poppa came into my room and sat on my bed. He started crying, then hugged me for a long time. He didn't say a word. He just kissed me on the forehead and walked out of the room. It was like watching my world divide and go into two directions at once."

"She must have been a wonderful person."

"The most wonderful I've ever known."

Without thinking he blurted, "You're the most wonderful person I've ever known."

She stepped close to him and reached up, cupping his face in her hands. "Aren't you going to kiss me?"

He flushed with embarrassment. "I don't know how."

She pulled his face to hers, and lightly kissed his lips. "It's easy. You just press your mouth against mine and hold me in your arms. Nature will take care of the rest."

He pulled her close, felt her warmth against his body, causing his knees to weaken. Never in his life had he felt such heat course through his body. Never had he felt such desire for another human being.

"Does this mean we're going steady?"

She smiled and kissed him lightly again. "Yes."

He chuckled. "I thought you'd prefer a Negro to a Colored man."

"I want a man. That's all that's important."

They stood by the car, embracing, kissing, the silent airfield in the distance.

23

✲ ✲ ✲

Nearly two weeks had passed since Thanksgiving, and on a chilly Saturday evening Samuel took Shania to the theater. It was her idea to walk. "The cool night air will feel good."

The theater had one ticket booth to serve customers; behind the booth were two doors, one marked WHITE, the other COLORED, to keep the races separate in the seating arrangements.

They stood in line in the cold, waiting their turn. They reached the window when a white man stepped in front of Samuel and laid his money on the counter. The ticket seller took the money.

"Excuse me, sir. We were in line first," Samuel said.

The man's eyes widened. His hand came up, arced, and came straight for Samuel's face. Instinctively, he blocked the slap, and in doing so used too much force and sent the man crashing to the pavement.

A chorus of groans rose up from the Coloreds congregated behind him, with shouts of "Lord have mercy," "The boy's gone crazy!" and the one he would never forget, "The nigger's gonna be lynched for sure!"

Samuel looked around and for a frozen moment, his eyes were welded to the group of Coloreds. Then, as if a great storm blew along the street, they scattered like straw in the wind. He and Shania were left standing alone as he tried to help the man to his feet.

"Get your filthy hands off me, you nigger bastard!" the man shouted. He pulled himself to his feet, straightened his coat as the theater manager arrived.

"Boy, have you lost your mind?" he shouted.

Through the din Samuel could hear Shania's voice pleading for them to leave. But other voices, angry and vile, filled the air as word spread into the theater, emptying the white moviegoers onto the street. Surrounded on all sides, he was alone, except for Shania, who stood by his side, trembling.

The crowd inched forward, the men with their fist balled, the women slipping to the rear but watching with anticipation.

Samuel remembered his father teaching him that there would be times in a man's life when he knew he would face death, and there was no advice he could give. Each man faces death his own way.

He heard the squeal of braking tires, the clatter of heavy boots on the pavement, and a calm voice saying, "Excuse me, folks. Excuse me. Please let me through."

Samuel saw a white man wearing an army uniform easing his way through the crowd. He wore a black armband bearing the initials MP. On his hip was an army holster, the flap closed. Samuel started to say something, but was surprised to see two Colored MPs appear at his side, batons in hand. Both swung at the same time and hit him in the head. The last words Samuel heard before he lost consciousness, was someone shouting, "Get a rope!"

His eyes slowly opened to a bright light. He saw a man sitting on the edge of a cot where he lay. He started to move, then felt his hands were bound behind his back.

"Lie still, young man. I'll be through in a moment." The man shined a light into Samuel's eyes. "I don't think you have a concussion," he said. Samuel looked past the man and saw the white soldier from the theater. The two Colored MPs stood behind him. "In the future, Sergeant, you might instruct your men to swing their nightsticks with less fervor."

"Yes, sir."

"Who are you?" Samuel asked.

"I'm Captain Emerson, the flight surgeon here at Tuskegee Army Air Field." He motioned toward the white soldier. "Sergeant Mc-Nally told me what was happening. You're lucky. He probably saved your life."

Samuel tried to move, but couldn't. "What am I doing here?"

Sergeant Phillip McNally stepped forward. A heavyset man who looked like a middleweight boxer, he reached into his pocket and took out a small key and unlocked the handcuffs. Samuel sat up, rubbing his wrists.

"I don't understand."

Emerson said, "Sergeant McNally and his men were on patrol in Tuskegee when they saw what was happening and intervened. Sergeant McNally told the people you were a soldier at the airfield and that he would take you into custody and have you court-martialed for assault and disturbing the peace."

McNally looked at Samuel, a smirk on his face. "That seemed to satisfy their thirst for blood. My men threw you in the Jeep and we brought you here for your protection. Hell, son, you damn near got yourself lynched."

Samuel sat up, rubbed his head, and felt two bumps on his skull. He looked at the two Colored MPs, who didn't appear the least apologetic. "I appreciate your help, Sergeant." He started to rise when McNally said, "Where do you think you're going?"

"I left my car in Tuskegee, and there's a young lady that'll be worried."

"That would not be wise, young man."

"Samuel," he said. "My name is Samuel Sharps. I'm a student at the Institute."

"I figured as much. I also figured you're new here and that you're not from the South."

"I'm from Arizona."

McNally and Emerson exchanged glances. "I suggest you stay here a few days," Emerson said. "Give things a little time to blow over in town. There's a lot of racial tension between white Tuskegee and the Negro soldiers here at the airfield. But they know better than to lynch a soldier in the middle of town. Take a few days, and you'll be able to go back without any problems."

"Why did you help me, Sergeant?" Samuel asked McNally.

"I've been in the army twenty years. Civilians treat soldiers like dirt, especially Colored troops. I don't like civilian authority, especially a lynch mob. The townspeople don't like to see Colored MPs carrying pistols. A few weeks ago two of my men went to the jail to pick up one of our Colored troops for drunk and disorderly. We usually get called when it's one of our boys. The local sheriff would rather see the army handle the matter. They figure it keeps from wasting the county's time and jail space. When my men arrived wearing sidearms, the deputies confiscated their weapons. A little tussle followed, and soon there was a mob gathered in front of the jail. I don't like my men being treated like that."

"You thought I was a soldier?"

"He did," Emerson interrupted. The doctor looked at McNally. "Can you find him a billet?"

"That would be against regulations, sir."

"It's my opinion this man requires further evaluation. I don't think the regulations prevent us from carrying out our responsibilities."

McNally said nothing more. Might as well give the kid a billet, he thought. At least he had the guts to stand up for what he believed was right.

The first time Samuel walked into an army barracks was with his father, when they went to Fort Huachuca to visit one of Adrian's old army buddies. He remembered the bunks lined in a perfect row, equipment hung by the wall locker, where neatly folded clothes waited at the ready for inspection. The rifle rack was filled with Springfield .03 rifles; the Doughboy "soup-bowl" helmets hung over field packs packed and ready for action.

But the one unforgettable characteristic of that barracks was its smell. It smelled of men from different walks of life, their individual history and passage leaving a small part of themselves within the fabric of the walls. The corrosive effect man has on an environment: floors splintered from heavy hobnailed boots; a puncture in the wall where a bayonet had left its mark; the walls and ceilings, caretakers of the conversation that is uniquely that of soldiers. Harsh. Bitter. Joyful. Prayerful. Lewd.

Not this barracks. This one was a large hospital tent with rough, wooden planks for flooring. There was no smell of history.

"Watch your step," the night charge-of-quarters whispered as he led Samuel through the center aisle, his flashlight dancing off the bunks. Samuel saw the heads of Colored men on the pillows, most asleep, some rising to investigate the commotion. He was led to a bunk at the end of the aisle, and heard the CQ whisper, "Reveille is at zero-five-hundred. Chow at zero-five-thirty."

Samuel whispered, "What does that mean?"

The CQ shined his flashlight in Samuel's face. "Five o'clock and five-thirty in the morning." He looked at him oddly, then said, "You're not in the army, are you?"

"No. I got into some trouble in town with some white folks. A sergeant and two Colored MPs rescued me. They brought me to the flight surgeon, and he thought I should stay here for a few days. Until things cool off in town."

The CQ sat on the edge of the bunk. "You a student at the Institute?"

"Yes. I'm a freshman."

"What did you do? Kill a white man?"

"I didn't kill him. I just blocked his punch. He was going to slap me."

The CQ released a long sigh. "I know one thing: You sure ain't no Southern Colored."

Samuel laughed. "I'm from out West."

"You might not be safe anywhere in Macon County. Or the state, for that matter. Coloreds don't go hitting on white men, or stopping white men from hitting them. Not here. No, man. Not here. You'll get lynched for sure."

"You sound like you know more about being a Colored than I do. What would you do in my place?"

"Pack your grip and get the hell out of Alabama. That white man's going to find out who you are. Then, one night, you're going to get a visit from the local hunting club."

"Hunting club?"

"Yeah. That's what the KKK call themselves. Makes them think it dignifies their outfit."

The CQ jerked quickly to his feet, like someone who suddenly realizes he is in the wrong place. "I better make my fire-watch round. You get some sleep. You can think better after you've rested." He walked away, and Samuel laid his head on the pillow. He tossed and turned but couldn't get to sleep. He kept seeing visions of a man coming down the aisle, flashlight in one hand . . . a hangman's rope in the other.

24

The quiet of the barracks was ripped away by the shrill of reveille. Samuel had finally fallen asleep when the bugle brought the barracks to life with the sound of men's feet hitting the hardwood floor. Strings of obscenities knifed through the air as a long line began forming in the aisle, where the forty men of the platoon walked past him in their underwear, toward the sound of running water in the nearby latrine. As the men passed his bunk, carrying towels and shaving kits, he was stared at with momentary interest. He might be in a Colored barracks, he thought, but these men were trained soldiers, not college students.

He didn't have a shaving kit, but he had a towel draped on the bunk, and the appeal of a shower was overwhelming. He fell into the rear and followed the men into the latrine. There were no shower stalls, only a wall lined with spewing nozzles, where the men cleaned their bodies. They didn't linger; they washed their armpits, face, private parts, and rinsed. What his father called a "soldier's shower." In and out. Quick and clean.

Each man dropped his shorts and stepped into the shower, washed, dried, wrapped the towel around his waist, then went to a sink for a shave. Samuel did the same, except for the shave, and one peculiarity that caught everyone's eye. He took his shower with his socks on.

One of the men standing beside him looked at his stocking feet. "Man, do you always take a shower with your socks on?"

Samuel grinned sheepishly. "My momma said to always leave my socks on when I take a shower in a public facility."

"Why's that?"

"Prevents getting foot infection."

At his bunk he saw the man next to him making tight hospital corners on sheets and blanket, pillow fluffed and neat. He took a quarter and slammed it on the bunk. The quarter jumped one foot in the air. He caught the coin. "What do you say, young soldier? Will my bunk pass inspection?"

Samuel smiled for the first time since the theater. "I'm not a soldier. Not yet. I hope to be one someday."

"Are you crazy?" He was a tall man in his early twenties, with a thin mustache, and large, bright eyes. Samuel thought of a deer as he looked at him. "What you want to join the army for, man?"

"Why did you join?"

"No choice in the matter. The judge gave me two choices: four years in the army or four years on the chain gang. I took the army. I figured the food was better. But I was wrong. Prison food is better."

Samuel liked the man and his straightforward, friendly voice. "I'm Samuel Sharps. I'm an ROTC student at Tuskegee Institute."

"College boy, huh."

"Something wrong with going to college?"

He pointed at the Western hat. "Texas?"

"Arizona."

"Close enough." He offered his hand. "I'm Private Dexter Kane, but the ladies in Evangeline, Louisiana, call me 'Sugar.'" He looked at the bunk. "Come on, man. Get that bunk made up, and we can get some chow."

Samuel made his bed and followed Kane to the mess hall, where he stood in line with the other soldiers. His first taste of army food made him reconsider what Kane had said about prison food. He ate powdered eggs, drank powdered milk, had fatback instead of bacon, and chipped beef in gravy on toast. Kane pointed at the beef and toast. "In the army, we call that 'shit on a shingle.'"

Samuel took a bite. His face twisted into a funny mask, then he forced himself to swallow. But he was hungry. He hadn't eaten since the afternoon before at the boardinghouse. He wolfed down every morsel on his plate, to the surprise of Kane. "Boy, you eat like a grizzly bear."

They ate and talked, with Kane doing most of the talking, telling Samuel about being in the army. "When I finished basic training, I was assigned to maintenance training, with the Twenty-Fourth Infantry. I was a mechanic back home, and they gave me a test to find out what I know. I was working on tanks mostly, but an engine's an engine. So I volunteered to come here and try my hand at airplanes. It got me closer to my home. I guess the army figures there is going to eventually be a Colored fighter squadron, so they're getting some of us broken in to be ready for when we form our own support units."

"You're an aircraft mechanic?"

"Yeah. I wind them up; the pilots take them up. We trained on all the aircraft the squadron will be flying. PT-17. BT-15. AT-6. All training aircraft. But the war bird is the P-40 Warhawk. That is one quick airplane. It was the fighter used in China by General Claire Chennault's Flying Tigers."

"Can you take me to the flight line?"

Kane sat back and studied Samuel. "What's in it for me?"

"Are you married?"

"Married? Man, I ain't met a woman yet who can tie me down."

"Do you have a girlfriend?"

"Boy, I am the 'Sugar Kane' man from Evangeline. I have dozens of girlfriends." His mustache rose and fell arrogantly.

Samuel shook his head. "I mean, do you have a girlfriend in Tuskegee?"

"Naw, man. There ain't much to choose from in Tuskegee. Except at the Institute, and army privates can't even get past Lincoln Gate where the women are concerned."

"I can get you past the gate."

Kane was suddenly interested. "How you going to do that?"

"My girlfriend has quite a few female classmates at the Institute. I'm sure she can introduce you to a nice young lady. I have a car, and we can double date."

"You get me past the gate. I'll get you on the flight line."

*   *   *

The smell of the flight line was like a narcotic to Samuel, who walked directly to a P-40 parked in front of an incomplete hangar. Kane pointed at the Warhawk. "That big boy was flown in China by the Flying Tigers. There were fourteen Japanese flags painted on the fuselage when it arrived."

Samuel stood silent a moment. "Fourteen enemy planes shot down by this one plane. The pilot must have been a real terror in the sky."

Kane said, "Want to see something interesting about the pilot?"

"What is it?"

The soldier climbed onto the wing, motioning Samuel to join him, and slid back the canopy. He reached inside and removed what appeared to be a small ledger. "This is the maintenance log. It's the life story of an airplane. It also tells who were the pilots that've flown the bird. Look at this name."

Samuel looked, and shrugged. "It says Major Phillip Cochran."

Kane laughed. "Man, you don't know nothing. Major Cochran is the pilot that cartoon character Flip Corkin is modeled after in *Terry and the Pirates*. And we have one of the planes he flew in combat."

Samuel stared into the well of the cockpit, slowly scanning the stick, with its gun trigger, the compass, gunsight, and rudder controls. "It's too small. I can't fit into the cockpit."

"Come on. Let's find out." He jumped down from the plane, yelling over his shoulder, "Get down and wait. I'll be right back." Kane hurried toward the hangar, and returned directly, carrying a parachute. "Here, put this on."

Samuel took the parachute. "What do I do?"

Kane was patient, spreading the shoulder straps, and saying, "Slip your arms through here."

Samuel did, then Kane knelt and buckled the leg straps on the harness. "Climb back up on the wing."

Kane motioned to the cockpit. "Get in."

Samuel started to climb in, but his legs didn't seem to fit. "Not like that, man," said Kane. "Stand on the seat, then sit from that position. That's how we put a size-nine pilot into a size-six cockpit."

Samuel did as instructed and folded himself into the cockpit. He wasn't too tall after all. When Kane closed the cockpit, the snap of the locking device signaled that Samuel was sealed into the cockpit of the Warhawk. He extended his legs, pushed on the rudders; he worked the stick from side to side and flipped up the cover shield on the trigger mechanism, revealing a small switch painted red. He reached above his head and felt an inch of space between the glass of the canopy and the top of his head.

The feeling was overwhelming. He could smell the history of the plane; could imagine diving onto an enemy aircraft, squeezing the trigger, and watching the foe disintegrate in a ball of flame.

Kane watched with a broad smile. He liked this young man from Arizona. And more so, for the possibility of meeting young ladies from the Institute.

He motioned at Samuel to open the cockpit. "Come on, man. There's more to see than the Warhawk."

They walked around the flight line, along the edge of the runway, where they found a B-17 parked on the tarmac. The crew was white and was loading their equipment into the hull. Samuel stared at the barrels of the .50-caliber waist guns jutting from port and starboard openings; he knelt and studied the revolving bubble of the belly turret, then moved to the tail-gun position. The bomber had other heavy machine-gun positions on the top turret and at the nose, and with its complement of bombs stored in the belly, the airplane more than deserved its nickname, "Flying Fortress."

"What are you doing here, soldier?" A voice came from behind, and they turned to see a white captain dressed in an army flight suit. His service hat was crushed along the edges, driven into that shape, thought Samuel, by the constant wearing of radio headphones. Kane saluted, while Samuel said nothing.

Kane replied smartly, "I'm giving this civilian pilot trainee a tour of the flight line, sir."

"Pilot trainee, huh?" Samuel nodded as the officer's eyes roamed slowly over him. "Continue with your tour, Private. But make it snappy. We're taking off in ten minutes."

Before he knew what he was doing, Samuel said, "May I see the inside, Captain?"

The officer thought for a moment. "I don't see why not. Come with me."

They followed him to the belly, where he reached up through an opened port, gripped metal handles, swung his feet inside first, then pulled his body into the bomber. Kane followed, doing the maneuver expertly; Samuel took three tries before he finally pulled himself into the B-17.

Inside the bomber, the space appeared smaller than he had imagined. The cockpit was designed for pilot and copilot; below, the bombardier and nose-gunner's position was even tighter. The waist-gun positions offered more room, but the turret gunners on top, the belly, and tail, allowed little room for movement except for firing the weapons.

When it was time for the bomber to depart, Samuel and Kane descended to the tarmac and stood away while the massive engines groaned, then came alive with a thunderous roar. Samuel could feel the ground shaking as the huge Fortress slowly taxied toward the end of the runway. After completing the preflight runup, the B-17 lumbered along the runway, gaining speed by the second, then stormed into the air with a deafening noise. Moments later, they stood in silence, watching the bomber disappear on the horizon.

For Samuel, it was a wonderful moment, but the bomber was not what he wanted to fly. He wanted to fly fighters.

In the early afternoon, Samuel checked in with the flight surgeon, who examined the knots on his head and found them doing better, but insisted he remain on the base a few more days. Samuel was allowed to call Shania.

"Papa called President Patterson, but he can't do anything at the moment except pray the incident will be soon forgotten."

"I doubt there's much anybody can do. It's going to take a miracle to get out of this situation. I think the best thing is to pack up and slip out of Macon County at night. I don't think I'll be missed."

There was a pained sound in her voice. "I hate the thought of you leaving."

Then he heard the wail of sirens filling the air outside of the dispensary. There was the sound of boots hammering the wooden floor as men were rushing in and out of the dispensary. Voices were shouting on the street outside; and in the background of Shania's house, he heard LeBaron's voice calling to Shania.

There was a long silence on the phone. Samuel shouted, "Shania! Shania! Speak up. I can't hear you. What's going on?"

Her voice came back on. "My God. Oh, my dear sweet God!"

"What's wrong? Speak to me! What's wrong?"

"The Japanese have attacked the navy base at Pearl Harbor! In Hawaii!"

Samuel stared in shock at the telephone, then lowered the receiver to the cradle. A pang of guilt coursed through him as he saw the real possibility that his dream would come true.

25

☆ ☆ ☆

WAR!!!

The attack began at 0755, Honolulu time, while in Washington, Japanese General Hideki "the Razor" Tojo's emissaries, Saburo Kurusu and Admiral Kichisaburo Nomura, were en route to the State Department to meet with Secretary of State Cordell Hull. The meeting was scheduled for 1:45 P.M., but the two bland envoys arrived late at 2:05. An angry Hull made them wait an additional fifteen minutes before allowing them in his office. The moment he received them at 2:20, a flash arrived from Hawaii that the United States had been attacked at the Pearl Harbor navy base, Schofield army barracks, and the city of Honolulu.

At Sabre Ranch, Selona and Hannah drove into the front yard, where they saw Theresa running from her house. She wore the frightened look of a doe being pursued by a wolf. Her mouth was moving, but there were no words; she kept pointing over her shoulder at the house.

Selona watched Theresa draw near and felt a sudden chill. "Something's wrong. Maybe the house is on fire! Or something has happened to one of the men." Her first thoughts were of Adrian. He was in Mexico with Jonathan, making arrangements for another delivery of cattle and seafood to the processing plant.

Hannah saw John Parks sitting on the front porch of Selona's house; his head was bowed and he appeared in prayer.

"There's no fire. Something else is wrong. Something terrible," said Selona.

Theresa stopped at Hannah's window, where she tried to catch her breath, and when she finally spoke, her forced words formed unintelligible sentences.

"Japs . . . Pearl Harbor . . . Attacked . . . This morning."

Hannah came out of the car and braced Theresa's shoulders. "What are you saying?"

Theresa took a deep breath. "The Japanese have attacked our boys at the navy base at Pearl Harbor. In Hawaii. Thousands of our soldiers and sailors may be dead. My God, it's war for certain!"

They hurried into the house, followed by Parks, who could only shake his head in disbelief. "I don't understand this. Not at all. Why would the Japanese attack the United States?"

Hannah turned up the volume of the radio, taking off her coat while she sat on the couch. They listened intently to the reporter on the radio.

"—This morning, at approximately seven-fifty-five Honolulu time, Japanese fighters, torpedo-bombers, and high-level bombers attacked the United States naval base at Pearl Harbor. Wave after wave of airplanes filled the sky, destroying ships anchored in the harbor and airplanes parked on the runways. First reports indicate the battleship *Arizona* was sunk by a direct hit; six other battleships, including the *California,* were sunk, along with three destroyers, and half the military aircraft destroyed on the ground. The attack was devastatingly accurate, and losses in equipment and human life are heavy. The attack came with total surprise as our servicemen slept aboard ships or in barracks, attended church, or were ashore for the weekend."

The reporter continued, but Hannah sat numb.

Selona listened quietly, feeling a deep new hatred. She had hatred for the Rangers who had scalped her, the Indians who had killed her father, the Klansmen who had blown off the Sergeant Major's leg, and the Germans who had killed her son David. She thought of young Samuel. He had been right about the coming of war.

The *bastards!* she thought.

They killed our boys while they slept and prayed in church!

In Nogales, Adrian was sitting in the front seat of his car, the door open, listening to the radio announcer report the few details then known of the attack on Pearl Harbor. He recalled the day in 1917 when he learned that the United States had entered the Great War in France. He had been excited at the notion he might once again serve his country in battle. But he had no feeling of excitement at this moment. He had fought in Cuba and was raised in the military, and he saw nothing exciting. The United States would be at war with an Asian power soon. The Germans would align with the Japanese. America would have to fight on two world fronts.

Jonathan leaned against the hood, staring off into the distance; dust swirled about him as cattle were herded aboard trucks for the trip to Wilcox. He watched the Mexican *vaqueros;* they seemed oblivious to the earthshaking news.

Adrian turned off the radio. "The country will be in a rage over this attack, Jonathan. The people are going to want blood." He spit on the ground with disgust. "Damn. Why couldn't they have just declared war. Done it with honor. I don't think our people are going to rest until we burn Japan to the ground."

"What about the Germans? When do you think they'll take sides with the Japs?"

"Soon," Adrian replied. "I expect their diplomats are already talking with the Japanese."

Jonathan shook his head. "I sure wasn't expecting this to happen. The Germans, yes. But not the Japanese."

Adrian watched him walk to his car. "Where you going?"

"Back to Tucson. It's time to do more than talk about the war and making a profit."

"What are you going to do?"

"What you and my daddy did back in 1917: join the army!"

26

* * *

On December 8, 1941, President of the United States Franklin Delano Roosevelt spoke to Congress and a waiting nation, issuing the formal request for a declaration of war.

"Yesterday, December 7, 1941—a date that will live in infamy—the United States of America was suddenly and deliberately attacked by naval and air forces of the Empire of Japan.

"The United States was at peace with that nation and, at the solicitation of Japan, was still in conversation with the government and its emperor looking toward the maintenance of peace in the Pacific.

"Indeed, one hour after Japanese air squadrons had commenced bombing in Oahu, the Japanese ambassador to the United States and his colleagues delivered to the Secretary of State a formal reply to a recent American message. While this reply stated that it seemed useless to continue the existing diplomatic negotiations, it contained no threat or hint of armed attack.

"It will be recorded that the distance of Hawaii from Japan makes it obvious that the attack was deliberately planned many days or even weeks ago. During the intervening time, the

Japanese government has deliberately sought to deceive the United States by false statements and expressions of hope for continued peace.

"The attack yesterday on the Hawaiian Islands has caused severe damage to American naval and military forces. Very many American lives have been lost. In addition, American ships have been reported torpedoed on the high seas between San Francisco and Honolulu.

"Yesterday, the Japanese government also launched an attack against Malaya.

"Last night, Japanese forces attacked Hong Kong.

"Last night, Japanese forces attacked Guam.

"Last night, Japanese forces attacked the Philippine Islands.

"Last night, the Japanese attacked Wake Island.

"Last night, the Japanese attacked Midway Island.

"Japan has, therefore, undertaken a surprise offensive extending throughout the Pacific area. The facts of yesterday speak for themselves. The people of the United States have already formed their opinions and well understand the implications to the very life and safety of our nation.

"As commander in chief of the army and navy, I have directed that all measures be taken for our defense.

"Always we will remember the character of the onslaught against us.

"No matter how long it may take us to overcome this premeditated invasion, the American people in their righteous might will win through to absolute victory.

"I believe I interpret the will of the Congress and of the people when I assert that we will not only defend ourselves to the uttermost, but will make very certain that this form of treachery shall never endanger us again.

"Hostilities exist. There is no blinking at the fact that our people, our territory, and our interests are in grave danger.

"With confidence in our armed forces—with the unbounded determination of our people—we will gain the inevitable triumph—so help us God.

"I ask that Congress declare that since the unprovoked and dastardly attack by Japan on Sunday, December 7, a state of war has existed between the United States and the Japanese Empire."

With the exception of one vote—that of a congresswoman from Montana—the United States Congress voted approval of the declaration of war against Japan.

On December 11, 1941, President Roosevelt again spoke to the Congress, and the people of the United States:

"On the morning of December 11, the government of Germany, pursuing its course of world conquest, declared war against the United States.

"The long-known and long-expected has thus taken place. The forces endeavoring to enslave the entire world now are moving toward this hemisphere.

"Never before has there been a greater challenge to life, liberty, and civilization.

"Delay invites great danger. Rapid and united effort by all of the peoples of the world who are determined to remain free will ensure a world victory of the forces of justice and of righteousness over the forces of savagery and of barbarism.

"Italy also has declared war against the United States.

"I therefore request the Congress to recognize a state of war between the United States and Germany, and between the United States and Italy."

The following War Resolution was issued by the United States Congress:

"Declaring that a state of war exists between the government of Germany and the government and the people of the United States and making provision to prosecute the same.

"Whereas the government of Germany has formally declared war against the government and the people of the United States of America:

"Therefore, be it Resolved by the Senate and House of Representatives of the United States of America in Congress assembled, that the state of war between the United States and the government of Germany which has thus been thrust upon the United States is hereby formally declared; and the President is hereby authorized and directed to employ the entire naval and military forces of the government to carry on war against the government of Germany; and to bring the conflict to a successful termination, all of the resources of the country are hereby pledged by the Congress of the United States."

From December 8, to December 11, 1941—less than one hundred hours—the United States had been drawn into the Second Great War of human civilization.

27

★ ★ ★

Samuel felt a prisoner of war. The world was in chaos, and he was trapped on an army airfield, surrounded by fighting men and machines, and could do nothing. Irony and reality now controlled his life. He had come to Tuskegee to join the Army Air Corps as a pilot, knowing war was inevitable, and now he was on the airfield held hostage by events of the outside world. Telephone communications outside the base were impossible; only secured lines could be used, and those for official business. He couldn't walk off the base for fear he might be lynched by racists. He couldn't contact his family or Shania. He could only sit in the barracks and wait.

The radio in the orderly room had become his only link to what was going on beyond the main gate; that and the newspaper, which was filled with stories of the attack on Pearl Harbor and the declaration of war with Germany.

He had read every article he could find and learned the details of the surprise attack on the navy base. America was outraged; the soldiers at the base were at full alert.

Kane returned on the night of December 12, took off his doughboy helmet, and dropped onto his bunk. He had been on guard duty at the flight line for two days without rest. He lay silent, staring at the ceiling, smoking a cigarette, and exhaling heavily, his fatigue obvious. "Well, young pilot, you wanted to fly in combat. I reckon you're going to get your chance."

"How's that?" Samuel asked.

"The word is the Ninety-Ninth is going to a full war footing."

"What does that mean?"

Kane drew on his cigarette. "This whole program was called an 'experiment' in the beginning. A bone thrown to the Coloreds to keep everybody quiet while the army went about its normal business. I guess the war is changing all that. Rumor has it that Major Ellison is being transferred and we're getting a new base commander. A full bird colonel named Kimbell. He'll be here next month."

Major James Ellison had commanded Tuskegee Army Air Field since construction began earlier in the year. He was liked by the Negro soldiers, but disliked by the local white population since he didn't cater to their racist views.

"I don't get it," Samuel said.

"Look, man, this whole thing was just to shut up all the activists raising hell about equal opportunity for Colored aviation in the army. I doubt anybody thought there would really be a war. Now that it's come, the government is stuck with the fact that it's training a Colored aviation unit. That means we have to be taken seriously. The army is sending in a real backbreaker to take over the base."

"Do you think the Ninety-Ninth will be sent to the combat areas?"

Kane nodded. "A fellow I know over at headquarters said the program is going to be stepped up."

Samuel understood that. "The army will drop its quota and open up the recruitment of Colored pilots."

"That's the ticket. I guess you just might get your chance."

"Not sitting here on this bunk, I won't. I've got to get off this base and find Chief Anderson. He'll know what I need to do."

Kane thought that over. "Officially, you're a civilian. I reckon you can walk off the base anytime you want. But you still got the boys in white sheets waiting on the outside."

"I doubt I'm that important now that they have a whole nation of people with yellow skin to fight."

"Could be, young pilot. Could be." He paused. "You got a plan?"

Samuel stood up and extended his hand. "I'm going home, Dexter."

"To Arizona?"

Samuel shook his head. "To Tuskegee. I'm not going to hide on this base. I came here to be a fighter pilot, and now that there's a war, I'm going to be in it."

They shook hands and Kane watched in silence as Samuel walked down the aisle and disappeared from the barracks.

He walked to the main gate, where the MPs on guard checked his identification and, convinced he was a civilian, allowed him to leave the airfield. He walked until he reached the dirt road that led to the boardinghouse, where he found his car parked in the front. It was near daylight, and he walked inside. The house seemed empty.

There was a light in the kitchen, where he found Guillard dressed in his ROTC uniform, sitting at the table drinking coffee.

"What's for breakfast?" Samuel asked wryly.

Guillard stood and shook hands. "You if the hunting club gets hold of you."

Samuel laughed weakly. "How did my car get here?"

"Shania drove it here after things cooled off in town. Man, I thought you'd be halfway to Arizona by now."

"Don't seem to be anyplace to run, Guillard." He looked around and asked the obvious. "Where's everybody?"

"Gone home to enlist. Half the campus has joined up. Mostly army. A few in the navy. What about you? I heard about your trouble."

Samuel poured a cup of coffee and sat at the table. "I don't know what I'm going to do, Guillard. What about you?"

"I came here to fly airplanes. I think I'm going to get my chance. There's an ROTC meeting this morning at ten-thirty. I think you should be there."

"That might not be wise."

"Don't be foolish, man. There's a war on. Nobody's going to

care what happened last week. The world's gone insane, and there's no time for concerns over one Colored student at Tuskegee Institute. Of course, no sense in reminding them of trouble. I've got an idea." He got up and went to his room, then returned with scissors, a razor, and a soap cup.

"What are you going to do?"

"Shave your head." Guillard chuckled. "White folks say we all look alike. But just in case, let's change your appearance a bit."

Samuel started to protest, but realized his friend was right. Twenty minutes later Guillard held a mirror. "You're not as pretty as you once were, but you'll pass muster in front of the white folks."

"What about my muster?" The voice came from the door of the kitchen.

Samuel hurried forward and embraced Shania. She kissed him lightly on the mouth, then rubbed his smooth dome. "I'd say it's an improvement."

Samuel felt embarrassed. "My grandfather shaved his head." He remembered a photograph taken of Sergeant Major Sharps in his dress uniform. "I think I'll grow a mustache. That ought to complete the disguise."

The sound of the telephone ringing interrupted them. Guillard answered, then handed the receiver to Samuel. "It's your father."

Adrian sat in the kitchen, wearing his robe, a cup of coffee on the table, a look of relief on his face as he finally reached a long-distance operator. He had been trying to call Samuel since the news of Pearl Harbor, but the country's telephone circuits had been overloaded with the same calls he was making: frantic Americans trying to reach loved ones.

"Why in the hell haven't you called, son!" His voice boomed in the kitchen, nearly rattling the cup and saucer.

"I've had a bit of trouble, Pop."

"What kind of trouble?" Adrian's voice mellowed as he listened to Samuel explain the incident at the theater.

At that moment Hannah walked into the kitchen, standing beside him, her ear lowered and nearly touching Adrian's.

Hannah suddenly looked concerned. "Safe from what?" she whispered.

He shook his head, then said to Samuel, "I think you're right. But, for God sakes, be careful." He looked at Hannah. "Your mother wants to talk to you."

Hannah grabbed the phone and sat beside Adrian. "Samuel, why haven't you called?" She listened as he explained. She began to tremble. "Get into your car and come home. Leave that hateful place this minute."

"I'm staying, Momma. I came here to go to school and become an aviator. Now that there's a war, this country is going to need all its men to fight it. I suppose I have to stand with my feet on enemy ground in this country until I'm sent to enemy ground overseas."

Hannah was angry. "You're sure full of yourself, young man. Have you gone crazy! Those Kluxers might lynch you!"

Selona walked into the kitchen at that moment, catching only the last part of Hannah's words. "What Kluxers?" she asked Adrian. "Who's getting lynched?"

"No one's getting lynched, Momma. It's Samuel. He's had a bit of trouble with a white man."

Selona wagged her finger at Adrian. "I told you not to let that boy go down South. It's open season on Coloreds down there. Always has been."

Hannah's voice ripped the air. "Quiet! I can't hear over you two arguing." She went back to Samuel. "Please, son. Come home."

Her heart fell as she heard him say, "I can't, Momma. Don't worry. White folks have more to worry about right now than one Negro defending himself."

Hannah stared incredulously at the telephone, then asked, "Negro? When did you all of a sudden become a 'Negro'?"

The line crackled with static, but she heard him say, "Since I stood up to that white man. Millions of Coloreds will have to become Negroes if we're to stand up to the Germans. Joe Louis did it against Max Schmelling. Jessie Owens did it against the Third Reich. I guess it's time the rest of the Coloreds in this country stood alongside them and the men of the Ninety-Ninth Fighter Squadron. We can't be denied. Not now, Momma. We're fighting on two fronts. I'm going to make it into the Air Corps no matter the price. It would make me feel better knowing you and Grams were standing with me. I can't fight the Germans, the Japs, and the two of you at the same time."

There was a long pause from Hannah. Her eyes teared as she realized she wasn't the only mother in the country—white or Colored—having this same conversation with a son. The children of America had been raised to be proud, strong, and to fight for what was right. To refuse to stand by them would betray everything they had been raised to believe. She looked at Adrian, his sleeve empty, remembering when he went to war, remembering when he returned. She knew Samuel was right. The cruelty of war was upon the nation and the world. No one person would be exempt from the horror. Millions of mothers would cry before the last gun fell silent.

"I'll stand by you," she whispered in a choking voice. "We'll all stand by you both."

"Both?" Samuel said.

"Jonathan has joined the army. He left yesterday for basic training. He said he'll be safe. He's going to be a cook. I expect that's a safe enough job."

"He'll be safe."

"What's your plans?"

Samuel took a deep breath, trying to sort out everything as he talked. "There's a meeting this morning of the ROTC students. I intend to apply for Air Cadet training. I only need a few more hours of solo flying to take my private pilot's license test. That should give me a good chance of being accepted."

"What about college? I thought the Cadets had to have at least two years of college?"

"The army is going to need pilots, Momma. Lots of them. Not bookworms. I'll get in the Cadets."

Hannah thought about something she had never mentioned in the past. Ernst Bruner was a member of the U.S. House of Representatives. Perhaps he might be of help. His father had helped Adrian and David in 1917. Samuel had saved his son from being killed by a range bull. The Bruners were people who never forgot a debt owed is a debt to be paid. But she chose not to talk about that at the moment. She didn't want to get his hopes up and see him disappointed.

"Let me speak to him," Selona whispered into Hannah's ear.

She said, "You call in a few days and tell us what's going on. We need to know. You understand? Give my love to Shania. She must be a wonderful young lady if she's worth you staying in Alabama when you've had trouble with white folks."

Selona took the telephone. "I know it ain't going to do no good to tell you your business. You're as hardheaded as your granddaddy and your daddy. But you got to watch yourself with them Kluxers. They don't like to see Coloreds wearing uniforms. It riles them something fierce."

She heard his booming laughter coming through the line from Alabama. "Grams, you worry too much. I'm a grown man. I can take care of myself."

She half covered the phone, and asked in a whisper, "Have you got that Sharps loaded?"

Again there was his laughter as he told her he loved her and would call soon. When she hung up, Selona stared at the telephone for a long moment. Something was strange, yet familiar. It would take her nearly the whole day before she figured out the puzzle: Samuel's voice sounded identical to his grandfather's.

28

Samuel and Guillard wore their ROTC uniforms to the Institute that day, a Friday, their thoughts on the war, not education. Life on campus had changed; conversation had shifted from scholarly discussion to Pearl Harbor and the American territories attacked in the ensuing days by the Japanese military machine. Though Tuskegee Institute was small by college standards, the student and faculty population had not gone untouched by the war. Samuel knew of a science teacher whose brother had died aboard the *Arizona;* an ROTC student had received word the night before his older brother was killed on the parade ground at Schofield barracks.

Samuel was sitting in the classroom used for military-science courses. The numbers had thinned out since Roosevelt's declaration of war; most of the students had returned home to volunteer.

Sergeant First Class James Wynn entered briskly, bringing everyone to his feet. He motioned them to be seated, then spoke in curt, military fashion. Rumor had spread among the students that Wynn would be leaving for Fort Riley, Kansas, to join the 4th Cavalry Brigade, a mechanized unit composed partly of the 9th and 10th Cavalry Regiments.

A short, stocky man, Wynn had already begun growing his cavalryman's mustache and sideburns. He wore crisply starched riding breeches, tall black boots, and the "Smoky Bear" campaign hat. He had been wounded while serving with the 9th Cavalry in the Moro campaign, in the southern Philippines.

"Gentlemen, due to the national emergency, the army has been forced to rescind previous college requirements for application to Officer Candidate School," Wynn said. "You came to Tuskegee to become officers in the United States Army. Here is your chance to attend the Infantry School at Fort Benning without the required two years of college education." He began passing out forms to the ROTC cadets, pausing as he handed the applications to Samuel and Guillard, to whisper, "Fill in 'Air Corps' for your choice of training."

Samuel filled out the application and turned it in to Wynn. He and Guillard left the building and drove to Moton, where they found Chief Anderson in the flight-operations building. He wore a gabardine uniform with the propeller insignia of the Air Corps on its dark green, woolen collar.

"Morning, Chief."

Anderson studied Samuel. "Have you any idea what you've started? It seems the Colored population has taken sides with you in that little fracas you had at the theater."

"I don't understand what you're talking about, Chief."

Anderson poured a cup of coffee and sat at his desk. "Whether you know it or not, boycotts are illegal in Alabama. Coloreds boycotting businesses can be fined, even jailed."

"What does that mean?"

"It means the Coloreds of Tuskegee have quit going to the theater in town. You've stirred up a real hornets' nest."

"I guess I'm really in trouble."

"I doubt that, Samuel. As soon as the theater owner starts feeling the pinch on his pocketbook, we might see some change."

"What kind of change?"

"I would imagine we'll see a 'Colored Only' ticket booth at the theater. A small, unidentified group of Coloreds have sent an anonymous message to the owner stating there would not be Colored attendance at the theater until our people are treated equally."

"I had no idea," Samuel said.

The Chief raised his hand to his ear, as though listening to something in the distance. "I can hear the hammer hitting the nails as that booth is getting built." He laughed softly, then added, "It might seem a small victory, but it's small victories that win great wars."

"I don't want any more trouble, Chief."

"You won't have any more trouble, son. Not if the citizens of Tuskegee—whites especially—want to go to a movie theater without driving to Montgomery."

Guillard slapped him on the back. "Good for you, Samuel. I thought they'd hang you for sure. I guess the Kluxers will think twice before bothering you in the future. My money is betting they enjoy movies more than lynchings."

Anderson knew the reason the two had come to see him. "I know about the ROTC meeting this morning. I'm assuming you two have applied for Air Corps training."

They both nodded.

"There will be hundreds—thousands—of applications flowing into Washington by that time. Your chances of getting into the program will be better with your private license. If you're not accepted, you at least have the opportunity to finish college. You'll get a commission in the regular army once you graduate."

Samuel merely shook his head. For him, becoming a pilot was an all-or-nothing proposition. He had come to Tuskegee to fly airplanes. "One way or the other, I won't be in college next semester. If I'm not accepted into the Air Corps, I'm going to enlist. If I can't fly for my country, I can serve in the cavalry, like my grandfather. But I'm not going to sit in a classroom and study agriculture while my country is fighting a war."

"My thoughts exactly," said Guillard.

Anderson was proud of these two young men. They were a new breed, reminding him of early Colored aviation pioneers. He understood their love of flying and dedication to their country. Were he a younger man, he wouldn't be having this conversation. He would apply for the Air Corps as a pilot, instead of preparing younger men for battle.

Anderson looked over the rim of his cup. "Are you ready to take your private check ride?"

"You tell me, Chief. Am I ready?"

"Let me see your flight log." Samuel gave him his CAA flight logbook, and he quickly perused the pages, noting the hours of dual instruction, solo flight, and the notation that he had passed the written examination. "You need two more hours of solo, then you'll have the time requirement. Get those hours in today, and I'll write you off for the check ride." He looked at the schedule on the blackboard. "Tomorrow afternoon." He turned to Guillard. "How many hours do you need, Guillard?"

"Four hours and small change."

"Can you put in four by day after tomorrow?"

"The money's tight, but I'll find a way, even if I have to sell my photography equipment. I know a professional photographer in Montgomery who'll buy it. It might take a few days, but if you can hold me on the books for a week or two, I'll get you the money."

Anderson liked Guillard's answer, although he hated seeing the young man give up something so important to his life.

"I'll carry you on the books for whatever time you need, Thomas. In the meanwhile, get those hours completed and be ready on Monday." He looked at Samuel, saying, "You'll take your ride in the morning."

The two left under the watchful eye of Anderson, who stood at the window, watching them walk to a Stearman. Though separated by glass, time, and distance, he shared their enthusiasm for the future. The sad part was, he thought, that like most advances for the Negro in America—whether freedom from slavery, or simple human fairness—the price was required to be high.

The shameful reality was glaring: Young men would have to suffer and die so those who followed would be given the chance to live in dignity!

29

The next morning, Samuel met the Chief at Moton Field. After passing an oral exam and planning a cross-country flight, completing the final phase of the ground requirement, the Chief said, "Let's go flying, Samuel."

Shania and Guillard watched as Samuel followed the Chief to the Piper and did a preflight on the aircraft, explaining every procedure. When satisfied, both men climbed into the cockpit, Samuel fired up the engine, taxied the tiny trainer onto the grass runway, did a runup, checked the instruments to be certain the engine was running properly, and checked the ailerons and rudders.

"Nice and smooth." said the Chief. "I want a short-field takeoff over an obstacle."

Samuel stepped hard on the brakes, increased the throttle, and when the Piper seemed to want to break apart, released the brakes and felt the tiny craft lunge forward. Rolling fast, he steered the plane down the center of the field, watched for the imaginary obstacle, and when just above stall speed, pulled sharply back on the stick. The Piper shot upward, and when over the unseen obstacle, Samuel lowered the nose to begin building airspeed.

They climbed to three thousand feet, where he performed a take-off and departure stall, approach-to-landing stall, chandelle, turn-about-a-point, and all the required maneuvers required for the private pilot license.

After an hour Anderson said, "Take us home. Execute a side-slip to a landing."

Samuel landed with smooth precision, taxied to the hangar, and shut off the engine. He was sweating when he climbed out of the trainer.

Shania kissed him. "Think you passed?"

He turned to Chief Anderson. "Well, Chief?"

Anderson had a severe look on his face but extended his hand. "Congratulations. That was one of the best damn private check rides I've ever seen. Even better than Captain Benjamin O. Davis, Junior, which I will personally convey to him first thing Monday morning."

Guillard threw his arms around Samuel. "My turn next."

Samuel and Shania arrived home to find LeBaron sitting on the couch, staring aimlessly at his family photo album. She could see he was bothered, and sat beside him.

"Papa, what's the matter?"

"Your Aunt Tilly called. Her brother-in-law has taken ill in Richmond. She's going to have to see him."

Samuel looked questioningly at Shania.

"Aunt Tilly is my mother's sister in North Carolina. We were going there for the holidays." She said sadly. "I'm sorry, Papa."

LeBaron sighed. "I did want us to be with family this Christmas, especially with Aunt Tilly. I doubt she'll be here for another. She's not in good health, either."

Shania walked to kitchen and stared out of the window. Samuel saw her tremble and put his arms around her.

"Why are you crying?"

"I didn't want to go to North Carolina. I didn't want you to go to Arizona. I had prayed we could all stay here for Christmas. Now I have my wish. We're here. You're here. With the war and all, I'm afraid it might be the only chance we would have to spend Christmas together for a long while. I know you'll be going off to war . . ."

"You're the most unselfish person I know." He lifted her chin and kissed her on the lips.

At the boardinghouse he found Guillard practicing a cross-country flight with his map. He went to the telephone and asked the long-distance operator to connect him with his father's office. When his father was finally on the line, he said, "Pop . . . guess what?"

They talked for a long time and when he was finished, he cradled the telephone receiver and pulled off his right boot and peeled down his sock. He retrieved a wad of folded twenty-dollar bills, peeled off his other sock and pulled out another wad of folded twenties, and remembered what his mother had told him: "Carry your money in your socks! Thieves will look everywhere for your money . . . but not in your socks!" He chuckled at remembering the surprise on the soldier's face when he showered with his socks on at the airfield.

He went to his car and drove away. But not in the direction of Shania's house.

When he returned two hours later she was beside herself with worry. "I thought you might have gotten into trouble."

He shook his head. "Everything's fine. Let's go sit with your father. There's something I want to talk to you both about. It's very important."

30

$$\ast \quad \ast \quad \ast$$

Two days before Christmas, Adrian arrived later than usual, nearly giving Hannah cause for alarm. She was miserable enough, what with Samuel in Alabama for Christmas, Theresa heartsick that Jonathan was in basic training, Selona and John feeling poorly. She watched him walk from the car, looking like he was carrying another burden from the business. With Jonathan away, that burden had doubled.

He took off his coat and hung it up, turned slowly, and said, "Hannah, dear, I forgot my valise in the car. Will you fetch it for me?"

She looked at him curiously. "You always say, 'I got one good arm. I don't need any help.' What's wrong? Is your back ailing?" Adrian's back had been giving him trouble for several years, the spine being pulled out of line by the lack of skeletal and muscular balance from the amputation of his left arm.

He lit his pipe, then said kindly, "Just fetch my valise, dear."

She threw a shawl around her shoulders and went to the car where she opened the door, jumped back, then yelped with glee as Samuel reached up and pulled her into his arms. He climbed from the front passenger seat, still holding her. "Hello, Momma."

"What . . . what . . . how . . . what are you doing here?"

"We're home for Christmas."

Hannah pulled from his embrace. " 'We'?"

Samuel pointed to the backseat.

The woman in the backseat moved; the light of the moon shone onto her face. "I'm Shania." Sitting beside her was Patrice LeBaron, who nodded politely. "I hope our coming along is not upsetting to your holiday plans."

Hannah was speechless, and could only shake her head when, finally, the words flew from her mouth. "Mind? This is wonderful! The most wonderful Christmas present I've ever had."

She looked to the porch, where Adrian stood, the cloud of smoke from his pipe not large enough to conceal the grin on his face. "Merry Christmas, Hannah."

Shania stepped from the Packard into Hannah's embrace, then LeBaron embraced Hannah, and the four laced their arms and walked into the house. Suddenly, Hannah pulled the other three to a halt as she looked quickly at Samuel, stammering, "What about the presents we sent to Alabama? There won't be gifts for any of you for Christmas."

Samuel patted her hand. "We don't need gifts. This is the greatest Christmas present we could have."

Hannah turned to see the nodding agreement of Shania and LeBaron. Then they walked into the house, Hannah forgetting that she had not brought Adrian's valise.

The front room swelled with laughter and questions that night as Samuel explained the whole idea. "I called Pop and asked if the three of us could come together. He said that would be wonderful . . . but don't tell your momma."

Adrian said, "Samuel thought it too far to drive, and so I suggested the train."

Samuel added, "I went to Chehaw to buy the tickets, but the ticket office said we might have trouble getting seats. I called Pop back, and in two days he had pulled the strings with his contacts on the Southern Pacific. And now, here we are!"

Selona had a suspicious look in her eye as she said to Adrian, "I should have suspected something was afoot when I found that train schedule last week."

"How was the trip?" asked Hannah.

Samuel stretched his legs and yawned. "Very long and tiring. We boarded in Chehaw, near Tuskegee, and rode day and night for three days."

Selona asked, "Did you bring your granddaddy's rifle?"

"I left the Sharps at Professor LeBaron's house."

Selona smiled approvingly. "Good. A big, young Colored man might get hisself into trouble carrying a rifle on a train through Secesh country. Especially with a war going on."

Everyone laughed. Hannah didn't care for the humor. "I'll hear no more talk about war in this house while Samuel is home. It ain't fitting to talk about such a terrible thing when we're celebrating the birth of the Lord."

"I agree, Momma. We won't talk about the war."

Hannah's face suddenly froze as she realized a dilemma. "What about food? Lord have mercy, I don't have a big enough turkey for all these folks."

Adrian patted her hand. "Don't worry. I brought a side of beef from the packing plant. It's in the trunk. We'll have steak along with the turkey. There's plenty of food and lots of cooks. Besides, if we run low, Samuel can take the shotgun and bring home some prairie chickens." Adrian looked warily at Samuel, "With all your college and flying lessons, you haven't forgotten how to hunt, have you, son?"

Samuel shook his head. "No, Pop. I haven't forgotten."

They sat and talked through the night. That was when Hannah became fretful. "We don't have enough beds for everybody."

That was when Adrian pulled another trick from his Christmas sack. "Why do you think Theresa went to Tucson to stay with Benjamin and the children? But don't you worry, they're all coming over for Christmas Day."

Hannah understood. Adrian had driven her to Willcox that morning, where she took the train to Tucson. "You've just about figured it all out haven't you, Adrian Sharps?"

Adrian touched the bowl of his pipe with a match and nodded slowly; his eyes danced with a warm glow.

*   *   *

The next morning, Selona and the Reverend John Parks were sitting in the front room, both wrapped in shawls. The weather was crisp, but not as cold as other years she had known.

"The war's changed the plans of the whole world," Selona said. Only the sudden crackle of the burning logs in the fireplace occasionally interrupted. She would pause, look out the window toward the stable, and shake her head sadly. "All these young Coloreds wanting to go off to war." Her eyes followed Samuel leading a saddled horse, Shania following. Selona shook her head sadly as she watched them climb onto their horses and ride away. "It don't make no sense."

Parks rose and stoked the fire. "It's meant to be that way, Miss Selona. I recall feeling the same way back in 'seventeen. I couldn't get to that army recruiter fast enough."

"You all right?" she asked. "You're looking poorly this morning."

He dabbed at his mouth with his handkerchief. "Just a touch of my consumption."

Selona grumped. "Consumption! You got 'mustard lung.' Now, my momma had consumption. That old 'black lung.' Had it real bad, too, even as a little girl. Took her to the grave as a young woman. Didn't have no penicillin or other doctoring suchlike for consumption. Just cough, spit, and get ready for the next attack." Her eyes followed one of the riders as he rode from her sight, and mused aloud, "I wonder what he'll get?"

"Won't get mustard lung." Parks snorted. "Those Germans are using gas more terrible than mustard gas in the Great War." He paused, then asked, "Did he say why he came back from college?"

Hannah came into the room and, having overheard, said, "To break his leg . . . I hope. Then he won't be going off to that foolishness."

"That won't stop him," Parks reflected. "Broken bones heal, especially with the young."

Hannah stood by the fire, warming her hands, then turned, facing the two. "He's mighty smitten with that young lady. Maybe that's enough to make him show that he's got some sense."

Selona looked at her, then remembered something from years

ago, during a war. "Adrian was smitten with you, as I recall. I didn't see you holding him back when the boys went marching off to France."

Samuel drew his horse to a stop on a hill overlooking Sabre Ranch and stared silently at the family spread. In the distance he could see the dusty rooster tail from his father's car winding toward Bonita. Since returning from France, his father always made the trip to town every Christmas Eve. On this trip, he took LeBaron, to show him the sights of the little mining town.

"Where does he go?" Shania asked.

Samuel pulled back his hat, then closed the collar on his coat. "To church."

Shania looked at him quizzically. "You once told me your father didn't go to church. Not since those people in Tennessee stood by while Kluxers shot your grandfather."

Samuel tightened the reins in his gloved hand. "He goes once a year to the little mission church in Bonita. But he doesn't go there to pray. He goes there to give a donation to the priest. It's for the poor people of the town. He once said, 'That gift gives me more gratification than any Sunday-go-to-meeting on earth. But most of all, it keeps your momma and Grams off me for the rest of the year!'"

She spurred the horse. He took after her, watching her hair trail behind, amazed at how well she rode. He shouted, "I didn't know you could ride."

She looked back, her smile mysterious as she yelled, "I can't."

Samuel spurred his horse, caught up with her, and gripped the halter until he brought the horse to a walk. He jumped from the saddle and pulled her down into his arms and they kissed. The words reverberated in her mouth, and she thought she understood, but had to ask, "What did you say?"

He looked sheepish, then said aloud, as though talking to the open desert: "Do you think you might consider becoming my wife?"

She took his big hand and kissed his gloved knuckles. "I've been considering that since I first met you."

He looked dumbfounded. "Does that mean yes or no?"

She laughed. "You really don't know anything about women, do you, Samuel Sharps?"

He looked embarrassed. "I guess not. But if you say 'yes,' then I figure you'll give me a chance to learn."

She swung into the saddle, spurred the horse, and yelled over her shoulder, "The answer is . . . yes!"

Samuel took off in pursuit, his hat flapping in the breeze. Nearby, a tarantula hawk wasp lit beside its mate on a saguaro and ruffled its wings, its keen eyes oblivious to the young lovers.

They rode into the ranch giggling and laughing, anxious to share the news with their families. They were so excited, they didn't unsaddle the horses, but tied both mounts to a hitching post and hurried through the door. The moment Samuel stepped into the front room he knew something was wrong. Selona sat on the sofa, staring emptily through the window. The Reverend John Parks was leaning against the fireplace. From the kitchen there was the sound of Hannah weeping.

"What's wrong, Grams?"

Selona was motionless as she said, "We got a telephone call from Benjamin. Your Aunt Theresa has passed away. They found her in bed this morning. The doctor figures she must have passed sometime during the night."

Samuel turned and walked through the door. Shania watched him leave. "Where's he going?"

"He's getting a shovel, child. There's a burying to be done."

Shania sat beside Selona and took her hands into hers, noting the difference marked by age. Shania's slender fingers surrounded Selona's short, stumpy fingers; long fingernails entwined with blunted, worn nails. Selona's fingers were stiff and twisted, like vine; Shania's straight and supple. It was as though time—today and tomorrow—lay in her palms, a road map of life. "I'm so sorry; I know you loved her dearly."

"We all got to come and go, child. One day, each and all of us. The going ain't important, at least, not in the when or the how, or the way. What's important is the 'leaving.' What you leave behind.

Theresa had a hard, lonely woman's life, but she never complained. Not for a bit. When she heard my boy David was killed over in France, she took a shovel and dug his grave. A grave we knew would be empty of body, but full of soul. The Sergeant Major wanted to dig the grave, but she said 'No, sir. Children bury their fathers and mothers. Mothers and fathers don't bury their children. Me and his children'll bury him. That's the natural order of things.' "

Shania followed Selona's eyes through the window to where she could see Samuel walking—a shovel in his hand—toward the cemetery.

31

✫　✫　✫

The engagement had come as no surprise to either LeBaron or
Samuel's family. All the parents were pleased with the notion
the two families would be joined. Being a practical woman and not
wanting the holidays to end in sadness, Hannah had a thought that
she shared with Benjamin the day after Christmas, when he and his
family arrived at Sabre Ranch to bury Theresa Gibbs Sharps.

Benjamin and his wife Francine sat at the kitchen table listening
to Hannah's plan. "I married Adrian the same day your mother
married your father. I had no family, and it was the only chance for
us all to be together before they shipped over to France."

"You want Samuel and Shania to get married before they go
back to Alabama," Benjamin said.

She nodded. "I do, but I don't want to offend you and your family. It don't seem right to bury a loved one, then turn around and cel-
ebrate a new beginning."

"I think it would be medicine for us all. Like you say, it's probably the only time we'll be together for a wedding." He looked to the
front room where his mother's casket sat. "I think Momma would
be pleased. She was a woman for the moment, but always looking
ahead. Does that make any sense?"

Hannah reached and cupped Benjamin's face in her hands and
kissed him lightly on the forehead. "More than you could ever

know. She didn't have a selfish bone in her body—except for her family. And rightfully so. I know your father—and mother—would be very proud."

"Just one promise?" Benjamin said.

"Anything."

"I think Momma would be proud to have Shania wear her wedding dress. I know you and Grams didn't have a proper wedding dress when you were married. I know my mother's wedding dress was made by my grandmother when she married my father."

"I think that would be wonderful." She stood and walked to the casket and kissed her sister-in-law on the cheek.

When the funeral for Theresa ended, Selona went to the house she had built for Vina Gibbs; where her son David had married Theresa. In the back room she knelt in front of a cedar chest and took out the wedding dress. In the front room, Hannah stopped in front of a fireplace much like the one in Selona's house. She reached above the mantel and removed a long, curved cavalry sabre that had belonged to Sergeant Darcy Gibbs. The same sabre David had carried to France.

The two women left with the memories of the past, and solid mementos that joined the two generations, not looking back, thinking only of the now, and the tomorrow. And, thought Selona, with a little of the yesterday. The yesterday was good—solid, careful, but always dangerous. The now was uncertain. But tomorrow? Who knew?

Yet, one thing she was sure of: If you're a bride going into the uncertain, wear a white dress that was never tainted with regret.

That afternoon, with the grave of Theresa Gibbs Sharps still fresh, Shania and Samuel passed beneath the apex of the two Buffalo Soldiers sabres—held by Adrian and John—into the uncertainty of the future, untainted . . . and with honor.

32

The sun shone brightly on the first day of April in Washington, D.C., where a slight breeze greeted Congressman Ernst Bruner, Jr. as he stepped from a taxi in front of the Willard Hotel. It was the same hotel where his father had once met with Theodore Roosevelt and William F. "Buffalo Bill" Cody to discuss the future of the plainsman's Wild West Show. On that morning in 1898, a particular person was discussed regarding the representation of Colored soldiers in the show. The person was Sergeant Major Augustus Sharps, a longtime friend of the Bruner family. Now it was time to discuss that person's grandson in a new historical context.

The congressman went inside and sat in the restaurant, where he waited for the one man he thought might offer assistance. He ordered coffee and toast, then browsed through the newspaper, which was filled with stories about the war in Europe and the Pacific. The news was all bad, especially in the Pacific, where the Japanese controlled most of the Pacific Rim. In Europe, the Axis Powers controlled most of the continent, including a major portion of North Africa and the Middle East.

"Good morning, Congressman." The man standing before Bruner spoke in a high-pitched voice that twanged with a Southern accent.

Bruner folded his paper and laid it on the table, then rose and offered his hand. "Good morning, Senator." He motioned to a chair, and the small man with the bow tie and wire-framed glasses seated himself.

The senator was a dapper man, a Missourian who had served in the Great War as a field artillery officer. He removed his glasses, wiped them slowly with his handkerchief, while watching the congressman from Arizona. "My apologies for being late. It's impossible to get a taxi these days, even if you are a senator."

Bruner understood the dilemma. Washington was overflowing with people since the outbreak of the war, and, with the rationing of petroleum, taxi service was in great demand. "That's quite all right, Senator. Frankly, I wish I could ride my horse these days. Travel would be faster."

The politician poured a cup of coffee then sat back in his chair. "How can I help you, Congressman Bruner?"

Bruner knew that the man was a strong civil-rights advocate and one of the early supporters of Negro aviation in the military. "I'm here as a representative for one of the families in my state. They are Colored, highly respected in the community. A business family with a restaurant and meatpacking interests. The man I'm representing served in the Great War with the Ninety-Third Division, where he lost an arm and a brother in the Meuse-Argonne. His father served with the Colored cavalry in the west."

The Senator smiled softly. "I remember the Colored soldiers in France. They did a wonderful job, though history hasn't been fair in chronicling their contribution."

Bruner nodded in agreement. "His son is an ROTC student at Tuskegee Institute, and has his private pilot's license. At the outbreak of the war he applied for flight training in the Army Air Corps, but hasn't received any notification from the War Department on his application. I've written several letters supporting his selection, but so far there's been no progress."

The senator was a man with well-known political ambitions that many felt included a watchful eye on the White House. He also knew the political arena was much like war, another arena where strength was enhanced by having allies. "Give me the young man's name, Congressman Bruner. I'll see what I can do for your constituents."

Bruner slid a piece of paper across the table and watched him read. "Sharps. That's an interesting name."

"An interesting family. His grandfather saved my grandfather's life by rescuing him from Comancheros. The grandmother shot a bank robber off his horse and saved the town's money. He's passed on, but she's still alive and feisty as ever."

"Sounds like a great family."

Bruner chuckled, then added, "He won a race last year against an army tank."

Truman nodded approvingly. "The young man sounds like a good horseman."

Bruner laughed. "No, Mr. Senator. He was riding a Missouri mule."

The senator laughed aloud, and said, "We Great War veterans have to look after one another, even now, in these trying times. Especially, when a young man has an affection for good mules."

The two shook hands, then the senator rose and left, stopping at a few tables to greet other members of Congress. Bruner left a few minutes later, went to his office, and dictated a letter to his friend Adrian Sharps.

Senator Harry S. Truman did the same; his letter was dictated to Henry L. Stimson, Secretary of War.

33

*　*　*

After returning to Tuskegee from Bonita, Samuel and Shania had attended classes while staying at her father's home. The boardinghouse was now filled with military families, and LeBaron was again seeing a solid financial return on his investment.

By April, the country was on a war footing, rationing critical goods necessary to fight a world war on two fronts. Samuel's car sat idle most of the time, except for special occasions; bicycles became the primary means of transportation to campus and town. The rationing had an effect on food production, making LeBaron's truck farm more important to the local economy.

Creed Shilton was captured by the state police in Mississippi and returned to Tuskegee. After two hours in the back room of the sheriff's office—where he was beaten with a rubber hose—he confessed, then led the sheriff to the barn where Munson's grisly remains were unearthed. He was tried in the Macon County courthouse and found guilty, then sentenced to die by hanging.

LeBaron leased the acreage that was once Chilton's and expanded his operation, with a greater focus on produce needed by the soldiers at the expanding Tuskegee Air Field.

The day LeBaron drove to the base he was accompanied by Samuel, who had not been at TAAF since the attack on Pearl Harbor. The McKissack construction crews worked feverishly beneath the blistering sun to complete the base as quickly as possible. The tent barracks had been replaced by wooden buildings; the administrative and support structures had been completed, though the interiors were still devoid of walls, allowing sound to travel throughout the building. This created a great deal of confusion, especially where the cadets attended classes.

While LeBaron met with the Quartermaster, Samuel, dressed in his ROTC uniform, strolled around the base. His first stop was Kane's barracks, where he learned that the men of his company had been sent to Chanute Army Air Field, Illinois, for advanced training. For Samuel, it was the first time he felt like a soldier, saluting officers, feeling a part of the environment.

But it was the drone of aircraft that drew him to the airfield, where he watched cadets practicing takeoffs and landings. The air buzzed as though filled with a swarm of bees, punctuated by an occasional obscenity from the ground personnel working on aircraft in a nearby hangar. The smell of aviation fuel permeated his senses, burning his eyes and stinging his mouth with its acrid taste.

He felt he was home.

The squeal of tires turned his attention to a jeep coming to an abrupt halt and an officer climbed from behind the steering wheel. Samuel snapped to attention and saluted. "Good morning, sir."

Captain Benjamin Davis, dressed in flight suit and carrying a parachute, returned the salute and started for the flight line. He paused, then walked back to Samuel. He studied Samuel for a long moment then asked, "Have we met?"

Samuel nodded, then replied, "Last fall, sir. You were having lunch with Chief Anderson at Tuskegee Institute."

"Yes, I remember. You are the young man who thought flying was more important than an education."

Samuel felt momentarily embarassed. "Yes, sir."

"Do you still feel that way, young man?"

Samuel's mouth tightened. "Yes, sir. Especially now that we're at war."

"Are you aware that the War Department is only allocating ten cadet positions every five weeks?" Davis said.

"Yes, sir."

"Which means you could be drafted before your application is approved. If approved."

"I understand that possibility, sir. But I still want to be an aviator."

Davis said nothing more. He turned and walked toward a P-40 Warhawk parked on the tarmac.

Samuel stayed long enough to watch the fighter take off, then he returned to the Quartermaster's, where he found LeBaron waiting beside his automobile. His father-in-law was wearing a broad smile and leaned with an unaccustomed arrogance against the vehicle. He touched a flaming match to the bowl of his pipe, looked around, then exhaled a cloud of smoke.

Samuel understood immediately. "You've been given another contract."

LeBaron nodded slowly, then drew another puff from the pipe. "A most lucrative opportunity. Major Masterson wants all the produce we can grow. Which means there is a great deal of work to be done."

The two men climbed into the automobile and drove away to the sound of heavy boots tramping in cadence as a class of cadets double-timed toward the classrooms. Samuel couldn't help but notice that the class, which would have originally numbered ten, was composed of only six cadets.

That night Samuel and Shania sat outside, the sounds of neighborhood chatter wafting from front porches. The war had drawn people closer as every family was affected by the conflict; the absence of young men had become more noticeable as the draft continued to drain the population.

Sitting on the front steps, Shania casually eased under his arm and nestled against his chest. Samuel had noticed that she had been acting strange of late, often going for long walks by herself in the evenings. She even wore a mysterious smile, as though there was some great secret known only to her.

Then, he felt her release a long sigh. She straightened and took his hands and held them gently, toying with his fingers, the way she did when she had something important to share.

"You all right, baby?" Samuel said.

Shania nodded, then he felt her grip tighten. "I saw Dr. Reynolds this morning."

This alarmed Samuel. He put his hands on her shoulders and held her at arms length. "Are you sick?"

There was a short pause from her, then she said calmly, "We're going to have a baby."

Samuel nearly fell off the step. He jerked to his feet, dragging her with him, his eyes wide and filled with surprise. "A baby? How? When?" He was stammering, unable to find the right words.

She giggled. "I expect you know 'how.' The 'when' will be sometime in October."

He felt a rush of elation and joy, mixed with the sudden reality of the desperate situation facing them and the world. "A baby. My God. We're at war, and I'm going to have to go into the military, and you'll have to be alone with a child."

"I won't be alone. Poppa will be here. Besides, you probably won't get called up before you start your flight training. That gives us at least another year together. The war will probably be over by the time the baby is born."

Samuel didn't share her feelings on the war's longevity. "It's going to be a long war, Shania. Like the Great War in Europe."

She took his hand and led him into the house, saying, "Let's not talk about war any more tonight. We have family to contact."

Suddenly, he swept her in his arms and started toward the front door, where he paused and kissed her lightly on the mouth, and whispered, "I love you."

Samuel called home and shared the news with his parents, whose excitement could be heard in the background. LeBaron sat listening from the couch, his chest swelled with pride like a banty rooster.

Samuel and Shania stood with the telephone pinned between their heads, both talking with such excitedness their words were barely understood in Arizona.

At the ranch, Hannah was the last to speak with Samuel and Shania, and hanging up the telephone she watched Adrian take his pipe and walk outside with John Parks. She and Selona joined the men, who stood talking in the last remnants of the fading sunlight. She helped Selona into her rocking chair and draped a shawl around the old woman's shoulders, then sat beside her.

"I hope it's a boy," Selona said.

Hannah dabbed a handkerchief at her eyes. "I don't care if it's a boy or a girl. All I want is a healthy grandchild."

"That's right," Adrian said.

Selona touched the flame of her new Zippo lighter to the bowl of her pipe and inhaled until smoke appeared. She took several more puffs, and when certain the tobacco was burning, snapped the cover of the lighter closed with such gusto it drew the others' attention. "Got to be a boy," Selona said flatly. "Girl can come later. We need us a boy."

"Why on earth is a boy so important, Grams?" Hannah asked.

Selona rocked a little faster, puffing furiously, the smoke rising in thick clouds. "We need a boy to carry on the Sergeant Major's bloodline." She stared intently into the distance, her puffing becoming rhythmic with the pace of the rocking.

"I don't care what it—" Hannah stopped suddenly. A cold chill threaded along her spine. She understood Selona's meaning. "You mean if he gets killed in the war without a son, the Sergeant Major's bloodline stops with him."

Adrian stood silent, watching her face twist into a mask of sadness. "Come inside, Hannah. Momma is just talking out loud. Nothing's going to happen to Samuel."

"It'll be the end of our family line. I love the other grandchildren, you know that without question. But that don't change the facts. The Sharps name will either be extended by Samuel's sons, or die with his death."

Hannah said nothing. She stood and hurried into the house. Adrian stared hard at his mother. "You could have waited, Momma." He walked into the house, followed by Parks, who paused and shook his head shamefully at Selona.

She said nothing. She knew that in war, the truth could be cruel.

34

The planting of LeBaron's acreage was nearly completed by the end of April, and as final exams approached, Samuel and Shania were busy preparing for what he believed would be his last days at the Institute. He couldn't keep his thoughts focused on the examinations since Shania was carrying their first child and the uncertainty of his military future was his major preoccupation.

Samuel was determined to do well on his final exams, knowing that if he were not accepted into flight training by the end of summer, he would enlist in the regular army. Having at least one year of college would give him a better chance of applying for Officer Candidate School, if he wasn't selected for the Air Corps.

He was sitting at the dining-room table, studying with Shania when a loud knock came at the front door. He rose quickly and went to a closet, where he took his Sharps, still mindful there were people in Tuskegee who had not forgotten the incident at the theater. He looked through the front window and saw Guillard standing on the porch.

Samuel opened the door, and Guillard entered without being invited. There was such excitement on his face and in his words, he didn't even offer a greeting. He came straight to the point, waving an envelope for both to see.

"I received my letter from the War Department." Guillard's voice was nearly a shout.

Samuel didn't have to ask the contents. "You made it into the program."

Guillard nodded wildly as he opened the envelope and pulled out the letter. "I've been ordered to report for training in two weeks!"

Samuel was so excited for his friend he momentarily forgot about his own dream of being accepted. He thrust out his hand, saying, "Congratulations, Thomas."

Shania threw her arms around him and they hugged while he still gripped Samuel's hand. His eyes danced with the sheer joy he felt throughout.

They went into the dining room where Samuel read the letter aloud. When finished, he folded the letter and handed it to Guillard. There was no hiding the disappointment on his face.

Thomas tucked the letter into the envelope then offered words of encouragement. "You'll be hearing from the War Department soon, Samuel. I can feel it in my bones. We're both going to get into the Air Corps."

Samuel wasn't as confident as Guillard. He knew that with every tick of the clock he drew farther from his dream of being an army aviator . . . and closer to being drafted.

The next morning, as he had done every morning for months, Samuel's first stop on campus was the post office. On this morning he went with refreshed hope, knowing that he and Guillard had applied from the same location and date. Perhaps, he thought, today there would be a letter for him.

He opened the mailbox and looked inside. There was nothing. He closed the box and stared at the small door for a long moment, then turned and walked to his first class. While walking across campus he recalled his mother always saying that "no news is good news."

His first class of the day was military science, the size of the group now diminished in numbers by the eagerness of many of the young men to serve their country in time of war. The ROTC class was shown a film on personal hygiene and venereal disease. The hygiene film was boring, depicting a white soldier going through the routine of shaving, showering, along with an explanation of why it's essential for a soldier's hair to be cut short.

The film on venereal disease was the one the students hoped would be more interesting; however, it proved to be insulting. Most of the soldiers were Negro, and shown with women who appeared to be prostitutes.

A slow rumble of anger began to rise from the students, who sat staring with loathing. The message was not lost on the use of Negroes, who were considered to be less than human in many parts of the country. But it seemed spiteful to portray men willing to die for their country as nothing more than degenerates who might infect others with disease.

When the film ended, the students walked out in silence.

The afternoon was hot and sultry. A typical Alabama sun beat mercilessly on Macon County, where heat waves wafted into the clear sky above the fields where Samuel and LeBaron labored. He had done terribly on his exams, and knew he had barely passed. However, that did not bother him. He had read somewhere that Winston Churchill, the feisty prime minister of Great Britain, had been a terrible student. That gave him some comfort. Some were good at taking tests. Others more designed for being put to the test.

He was weeding a row of corn when he heard a car pull into the front. It was his DeSoto, with Shania driving. That was unusual since the gas rationing required that the use of the auto be minimal. She practically flew from the car and began running toward him, an envelope clutched in her hand. Breathless, she stopped and extended her hand.

Samuel looked at the envelope for a long moment, then took it from her. In the corner was the official seal of the War Department. He opened the envelope and quickly read the letter.

A broad smile suddenly filled his face. "I've been accepted into the Air Corps."

PART 2

99TH PURSUIT SQUADRON

35

On April 2, 1943, the 99th Pursuit Squadron left Chehaw train station for New York, where, in the early morning hours of April 15, the 99th moved from their billets at Camp Shanks, New York, to the pier at the Brooklyn Naval Yard. There they joined nearly four thousand troops boarding the *USS Mariposa,* a former luxury liner pressed into service for transport of troops to North Africa. Gone was the splendor of the promenade deck, the elegant dining rooms, the dance floors that once vibrated with music, laughter, and clattering feet. Now there were cold gray walls and deckling dining tables that were constantly filled with either the men eating their two meals per day, or the KP crews preparing for the next hungry onslaught.

Prior to departure, Lieutenant Colonel Davis had been selected as executive transport officer, the first Negro in American military history to command both white and Negro troops. Davis quickly organized a staff, including an adjutant, mess officer, provost marshal, and police officer in order to carry out his orders.

Before sunrise, the ship slipped from the harbor and joined a convoy off the East Coast for the journey to North Africa. The decks of the transport were packed with troops watching the skyline of New York City gradually fade from the western horizon.

On the morning of the twenty-fourth, the sound all had waited

to hear was heard: "Land!" The sound became tumultuous, syn-
chronized into a chant until the bowels of the ship emptied onto the
decks. In the distance, beneath the rising sun, a thin strip of land
could be seen etched above the darkness of the ocean.

That afternoon, the *Mariposa* dropped anchor in the port near
Casablanca, where the slow debarkation of the arriving soldiers
drew a throng of Arabs, all begging for anything the soldiers might
offer.

The long line of soldiers, duffels over their shoulders, rifles slung,
tramped onto the deck and fell into formations. Convoys of trucks
arrived and departed constantly, slowly exhausting the human cargo
from the *Mariposa* until it was the 99th's turn to disembark.

The group loaded into army trucks, then slowly wound its way
from the port through Casablanca, to the cheers of Arabs crowding
the narrow streets. For the Americans, the white buildings, green
squares, and Colonials sitting at sidewalk cafés was the most fasci-
nating sight in their life. Even as dust rose in dense clouds the
brightly colored robes and turbans shone through like bright pebbles glistening from the bottom of a sandy creek.

The squadron bivouacked that night in the desert, beneath a
charcoal black sky. The next day was spent drawing equipment,
writing letters, getting their land legs back after spending nine days
aboard the transport.

Two days later, the word came down that the squadron was moving to its training station near Fez. After a horrendous seventeen-
hour train journey, the squadron arrived at an Arab village named
OuedN'ja. The squadron was met with friendliness by the local citizens, and were even entertained by the great Negro Parisian cabaret
singer Josephine Baker. With the arrival of their new P-40s, the pilots began their training in earnest. One of the thrills was to meet
Lieutenant Colonel Phillip Cochran—the pilot used as a model for
the character Flip Corkin in the cartoon strip *Terry and the Pirates*.
Cochran, considered one of the greatest dive-bomber pilots, provided invaluable training in dive-bombing techniques while estab-
lishing a warm rapport with the squadron.

After a month of training the squadron was moved to Fardjouna,
near the Mediterranean, where the first combat assignment came on

June 2, 1943, a strafing mission against the heavily fortified island of Pantelleria

On June 9, Lt. Charles Dryden engaged an enemy aircraft, a first in the squadron's history.

On July 2, Lt. Charles B. Hall scored the squadron's first air-combat victory over Castelvetrano, Sicily, destroying a Focke-Wulf 190. After performing a victory roll over the airfield, he was met by his jubilant comrades, who presented him with a bottle of precious Coca-Cola. Later that day, Generals Dwight D. Eisenhower, Carl Spaatz, James Doolittle, and John Cannon visited the squadron to pay their personal congratulations.

On July, 25, 1943, having completed his training, and with more than a year of continuous flight training at Tuskegee AAF, Second Lieutenant Samuel Sharps, received his orders for the European Theater. He would ship out for North Africa following a thirty-day leave.

36

On the morning of August 10, 1943, Selona Sharps, now age eighty-six, was pulled from a deep sleep by the sound of footsteps on the hardwood floor of her home at Sabre Ranch. She rose from the thick feather bed and, through squinting eyes, could see the outline of a tall man framed in the door.

She reached to her nightstand for her spectacles then smiled as the image came into sharp focus.

"Good morning, Grandmother," said Samuel.

She slid over slightly, then patted the bed, saying, "Good morning, baby. Now you come and sit with your grams."

At twenty-three, Second Lieutenant Samuel Sharps wore the uniform of the United States Army Air Corps; on his left breast were the wings of an army aviator.

Selona's eyes brightened as two more people came into the room. Shania carried in her arms their son, Adrian Samuel Sharps, Jr.

Samuel stood as Selona reached up and Shania gently placed the baby in her arms. Her ancient eyes joined those of the baby for a long moment, then she kissed him softly on the forehead. Momentarily she lifted the baby to Shania.

"I'm going to give him a bottle, honey," Shania said, then she left the room.

Selona looked quickly at Samuel. "Are you hungry?"

Samuel patted his stomach. "Momma fed us. If I eat another bite, my uniform will start popping buttons."

She laughed, and her mind tumbled back over more than seven decades to another young soldier she had once fed.

"You look just like your granddaddy."

He sat on the edge of the bed and took her hands. "The Sergeant Major? Why, Grandmother, you know I'm better-looking than he was."

She slapped playfully at his hands. "You hush now. He was the handsomest man God ever put on this earth." Then she paused for effect, and added, "Well, one of the best. You've done right well for yourself in the looks department."

He smiled. "I come from good stock."

Her eyes drifted toward the light bending through the window. "I expect you'll be leaving this morning."

He gathered her frail hand in his long fingers. "Yes. Pop is going to drive me to Willcox. I'll catch the train this afternoon."

"I'm so glad Shania and the baby are staying here at the ranch while you're away."

Samuel recalled something, then said, "It seems to be a family tradition. Momma and Aunt Theresa stayed here while Pop and Uncle David were in France."

She looked at him suspiciously. "You're sure her daddy don't mind?"

Samuel shook his head. "He doesn't mind."

She thought for a long moment. "Seems the men in my life are always catching a train to go off to war." Her voice cracked. "Your daddy went off to war from that same train station. That old platform's done seen a lot of Sharps men go off to war. Even the same platform where they brought Darcy Gibbs' body when he was killed by old Geronimo's warriors."

Samuel nodded slowly. "At least Shania and the baby will be here to keep you all busy."

"There's some comfort in that." She sighed, then said, "I expect you'll be going over there and fighting them Germans."

"Yes, ma'am. I've been assigned to the Ninety-Ninth Fighter Pursuit Squadron."

"The whole world has done gone and got itself into another ruckus."

"That it has."

"You got to promise me one thing," she said.

"Anything for you."

"You come back safe and sound. Don't go getting crazy and try to be a hero. Do you understand?"

He nodded. "I understand."

She took a deep breath. "Now, you go on and get on over there and help stop this war."

He leaned and kissed her gently on the forehead, then held her in his arms, knowing it might be the last time he would see her alive.

He stood, bowed slightly, and said, "I'll see you again."

Then he walked out of the bedroom, not seeing the tears in her eyes. Nor did she see the tears in his.

All morning Hannah had found things to do to keep her mind off the coming sadness. Now fifty-one, she had nothing but gratitude to God for the good life He had given her. Adrian had come home from his war twenty-four years ago and she could remember few occasions since when she did not wake up looking forward to the day. Adrian, still the dashing Adrian she had married before the Great War, had made a success in the real-estate business and was still Bonita's great war hero, and long ago she had taken over responsibility for Selona's restaurant business and had her own success and satisfaction. Yes, the passing years had been good—even during the Great Depression, when she had become a sort of local legend for giving away more food than she sold.

But now she had to face the heart-tearing moment she had hoped never to experience again after she had said good-bye to Adrian back in 1917. Selona had to do it countless times when the Sergeant Major saddled up when duty called; now it was Shania's turn, and Hannah's heart ached for her daughter-in-law.

So now she puttered in her kitchen as if keeping busy would delay the moment. But through the window she could see Adrian and Samuel walking toward the cemetery, and she knew what that meant: It was Sharps family tradition to say farewell to the gallant men, and the gallant woman Vina Gibbs, who lay at rest there.

She watched them talk a while, then start back toward the house. She knew what would come next.

Hannah put away the last of the washed breakfast dishes, wiped her hands on her apron, and went into the sitting room. Shania was sitting on a divan, feeding the baby, when Samuel and Adrian entered.

Samuel's heavy military suitcase was packed and sitting by the front door.

Adrian said nothing as he walked to the mantel, where he reached up and removed the dented, battered sabre from the two wooden pegs.

"Samuel, your grandfather carried this for nearly forty years in the defense of this country. It was given to me when I went to war in France. Now it belongs to you. I know you will carry it with honor."

Samuel turned his palms upward and received the sabre, and as the metal touched his skin, he thought he could feel the presence of the Sergeant Major.

"I will, Pop."

Samuel placed the sabre on his suitcase. Adrian looked at Hannah, and said, "I guess I'll load his gear into the car."

Hannah came to Samuel and put her arms around him. "You be careful. If you get hurt, I'll break your arm!" Tears began to streak her face as she held her only remaining child.

He hugged her, kissed her forehead, then turned and left quickly, followed by Shania, who carried the baby.

She watched him until the door closed, then went into the kitchen and sat at the table, listening to the doors slam, the engine start; then the car drove away.

From the bedroom Selona heard the familiar sound that echoed from her past on so many occasions.

She heard a mother weeping.

37

A lone C-47 transport banked sharply in the late hours of the night on September 28, 1943, and lined up on the runway at Barcellona, Sicily, on the north coast of the island. Code named *Avalanche,* the invasion of Italy was under way. The Germans had been driven off Sicily by Patton and Montgomery's lightning assault and now waited in Italy for the advancing Allied armies.

Samuel stepped down from the "Gooney Bird," tired, his uniform wrinkled, carrying one piece of baggage. Tied inside the handle grips of the bag was his grandfather's sabre.

He reported to flight operations, an old house on the flight line, where he found a white sergeant doing CQ duty, his crossed feet perched atop the desk. The man looked up momentarily, snickered, then returned to his comic book. "What can I do for you, boy?" he said.

Samuel felt his stomach tighten. "You can start by standing on your feet and calling me 'sir,' or 'Lieutenant.' Not 'boy.' "

The sergeant unfolded his feet and leaned forward in his chair. He laid the comic on the desk and slowly stood. "Yes, sir. How can I help you, Lieutenant?"

"I'm looking for the Ninety-Ninth."

The sergeant pointed beyond the window, and said, "Go outside, take a left. The nig—" He stopped. "The Ninety-Ninth is located about two hundred yards down the line."

Samuel picked up his bag and left. The sergeant sat down and chuckled, saying, "I should have told him to just follow the smell."

He found the headquarters tent of the 99th and went inside. A young corporal was listening to Lena Horne on the Victrola. He sprang to his feet upon seeing Samuel enter. "Good evening, sir. Corporal Kane, sir."

"Is that Kane, as in 'Sugar' Kane? From Evangeline, Louisiana?" A huge grin spread across Samuel's face. He still wore his head shaved and sported a thick brushy mustache that flowed into mutton chop whiskers, like those of the cavalry of the western frontier.

"Samuel!" Kane shouted. He roared around the table and threw his arms around his friend. Then, as quickly, he straightened to attention. "My apologies, sir." He was grinning from ear to ear.

"At ease, Corporal." They shook hands vigorously.

"Man, I never thought I'd see you again after Tuskegee," Kane said.

"After the day the Japanese attacked us at Pearl Harbor, we lost touch. I went and completed the flight training. I know your outfit went to Chanute Army Air Field. Where did you go to after that?"

"At Rantoul, Illinois, where Chanute is located, we spent twenty-two weeks, training day and night to form the fighter squadron's support group. I thought I was going to get back to Tuskegee, but I was so good at my job they made me a corporal and an instructor."

Kane told Samuel about the rigorous training of the support group. In March, 1942, the Adjutant General's office organized the 318th Air Base Squadron, the support element for the 99th Fighter Squadron. More than four hundred enlisted Negro men were sent to Chanute to begin their training. They were met by fourteen non-commissioned officers from the 24th and 25th Infantry Regiments, sent to Chanute to assist in the administration, training, and supervision of the trainees.

Five Negroes were selected as officer candidates, to be trained at Chanute and to become administrative members of the 318th upon receiving their commissions. These five cadets became the first

Negro Army Air Corps officers. Eight months later, on November 7, 1942, General Hap Arnold, Commander of the Army Air Corps—who had not believed the unit could be trained in less than one year—issued Order 263, activating the 318th. The unit was sent to Alabama to prepare for the pilots still in training at Tuskegee. The base was mostly a tent city, and since there were no flight operations other than training the first class—designated C-42—the 318th was put to work in the construction of the base. Nobody grumbled, since all the men knew they were building the barracks they would live in, facilities where they would work, and a squadron that could only go into combat when fully operational.

"So they made you an instructor at Chanute?"

"Beats the hell out of the chain gang!" Both laughed heartily.

"Good to see you," Samuel said, "damn good to see you, Dexter. I still remember that day on the flight line."

Kane looked at his wings. "Well, young lieutenant. You got those wings. Congratulations. Lord have mercy, I'm so proud of you! I heard they kept you guys training, training, and more training." He shook his head, then beamed. "But now you're here and there's a fight coming. We're taking it to the Jerries in Italy, after kicking their butts off this rock!"

"I can't wait. Remember that girlfriend I told you about?"

"The college student at the Institute? You never did get me that double date."

"Sorry about that. Anyway, we got married. I have a baby boy!"

Kane whooped. "Man, you have been busy!"

A voice boomed from behind them. "What's going on here, gentlemen?"

Both turned. Captain George S. "Spanky" Roberts stood at the tent entrance.

They snapped to attention. Kane said, "Sir, this is Lieutenant Samuel Sharps, one of the replacements."

Roberts studied him. "Welcome aboard, Sharps. We have a briefing at zero-six-hundred." He turned and left the tent.

"He's the new CO now that Lieutenant Colonel Davis has been sent Stateside."

"I remember Captain Roberts from Tuskegee, though I never met him there."

"One roaring, tear-ass squadron commander. Do your job, and you're OK, foul up, he'll eat you blood raw."

"I'll remember that." Samuel yawned.

"Damn, you must be tired." He grabbed Samuel's bag, then paused and looked at the sabre. "What in the hell is this?"

"My grandfather's cavalry sabre from his days soldiering on the western frontier with the Buffalo Soldiers. My father carried it in World War One. Now it's my turn."

Kane released a long, slow whistle. "Man, if this thing could talk." He handed Samuel the sabre. "Come on. Let's find you a bunk. You're going to need some sleep before the briefing."

Samuel followed Kane along a row of tents that housed the officers and the enlisted support personnel. Stopping at one, Kane opened the tent flap and shined a flashlight on an empty cot. "Sure ain't much, but I guess it beats sleeping on the ground."

"I could sleep on rocks right now, Dexter."

"Sit tight. I'll get over to supply and get you some bedding."

Samuel grabbed Kane by the arm. "No, that's all right. I won't know the difference. I'll pick that up tomorrow. There is one thing you could do for me."

"Name it, you've got it, my friend."

He told Kane. "I'll see to it before the sun rises," the corporal said.

Kane left and Samuel lay down on the cot. The tent held four, and as he listened to the others snoring fell asleep with his tie still around his collar.

The briefing was attended by all the pilots of the 99th, both veterans and replacements. The brightest moment was seeing Guillard, who had left the replacement training center the day before Samuel. They sat together and listened to Captain Roberts brief them on the morning mission.

Roberts turned to a map and ran a pointer along the Strait of Messina, separating the island from the mainland of Italy. "Our mission is to keep the shipping lanes open for transports to deliver supplies and equipment. There's not much expectation of encountering the enemy, but we need to be on our toes. We have two new men, Sharps and Guillard. Sharps will fly with Lieutenant Hall, Guillard with Lieutenant Dryden. You will all be briefed individually by your wingmen on the way to the aircraft. Gentlemen, good luck, and good hunting."

Roberts left, and the pilots departed for their aircraft. Samuel knew of Hall. He had scored the first air victory in United States Negro military aviation history. He was a tall man, with warm eyes and a soft smile. They talked for a few minutes about the mission, then went to the flight line, where Samuel found his own P-40 Warhawk waiting.

Kane had instructed one of the ground crew to paint a name beneath Samuel's, in bold letters: *Lady Shania.*

The moment Samuel had dreamed of for years had finally arrived. As he sat in his P-40, the propeller turning smoothly against the early-morning air at the dispersal area of the airfield, he recalled his first Stearman flight with Sparks Hamilton.

Now, he was a fighter pilot about to go into combat!

Heat waves boiled off the dusty runway, shrouding the airplanes, giving them ghostly looks, as the powerful engines created a storm cloud of gritty sand. Samuel pulled his goggles down, and S-turned, giving him some opportunity to see the aircraft to his front, allowing him some situational awareness. He knew Guillard was behind him, doing the same, and prayed he didn't hear—or feel—his tail section being chewed away by his propeller.

When the voice of the controller crackled over his radio, he turned ninety degrees to the port, shoved the throttle forward, and felt the engine's power vibrate through the Warhawk, causing the control stick to shake in his hand. He maintained a compass heading, hoping he was still on the runway, felt the tail section rise, giving him some increased visibility. Sweat poured into his eyes, but he couldn't wipe them since both hands were busy. When the airspeed indicator reached the proper speed, he eased back on the stick, felt the wheels break ground.

Suddenly, as though awaking from a foggy dream, he was above the dusty storm, roaring through a sky as clear and pristine as any he could remember in Arizona.

"Cowboy . . . you clear, man?" Guillard's voice called over the radio. "Cowboy" was Samuel's radio call sign.

Before Samuel could respond, he saw Guillard ease onto his starboard wing. Hall was on his left. Dryden to the starboard of Guillard. The two veterans had the rookies flying the inside slots.

Five hundred feet above, two other aircraft were turning a 360-degree holding pattern, waiting for the four to join them.

Samuel pointed to the two fighters, raised the nose, and flew toward the waiting Warhawks. When the six fighters were joined, they turned east from Barcellona and flew toward their mission arena: the Strait of Messina.

"Check your guns!" Hall's voice came over the radio. Samuel gripped the stick, pressed the red firing button, and felt the Warhawk shudder slightly as the guns stammered, spitting bullets into the empty sky.

"I'm clear," Samuel replied. He looked to the right, saw the smoke from Guillard's guns, then gave his wingman a "thumbs-up."

Samuel's first mission was a strafing and dive-bombing operation, requiring low-level flying at a steep angle of attack, a technique the replacements had practiced endlessly in the past weeks in North Africa after arriving there from the United States.

Guillard's voice came over the radio. "What do you think, Cowboy? Is this a sight to behold or what? Beats the hell out of Tuskegee any day."

Samuel had to agree. He missed his wife and baby, but the cerulean blue of the Mediterranean was majestic. In the distance he could see the coast of Italy. When they neared the eastern shore of Sicily, white signatures of ships etched the watery surface, appearing like scratch marks on blue paint.

"Beautiful. But I'd rather see a German fighter."

"That's the truth."

"You gentleman want to stop the chatter. The more you talk, the less you see. Keep your focus; otherwise, you might wind up a kill marking on a Jerry aircraft," Hall said.

The chatter stopped, and the six planes roared along the northern coast.

When they reached the strait they saw no sign of German fight-

ers; only calm water and white puffs of smoke splotched the coastline—artillery fire pounding the German positions.

Suddenly, Hall's voice snapped over the radio. "Jerries! Twelve
o'clock high!"

Samuel looked up, to the front, where he saw four black dots
against the blue sky.

"Focke-Wulf 190s," Hall shouted.

Samuel watched, mesmerized, as the dots grew larger, coming at
them from above, and with the sun at their backs. He had learned
that in air combat the first rule was . . . *get off the first shot.* He
picked one of the approaching fighters, took a line directly toward
the incoming fighter, then lowered his thumb to the red firing button. He watched, anxiously. His tactic simple: He would fire a
stream of bullets to the front of the Focke-Wulf, allowing the German to fly into the stream. When he felt the moment was right, he
pressed the firing button, felt the Warhawk shudder, and saw a
stream of .50-caliber bullets, their path marked by tracers, form a
white stream of molten lead in front of the German. But just as the
Focke approached the deadly stream, the enemy plane banked hard
left and evaded Samuel's volley.

The German banked again, this time toward the Warhawk, and
had the advantage since Samuel's nose was up, and he was flying off
the firing angle. The German swept toward him, his guns making
pinpricks of light, the path of his bullets directly to the front of
Samuel's Warhawk. Samuel raised the nose, winged over, and
avoided the deadly stream, but as he turned away from the enemy
fighter he knew the Jerry was on his tail.

He began jinking, kicking rudders, knowing the German was
staying on him, waiting for the moment to fire. He waited to see the
tracers pass him, giving him an idea of where the Focke was, but he
saw nothing. Then, he heard Hall's voice. "Damn . . . they just
swept through us. They're not here to fight!"

Later that afternoon, he lay on his cot, his eyes fixed to the ceiling,
trying to reenact what had happened. The engagement wasn't like
practice dogfights, where he could chase other pilots through the
air, make mistakes, have time to consider the situation, correct for

errors and try again. He realized that in this game—this game of air combat—there were no medals given for second place. If he was going to survive the war, he needed to learn to fly instinctively.

"You all right, man?" Guillard said as he entered the tent and sat on the edge of Samuel's bunk.

"I'm fine."

Guillard shook his head in disappointment. "At least you got to shoot at the suckers. All I saw was a blur rushing past. I didn't have time to get a good look at the bastards."

"Some shooting. I was wide by a mile. That German knew exactly what I was going to do before I did. He set me up beautifully. If he'd stayed on me, I'd be fish bait right now."

Guillard tapped him on the shoulder. "Let's go get some chow."

Samuel's stomach convulsed at the thought of food. "You go ahead. I'm not hungry."

He lay back, closed his eyes, and replayed the engagement over and over in his head. Before he realized it, reveille was sounding. He had refought the battle through the night, in his dreams and sleep.

38

☆ ☆ ☆

Samuel's father would always say: "The greatest contribution a soldier can make in battle was to save the lives of as many of his comrades as possible. You can't save them all, but you can bring back more than you will lose by proper leadership." To Samuel, none more exemplified this than the core of the 99th, men like Benjamin O. Davis, Jr., Charles Dryden, George Roberts, Spann Watson, Charles Hall, and countless others whom history would probably ignore for one reason or another. But there was a leader he would never forget.

Lieutenant Francis Hurd had enlisted in the army as a teenager and served with a mechanized reconnaissance unit at Fort Riley, Kansas, in the 10th Cavalry, modern-day descendants of the Buffalo Soldiers. He was a soft-spoken man, light-skinned, with laughing eyes that could turn into cold steel ball bearings when necessary. He was more than a flight leader; he was a soldier, and a teacher.

Samuel was standing by his P-40, talking with Kane, who had been assigned his crew chief, when Hurd approached. "Lieutenant Sharps, get your parachute on. We're going flying," he snapped, walking past the two without explanation.

"Seems like the first time we met I helped you strap on a parachute," said Kane.

"Yeah. But back then there wasn't any enemy waiting." He adjusted the leg straps and climbed into the cockpit. Minutes later the two fighters were roaring along the runway, then lifted into the sky.

Hurd's voice crackled over the radio. "I heard about what happened yesterday. You got your lunch eaten pretty good, didn't you, son?

"In the game of air combat . . . you better keep your business strapped tight . . . or you're going to die! It's as simple as that!" Hurd's voice crackled over the radio.

Hurd's Warhawk snapped with a wing-over, then disappeared from Samuel's sight. He looked around, but Hurd was gone.

"See me yet, young lieutenant?" Hurd's voice called.

He looked around. Nothing.

"Six high . . . on your ass!"

Samuel turned, looked back and up . . . he was only feet above Samuel's tail section.

"You have to think in the other man's mind. Know what he's going to do before he does. Then get there first!"

Hurd rolled right . . . Samuel rolled left, trying to get into Hurd's mind. Thinking. What would he do?

The sun! It was to Samuel's front. Hurd was going to come at an angle!

Samuel kicked the right rudder, banked hard right, turned ninety degrees, and there was Hurd. Hurd was coming straight at him.

"Good," Hurd said. "Now what you going to do?"

Get the angle on him!

Samuel banked left . . . then right, and had him at an angle.

"That's it!" Hurd shouted. "Now . . ." Then Hurd banked away.

Samuel swung onto his tail.

"What am I going to do next? You've got me on my tail," Hurd said.

Samuel felt he was going to go high. They were too low for him to go down. Hurd raised his nose . . . then Samuel raised his, but he was higher than the more experienced pilot. Come on, baby! Come on, baby! he told himself. I got your ass! "Rat-a-tat!" Samuel yelled. "I'm leading my fire for you to fly into it. I got you!"

Hurd laughed. "Return to base."

Samuel eased back on the throttle, saw Hurd waggle his wings, and for the first time since the Jerry, his stomach didn't feel tight.

The most important time was when mail arrived. He had three letters waiting. Two from Shania. One from his folks, which he read first, then settled onto his bunk and read the letters from his wife. The first was the most wonderful of all. She told him about her new job, teaching at the school in Bonita. But the second brought the most wonderful news of all.

Shania had spent the late afternoon walking in the desert near the ranch, carrying her pen and notepad, trying to find the right words, the sadness mixed with joy, creating a flood of conflicting emotions. She sat on a large rock, still uncertain whether to put the words to paper. She carefully wrote each word, knowing he was lonely, in the hellish nightmare of war, and with all that on his mind, she would now add to his burden:

"My dearest Samuel,

"Light of my life. It is so sad, to know you are so far away. I wanted to start this first letter by saying something. . . . You are my love, until my last breath . . . then beyond, into the forever.

"This war will end. You will come home to me. We will be together. Please be careful. Please . . . don't be too brave?

"We are all doing fine. The baby is growing, and eats like his father. Grams is forever spoiling him, when he's not being spoiled by your mother. I'm enjoying teaching, although it is sometimes a little difficult. The children are not quite used to having a Negro woman for a teacher, but they are polite, and behave well. I think the most satisfying part of the job is that it keeps me busy; otherwise, I would sit and cry, thinking of how much I miss you. With the war, so many women are now working outside the home. I think work is the only thing that keeps our sanity intact.

"There is something I need to discuss with you, sweetheart. I know you're busy, and you shouldn't be bothered by the trivial things at home, but . . . you're going to be a father, again!"

Samuel flew off his bunk, stood trembling while the words on the page blurred in his shaking hands. Before he realized it, he was standing outside his tent, oblivious to the roar of incoming aircraft.

"Samuel, ready to go to the briefing?" Guillard asked as he approached. He stopped suddenly. "Hey, man, are you all right?"

Samuel held out the letter. "We're going to have a baby."

The two hugged each other, then Samuel read him the letter as they walked to the briefing tent.

39

Selona had been born a slave, and by law, was not taught how to read or write. She would learn from an incredible white woman at Fort Davis, Texas, named Marcia O'Kelly. She learned her letters, then how to spell while learning to read.

Today, all that effort was to be put to its greatest test.

She sat at the kitchen table and wrote four letters to the people she loved most in the world. She took her time, since Hannah was at the restaurant, Shania at school, and Adrian in Willcox. Only the baby was there, and he was sleeping. She was alone, the way it was meant to be to write such letters.

She took her pencil and paper, and began. She wrote about her life, about where her family came from, about the first time she met the Sergeant Major. . . .

It was cold; wet snow fell. She wrote carefully, and hours passed. Each letter different, except the ending, where she closed by saying:

> ". . . And I've had all of you. David wasn't from my body, but he was from my heart. The day I heard he was killed in the Argonne, my soul was torn from me.
>
> "The day the Sergeant Major's horse rode in, without him in the saddle, I knew.
>
> "I expect I'm guilty of loving too much. I don't mind. It's been my pleasure. A pure treat.

"I'm going to say good-bye now. I love you. So much. Loving is a hard thing to do. It means you have to stay close. Stay loyal. Even when you're a long ways off."

She signed the letters, folded them, and placed them in their separate envelopes.

Then she went out to the "Remembering Bench" and sat in the warm sun.

Adrian was in a surly mood, as he had been all morning, and now, during the late-afternoon drive home, he continued to boil. Nothing had gone right since he walked into his office. Shipments were being delayed by the shortage of boxcars caused by the war effort; two of his employees had been drafted into the service, and his secretary had run off and married a sailor home on leave.

He pulled into the driveway at the ranch and saw his mother sitting on the front porch. He paused for a moment, composing himself. She was sitting in her rocker, puffing on her corncob pipe, staring into the distance.

"Momma. You all right?"

"I was thinking about those Apaches."

Adrian looked dumbfounded. "What Apaches?"

"That time we first come to Fort Grant. Lord, I was so scared. First time I ever seen Injuns up close. Thought I was going to die of fright."

Adrian lowered himself onto the porch, took his mother's hand. He could see it coming. Her grip was weak; her eyes hooded. "Momma, those were shining times."

"Yes. Life is mostly darkness. But it's the shining times that keeps the light burning in the heart."

He swallowed hard. "You always told us that. You always said, 'Don't be afraid of the dark, the light will come, and all will be safe.' "

"I'm sounding like an old woman."

He choked lightly. "No. You're sounding of your truth."

"You know, baby?"

"What, Momma?"

She looked away, as though searching for something lost. "I've seen the moments of the best of time."

"What were the best times, Momma?"

She pulled her shawl around her shoulders. "You. All of you. You were the shining that made the darkness just run from my eyes. You. Your daddy. Your brother . . ." She glanced over her shoulder. She didn't want to think about the empty grave not far away in the cemetery. "All of you."

Adrian forgot his troubles, listening to this woman of the western frontier who had struggled every day to keep him alive. "Tell me what you're thinking, Momma. I need your words. Your strength."

She looked at Adrian. "You don't need me, son. You have all the words carved into your heart. You have the strength, the love, the caring. That's all that matters. Anybody can be mean and evil, and stupid is the easiest. You have the difficult part—to be smart, good, and brave."

"I'm not any of those things, Momma."

She put her hand on his head. "You have all those things and the bravest heart of them all. Even the Sergeant Major."

He looked up astonished. "How can you say that?"

She explained. "He had no choice but to be brave. You chose to be brave. There's a difference."

"We were nothing but trouble."

She remembered him and David, scampering in the pinons at Fort Davis, running alongside the wagon going to Fort Grant, raising a ruckus with the rabbits with their slingshots. "You were a joy."

He could see she was growing tired. "Momma, come into the house. You need some rest."

Adrian helped her from the chair, and at that moment her pipe fell. He reached down and picked it up and handed it to her.

"I don't need it anymore," she said.

He said nothing as he led her toward the door. She turned and looked to the sun, watching its last traces stretch across the ground, running from the west like a red flood tide.

She smiled, then nodded, and said, "Let's go inside."

*   *   *

Selona had been a blossoming child when she first came to the western frontier in 1866. Now, in her eighties, she did what had she done every morning since she could remember: She rose early and went to the kitchen and fixed a pot of coffee.

There had not always been a kitchen; she had lived in tents, adobe huts, and even in an old army hospital wagon during the long trek from Fort Davis, Texas, to Fort Grant, Arizona, in 1885.

She did it the same, old way: ground up the rich, dark beans, put the fine grounds into the pot, added water, then boiled the mixture until it could be used for boot polish. Army coffee, she called it; stuck to the ribs and, in a pinch, could be used for oiling a Spencer rifle!

Her thoughts drifted from the kitchen, to the cemetery, where so much of her life lived in the quiet of death. She could see the markers, remembered getting one for her mother in Wallace, Kansas. Knew the one above David stood as a lone rememberance of his life. She stood there, looking into the vastness, the open desert, saw the stone reminders of her life.

Then, with her cup of coffee, she sat in a chair in her kitchen. An hour later, Adrian found her, slumped slightly, a smile on her face. She didn't move; she stared in silence at the wall, her spirit now joined with the loved ones in the ground.

Not far away.

Adrian stood silent, staring at the mound of fresh dirt, trying to remember what she looked like when he was a boy. And he saw her. Rising from nothing, raped and scalped by Texas Rangers, wearing that buffalo fur wig, big pistol in hand when she shot the rattler at Fort Davis, starting her cooking business with nothing more than the dream of owning a piece of land, facing down the Apaches on the long trek to Fort Grant, whipping the long rifle from a saddle scabbard and shooting the bank robber off his horse on the streets of Bonita. Saving the town.

Every time . . . she saved the day!

Hannah's hand touched his shoulder, then she whispered softly, "She's still with us, baby. She'll always be with us."

He said nothing. The flood of memories kept running through his mind. The memories, he knew, were like being lost . . . lost in time. But his momma had once told him, " 'Being lost . . . then finding your way . . . makes the lost worth the finding your way, and coming home.' "

Her words kept coming back, like sunlight filling the morning darkness. " 'The journey . . . not where you're going . . . it's the journey . . . that's what matters most.' "

Now, he wondered how he would continue his journey without her there, carrying the lamp, leading the way.

As she had always done.

He took a deep breath, one last look, then went into the house, knowing the answer.

She would always be with him!

Samuel received the letter from Shania two weeks later. As he read the words, he sat numb, reading the letter again and again. He had cried his tears, lost his thoughts in the reflections, then come back to the reality that only comes with pain. The reality of life.

In the background was that reality; the churning sound of war machines winding up their engines, groaning toward the flight line, preparing to go to war. Young men going to fight . . . maybe die . . . in a world gone insane!

He folded up the letter, stuck it in his Bible, then took his helmet and walked through the flap of the tent.

Toward the insanity.

Adrian stood at the gate of the cemetery, staring at the graves of his mother and father. Above his head, the sabres glistened in the moonlight, as his thoughts focused on the history that lay buried beneath this hallowed piece of ground.

"Come inside, honey," Hannah's voice called from behind him. He turned and saw her standing there, unsure of what to say.

"You've been out here every night. It's time to get on with living."

Adrian turned and started toward the house. He paused at the back door, glanced back one more time.

* * *

Teddy Bruner came by the next afternoon, his limp not as exaggerated as before, but his leg damaged enough to keep him out of the service. Adrian had noticed a sadness in the young man, one that he had carried since the outbreak of the war.

Bruner sat down heavily on the front porch. "I got a letter from Samuel." He held out the letter.

Adrian read, tears streaming down his cheeks.

"I think he wanted to say some things from his heart. Things he didn't want to say to you because he was afraid it would upset you more."

Adrian nodded, then folded the letter and gave it to Teddy. Teddy shook his head, saying, "I want you to have it. I think he meant it that way."

"You know, Teddy. Your family and mine have been a big part of building this part of the country. When I served with your granddaddy in the Rough Riders . . . he was one of the few men I knew I could trust. White folks didn't care much for Coloreds back in ninety-eight."

"Things haven't changed much, have they?"

Adrian rubbed his hands together. "Not much."

The news report in the September issue of the *Pittsburgh Courier* was distressing to Adrian. Black pilots were being treated with great disrespect at Selfridge Air Base, near Detroit, where Lieutenant Colonel Benjamin O. Davis, Jr. had returned to the United States to train the newly formed 332nd Fighter Group.

Coincidentally, *Time* magazine had come out with a scathing article titled "Experiment Proved?" an article that not only questioned the performance and leadership of the 99th, but raised sociological and physiological questions regarding the Negro's ability to ably fly in combat. Information for this article was supplied by "unofficial sources" from an army report in the Mediterranean theater.

He crumpled the newspaper and threw it into the garbage. In the front room, where he sat on the couch, staring at the empty pegs where his father's sabre and the Sharps rifle had hung.

40

☆ ☆ ☆

The first all-Negro fighter group in American military history had been formed, led by Colonel Benjamin O. Davis, Jr., who returned from Selfridge to take command of the group for the final push against the Axis Powers in 1944.

The Nazi's had disproved the *Time* article. Pilots from the 99th, on January 24, 1944, engaged the enemy with odds at two-to-one against the 99th.

Led by Captain Clarence Samisen, of Cleveland, Ohio, the Red-Tails shot down five enemy aircraft and watched the still-outnumbering Jerrie scurry for home.

The second wave, led by Lieutenant James T. Wiley . . . shot down three.

The Red-Tails did not lose a single aircraft in the engagement.

Samuel made his first victory roll over the airstrip, along with eleven other pilots, then landed to the jubilation of every member of the squadron support group.

Kane broke protocol and threw his arms around Samuel when he climbed down from the cockpit. He quickly recovered his composure, saluted, then, with a big smile, said, "Good job, sir. You've made us proud!"

Samuel's words stumbled awkwardly from Samuel's mouth. Almost apologetically, he said, "I got my first kill."

He walked away, the buzz of battle still in his ears, the fog of war in his brain.

He walked with an empty feeling inside. He wanted to lie down, to forget the victory. He had to prepare himself for the next encounter. Not handshakes and shouts; tomorrow he would need to do it again, and he needed to keep the edge.

In his tent he sat on his cot, took his notebook, and began writing. He wrote with an intensity he had never known; with a passion he had never felt. He wrote with a feeling he never thought possible.

He wrote with hatred!

After Shania received his letter, she saddled her horse and rode west into the desert, as she always did when a letter came from her husband.

Shania had found a book Samuel had told her about. *The Prophet,* by Kahlil Gibran. She wrote him a passage from the book:

" 'Much of your pain is self chosen,
"It is the bitter potion by which the physician within you heals your sick self.
"Therefore trust the physician, and drink his remedy in silence and tranquility:
"For his hand, though heavy and hard, is guided by the tender hand of the unseen.
"And the cup he brings, though it burn your lips, has been fashioned of the clay which the Potter has moistened with his own sacred tears.' "

Then she sat by the tall cactus where Samuel had proposed to her and wept. Not for herself. Not for him. Not even for their child.

She wept, thinking of all the dying . . . while creating life.

41

H is name was Captain Wylie Patterson. He had seven kills and
was an ace. He was from Macon, Georgia, and grew up with
a Negro nanny and sat looking surprised when the pilots from the
99th came into the briefing. The "Red-Tail Angels," as they had
come to be called, had joined the 79th Fighter Squadron at Fóggia,
Italy.

Colonel Earl Bates, squadron commander of the 79th, stepped to
the map and nodded at Captain Roberts when he came into the
tent, followed by his pilots of the 99th Fighter Squadron.

"Gentlemen, we are now joined by the Ninety-Ninth Pursuit
Squadron. We will coordinate this mission with their element."

The 99th pilots seated themselves. Patterson saw a tall pilot, and
turned back to the map, where Bates was giving the day's mission.

"We suspect a communication and fuel depot has been established here, in the Chieti area. The mission will call for low-level
bombing and strafing. Put your ordnance here"—he pointed at
what appeared to be a wooded area—"and here." Another wooded
area.

Bates looked at Roberts, who nodded. "Any questions, gentlemen?" Bates asked. There were none. The pilots stood, ready to
leave.

There was a moment of tension as the white pilots stared at the men of the 99th.

Patterson walked up to the tall Negro pilot and extended his hand. "I'm Wylie Patterson. Call sign is 'Hawkeye.' "

"Mine is 'Cowboy,' " Samuel said as he shook hands with Patterson.

"Where you from?"

"Arizona, sir."

"Drop the 'sir,' crap. We're fighter pilots. Not prima donnas at a high-school prom."

Samuel loosened up. He liked the man immediately.

"Thank you . . . Hawkeye!"

"Your guys ready for this?"

Samuel looked around. The 99th pilots were shaking hands with the 79th pilots. He had a good feeling. "I think we're ready for anything the Jerries can throw at us."

Patterson knew the history of the 99th. "Welcome to the war!"

When Samuel saw Patterson's P-40 Warhawk, he could only stand in absolute silence, and awe. Seven black Swastikas were painted on the fuselage.

"I understand you have an air victory," Patterson said.

Samuel nodded. "But nothing like you. Man, you're an ace."

Patterson clapped him on the back, and said, "You'll be one, too. Stay tight on my port wing. We'll go on them together. Double up on the bastards!"

They did what is called the "bump." They touched helmets, a significant gesture between fighter pilots that meant "good luck," and "good-bye."

An entirely different mood existed in the minds of the Red-Tails. They were integrated with the 79th, and were being shown respect. Not like with the 33rd, and Colonel Momyer, who wrote them off as being practically unfit for combat.

Samuel looked to the right side of his cockpit. The sabre was tucked in tight and secure. He thought about his grandfather, and the charge at Rattlesnake Springs, his father, and the sabre buried at the Meuse-Argonne.

Then, in the pristine sky above Chieti, he shoved the nose forward and began his bomb run, with a white man from Georgia on his wing.

Samuel and Patterson sat and drank cans of beer before a setting sun. Neither said anything at first. When they finally began to talk, they talked about their families. They talked about their lives. They talked . . . and became friends.

"Do you ever get scared?" Samuel said.

"No. I can't afford the luxury. Do you?"

Samuel drained the can of beer. "My first time against them, I threw up."

Patterson laughed. "Me too."

"Really?"

Patterson took the church key and opened another can of beer. He handed it to Samuel, then opened one for himself.

"Really. I dumped my first one over North Africa. Lucky kill, if you want to know the truth. I puked all the way back to the base."

Samuel understood something only he and others like him would know. "Then something happened inside?"

Patterson took a long pull from the can of beer. "Yes. A part of me died. I was no longer scared. You?"

Samuel took a long drink from his beer. "I hated them for what they made me become. And the answer is no. I'm not scared anymore."

"I know." Patterson leaned forward and drew a squiggly picture in the dirt with the church key. "They have reduced us to their level. Now we have to destroy them."

Samuel took a long, deep breath. "Do you think we could have been friends with them. Say, if we met on the Champs-Élysées?"

Patterson nodded, then drained the beer. "I like to think so."

Samuel finished off his beer and threw the can at the ground. "Do you think this war is ever going to end?"

Patterson just shook his head and said nothing. But Samuel knew that in the man's silence, the question had been answered.

The war would never end.

They would fight the war until their dying breath, even after the shooting had ended.

Then they sat in the quiet, as friends and comrades, and drank beer and talked about flying.

Patterson talked about his wife, Linda, and stared with empty eyes at the setting sun.

Samuel talked about Shania, and the new child she carried.

Neither man knew if they would ever see their families again.

It was men's talk. The slow, easy talk that nurtured the heart and allowed the soul to open up, and let the pain in.

The kind of talk that proved they were both still alive.

42

☆ ☆ ☆

Ernie Pyle wrote about Anzio in a newspaper article: ". . . On the beachhead, every inch of our territory was under German artillery fire. Rear area echelons were not immune, as in most battle zones. They could reach us with the 88's, and they used everything from that on up. The land of the Anzio beachhead is flat and our soldiers felt strange and naked with no rocks to take cover behind, no mountains to provide slopes for protection. It was a new kind of warfare for us. Distances were short and space was confined. The whole beachhead was the front line, so small that we could stand on high ground in the middle of it and see clear around the thing. That's the truth, and it was no picnic feeling either. . . ."

Samuel could see the beachhead. The soldiers rushing forward appeared like ants sweeping across a vast plain, turning the ground dark with their bodies and blood. On X-Ray and Peter Beaches, young Americans fought and fell, never turning back, for they knew there was nothing to turn back to. Except the water. He thought of that and, pushing the nose over and beginning a strafing run, knew that for him, too, there was no going back!

The shipping lanes from Ponzione Island to Anzio were clogged with troop transports.

Then, they appeared out of the sky. Gray, with black markings. Two Focke-Wulfs at ten thousand feet. Samuel jettisoned his belly tanks and cut an angle line on one of the Germans. The Jerry, knowing he was outnumbered, turned and tried to run. But Samuel stayed on him, flipped the hood, hit the switch, and sent a stream of molten lead on a death course.

The FW-190 exploded. It came apart in three pieces. Samuel saw the pilot spit out of the cockpit, fall for a few moments, then his parachute opened and he had silk over his head.

Samuel put the nose on the canopy and had his thumb on the trigger.

Then he backed off. He could kill. But not murder. There was a difference.

He landed at Capodichino, the squadron's new base, near Naples, and rolled to a stop, with Kane smiling at him.

"Good job, sir. The boys in commo flashed me the word that you got yourself another kill."

Samuel nodded, then walked past Kane and went to his tent. He was tired, needed a shower, but only wanted to lie on his cot and sleep.

When he woke up, it was late, and he was hungry. The mess hall had closed, so he went to the motor pool and signed off for a Jeep. He drove through the cool night until he reached the outskirts of the town. He parked and went inside a small restaurant, where the aroma of food struck his senses with a fury. He instantly thought of his mother's restaurant.

He took a table in the corner, and ordered wine and veal parmigiana. The atmosphere was pleasant, until a group of soldiers came in. They were red faced from drinking, and loud, the way soldiers can be on leave. There were three of them and they eyed him with contempt, but he ignored their stares.

His food was delivered, and as he started to eat, the door opened and a woman came in. She had long dark hair, olive skin, and Samuel was overwhelmed by her resemblance to Shania.

"What you looking at, boy?" a voice asked.

One of the soldiers, wearing corporal's stripes, leaned on Samuel's table.

"I'm not a boy. I'm an officer. And I suggest you return to your table and friends."

The corporal's words were slurred. "You're a nigger with looey bars on. That's all." He reached and ripped Samuel's flight wings from his blouse.

The fist flew up from the hip, but Samuel was ready. He drove the palm of his hand into the corporal's chest. There was a rush of air as he tumbled backwards and crashed into the table shared with his buddies.

The soldier roared, and charged head down toward Samuel, who stepped to one side, drove his knee into the soldier's jaw and watched him spiral into a wall. The corporal slid quickly down the wall to the floor, where he lay silent and still.

He heard the sound of glass breaking; he turned and faced the other two soldiers, both held jagged wine bottles. They moved cat-like, one to his right. The other to his left, moving in carefully and with menacing eyes and confident grins.

"Never skinned me a nigger before," one said.

"Me neither," said the other.

Samuel reached into his pocket and took out a strange-looking piece of metal and slipped it on the middle finger of his right hand. It had belonged to the Sergeant Major, something the Buffalo Soldiers called "drinking jewelry." It was a bent horseshoe nail, with two spike tips, that fit his finger perfectly. His grandmother had given it to him before he left for Europe. He took the tablecloth and wrapped it around his left wrist.

"This can end right now. We can forget it and go on our way. But I will kill you if you come one step closer."

One soldier took a step closer, then a loud boom shook the restaurant. Samuel looked to see a small, Italian man holding a sawed-off shotgun. A hole was in the ceiling, and smoke wafted from the right barrel of the weapon. He walked toward them, then pointed the weapon at the white soldiers, and said, very calmly, "Take your injured friend and leave. This moment. I have suffered Mussolini, Hitler, and I will suffer no more. Go, or I will kill you where you stand."

The two soldiers took the slumped corporal and dragged him from the restaurant. The smoke of the discharge still danced lightly in the air above the tables. The pretty woman who reminded Samuel of Shania slowly eased from beneath her table, wide-eyed and trembling.

The Maquis

43

☆ ☆ ☆

On May 2, 1944, Samuel and Shania's second child was born. He was named Franklin LeBaron Sharps.

On June 6, 1944, the Allied forces invaded western France at Normandy, a long stretch of beaches designated Omaha, Gold, Sword, and Juno. The operation was code-named *Overlord*.

On August 15, the invasion of southern France began. This operation was code-named *Anvil*.

The 99th had now joined with the 332nd, forming the first Negro combat aviation group in American military history. Benjamin O. Davis, Jr., became the Group commander, having been promoted to full colonel. Only his father had a higher rank among Negroes in the US military.

The P-51 Mustang was now the aircraft of the squadron. The tail sections were painted bright red, giving them instant visual identification to friend and enemy. Bomber cover was the squadron's new assignment, and they prided themselves on the accomplishment no other squadron or group could claim: They had not lost a single bomber to enemy aircraft.

The massive bombing campaign was first directed at Marseilles, the coastal area where the invasion force would begin its assault.

Samuel was part of a bombing mission directed at Montpelier, the Bezier rail yards, and Toulon. Inbound to the target there were no Nazi aircraft to meet them, and he felt the mission would go well, when he saw the gray-black puffs of flak in front of him. Fighter pilots were more terrified of flak than of fighters. They could fight the enemy planes; they could only hold their breath when they flew through flak. Flak, antiaircraft fire, knew no human distinction, and created hell for a few moments in one spot.

It was on that day in August, when he felt his aircraft suddenly bounce hard, pull to the right, and start to spin earthward, that his luck ran out. Looking to his right, he saw that half of his right wing had been sheared off.

He pulled the canopy back, cut the engine, disconnected his belt harness, and grabbed the Sergeant Major's sabre before he rolled hard right stick and rudder to the inverted position. He fell from the cockpit like a rag doll caught in a tornado, turning, twisting, falling, the earth above his head instead of beneath his feet. Concentrating, holding desperately to the sabre, he reached for the rip cord, pulled hard, felt himself slow, then was jerked upright as the canopy deployed.

It had happened so fast he had not had time to give thought to anything, especially the fact he was now drifting earthward, toward ground held by the enemy.

Yet, he couldn't believe the silence, except for the erupting of flak, which was now above him. He looked up, saw the dark spots etching the blue sky, the bombers releasing their bombs. Moments later he saw the bombs strike the earth, leaving momentary signatures on the terrain. For the first time since he entered the war, he had a front-row seat as he watched, and thought about the human carnage that was happening at that very moment. Down he drifted, drawing closer to the ground; he saw a farmhouse and looked quickly to the sun, acquiring a reference.

He landed in a tree, his big body tearing through the limbs with such force his goggles were ripped away. He could feel his flight suit shred as he covered his eyes and raised his knees to protect his groin.

Then, he snapped to an abrupt stop. Looking down, he could see he was only a few feet from the ground. And he realized he had dropped the sabre.

Samuel reached down and unbuckled the leg straps and fell to the ground. He scurried around for a few minutes, and saw, lying in a small bush, the burnished scabbard.

With the sabre in one hand, his drawn Colt .45 in the other, he started in the direction of the farmhouse.

Anton Charpentier was a twelve-year-old boy whose eyes had seen too much and appeared ancient. His body was wracked by the corrosion of malnutrition, his brain filled with the agony of remembrance. Remembrance—that gnawing disease God had given all to carry with them forever. What he hated was that there were no good memories—only bad. Why? he often asked himself. Why could he not have pleasurable remembrances?

There was no answer. Only the biting pain of the Germans invading his country. Then, his parents were murdered by storm troopers. Finally, his brother and sister were executed for being members of the resistance.

He wondered what he had done to deserve such punishment. He often shouted that question to the gray morning from the farmhouse where he grew up in a small village in the south of France.

He wore a goatskin coat and leather boots too large, a double-barreled shotgun slung to his shoulder, as he sat against a rock wall near his farm and squinted toward the horizon. Raising a leather flask above his head, he squeezed until a stream of water flowed into his mouth. That was just before the sky shook, and he felt the ground tremble. Looking up, he turned quickly to the south. From the shadows beneath the clouds a dark image had appeared. A bird? Perhaps a vulture, there were many above the shattered fields north of Toulon.

A low, piercing whine bored through his brain; his ears ached, and he thought his heart would explode as the black shape suddenly veered off, as if the hand of God had turned the machine from the path aimed directly at him.

Like lightning, the image was there—then gone—swooping behind a tall stand of trees. Anton's legs pulled his weight upward, then pushed him along the craggy ground. Ahead stood the trees. He raced with all his strength toward what seemed to be the screams of a thousand demons echoing through the early-morning air; sounds of trees breaking, metal shrieking.

Then silence.

Rounding the promontory, he stood in the shadows of the tall tree formation, watching the place where the dark intruder had crash-landed. Smoke billowed from the earth, masking the outline of whatever it was.

He watched for several long minutes, not moving, barely breathing, allowing the pace of his heart to settle. The machine made many noises: Sparks shot out from the rear; there was a whirring sound he recognized.

Finally, he began walking forward; half-crouched, his shotgun extended, he neared the cloud of smoke.

Suddenly he stopped. The barrel of the shotgun rose to greet the shadowy figure approaching through the smoke.

Samuel had hidden behind a rock wall that marked the boundary of the farm. Just when he was about over the wall, he froze. A familiar sound—the sound of a hammer drawing back on a weapon. He turned slowly to see a boy of no more than twelve standing before him, a double-barreled shotgun aimed at him. Slowly, he laid the pistol down, then the sabre. And for some odd reason he could not understand, he sat on the ground, crossed his legs, folded his arms, and said, "Hello. My name is Samuel. What is yours?"

The boy looked confused, and Samuel tried his awkward French. *"Je suis Samuel. Vous?"*

The boy stared at him incredibly, then a slow smile filled his face.

Samuel nodded, then extended his hand, and said, "American."

The boy had dark eyes and soft skin. He had a look about him that said he was scared, but not afraid, which made Samuel feel uneasy, since he couldn't be sure exactly what to expect. Then he motioned him to his feet with a jerk of the barrel and pointed toward the farmhouse and picked up the pistol and shoved it in his belt.

The boy looked at the sabre and motioned Samuel toward the weapon.

Samuel picked up the sabre, then they walked to the house without saying a word. He wasn't sure what to expect, but he felt safe.

When they reached the farmhouse the boy tapped four times on the door, then twice, then once. The door opened, and the boy motioned him inside. The house was dark, and he went in as though entering a cave, unsure of what he would find.

A voice asked, "What squadron?"

The voice was clearly that of an American.

"The Three-Thirty-Second Group. The Red-Tails."

"Name?"

"Sharps. Samuel Sharps. You?"

"Patterson. Captain Wylie Patterson."

Suddenly, a candle was lit and Samuel saw Wylie Patterson, his arm in a sling, wearing a growth of beard, and grinning from ear to ear.

"Hello, Samuel," he said.

Three other American pilots sat eating bread and drinking red wine. One had a broken leg, another had a bandage over his eye, and said little. The third looked as though he were in a daze. He stared at the candle and didn't eat or drink.

Samuel sat on the dirt floor beside Patterson. "What happened to you?"

He shrugged. "Took a burst up my ass and had to crash-land. I was on the ground for three days before I was found by the Maquis."

"The French resistance?"

Wylie took a drink from a wine bottle and handed it to Samuel. "They're good people. They hate the Germans worse than we do."

Samuel took a sip and tore off a piece of bread. "I thought that kid was going to shoot me."

"I thought the same thing. He hasn't spoken a word in two years. He watched his mother, father, brother and sister executed by the Germans."

Samuel could only shake his head in disgust. "Damn. I was going on picnics and high-school games at that age."

"Me too," Wylie said. "Looks different on the ground than on a briefing map."

44

☆ ☆ ☆

Guillard sat stunned on his cot, thinking about Samuel seeing spiral toward earth, then watching his parachute open, and feeling utterly helpless. Then he looked up as Kane entered, tears streaming down his face.

"Is it true?" the young crew chief asked.

Guillard said nothing; he merely lowered his face to his hands.

"He'll be back to us," Kane said.

"Can you stay for a moment?"

Kane nodded.

Guillard began writing a letter. When he was finished, he folded the letter neatly and handed it to Kane. "See that this letter gets mailed."

Kane saluted and left. Guillard lay back on his cot and fell into a restless sleep.

The Red-Tails had risen early, had their briefing, then mounted up their P-51 Mustangs, lifted off, and rendezvoused with a squadron of B-25s south of Marseilles just after sunrise. Guillard was flying wing for Hurd as the bombers appeared from their base in central Italy. Six more P-51s were assigned to ride herd on the convoy, and on the blue water of the Mediterranean he could see dozens of support ships and transports moving toward the coast.

Crossing the coastline, four ME-109s appeared in attack formation, which surprised Guillard. Most 109s were in rear areas or staying out of combat, forming a northern protective line for the German army, now in retreat.

He picked the Messerschmidt angling on the lead bomber and increased his power, easing the nose forward slightly to counteract the Mustang's climb, gaining airspeed while closing on the enemy. When he had the 109 in his sights he fired a three-second burst, saw the tracers miss to the aft, then banked left, trying to put himself between his countryman's plane and the enemy.

The two war machines came straight at each other, guns blazing. Just as Guillard saw his bullets strike the nose of the 109, he felt the slamming impact against his chest. He tightened, looked through the spiderweb holes in his cockpit, as his blood rose in his throat.

He looked down to see a large hole in his chest. Through the smoke now rising from his engine, he could see the Jerry 109 disintegrate in a ball of flame.

Then, Lieutenant Thomas Guillard went limp, his eyes open, but unseeing.

The bombers reached the target area, where the flak started speckling the sky as the B-25s began to drop their deadly payload. From the hayloft of the barn, Samuel and Patterson watched as the black-flecked sky became filled with inbound warplanes and bombers forced to fly through the deadly bursts of antiaircraft fire.

Wylie Patterson pointed to the aircraft now racing toward the earth. "They got one of ours."

"Yes, but he took one of the bastards with him!"

They sat like children lying under a circus tent stealing a peek at the three-ring show, watching in utter amazement and silence as the deadly ballet played to the music of the antiaircraft guns in the distance.

Finally, Augusts spoke. "Wylie? You ever see it from this angle?"

"Nope, only from up there."

"Man, we've got the best seat in the house."

While both men wondered if they would again see the war from the air, the barn shook as hundreds of bombs pounded the countryside.

45

* * *

Samuel knew that fear was the most powerful emotion to overcome from having faced fear while fighting the enemy. Fear was
personal, private, but manageable, so long as it was kept in per-
spective. Situational awareness was what fighter pilots used to overcome their fear. Retaining awareness gave one confidence in any
situation, especially in the cockpit, for that was the private, personal
world of the fighter pilot.

Outside the cockpit was different—situational awareness was reduced to the elements. Gone now was the swagger, the arrogance,
even the cockiness in himself and the other pilots. That was why
they all jerked in sudden fear at the appearance of four heavily
armed men.

One man, tall, carrying a German submachine gun, stepped forward and leaned into the candle, lighting a cigarette. His features
were dark, as were his eyes, and a thick scar ran from his left ear to
the edge of his mouth.

"Hello, gentlemen. I am Jean-Claude DeLantile. I am an officer
in the French resistance. We have to move you from this location to
one of our camps, where you will be safe until your countrymen arrive."

"When will that be?" Samuel said.

The Frenchman shrugged, then drew a long puff on the cigarette. "When they arrive, *mes amis.*"

Samuel looked at Patterson, and it was obvious they had many questions. But now was not the time to ask—now was the time to move and hope this man could be trusted.

"Let's do what the man tells us," Patterson said. "I don't think we have any other options."

Samuel merely nodded, then stood and started helping the others to follow the resistance fighter.

In the farmyard they climbed beneath a rick of straw piled onto a wagon, and though shoved close together, and barely able to hear themselves breathe, they could hear DeLentile's voice clearly say, "Do not move until you are told . . . or you will die."

An old man climbed onto the seat of the wagon and skipped the reins onto the back of a single horse. Samuel felt the wagon lurch forward and tasted the foul manure-soaked straw that covered their bodies.

He could not help but remember the stable at Sabre Ranch where he kept his horse. The smell was familiar, except that now, instead of the repugnant miasma of manure, he could taste the stench and the sweat of all their fear.

The wagon had bounced for what seemed to be an interminable length of time along a road that Samuel and the others knew was being traveled by German vehicles moving south to the new battlefield. There was no sense of time, only discomfort—and the fact, that as long as they kept moving . . . they were still alive.

Gradually, the sound of vehicles stopped, and sometime later the wagon came to a sudden halt. Samuel stiffened. Then he heard voices speaking in German. The men lay still as though dead, knowing that movement would give them away. He could tell there were three voices: two in German and the voice of the old man.

That was when a new, unfamiliar sound was heard. Like the cough of a young child in the night. Then another cough, followed by the lowered voice of the old man and another who spoke French.

Samuel nearly panicked as he felt the straw being pulled away. With each layer that was removed the light grew brighter and his fear greater.

That was when he saw DeLentile, who said softly, "Gentlemen, you must get out and sit on the ground."

The Americans sat on the ground in a circle, watching DeLentile and the old man change clothing with two dead German soldiers at what was obviously an enemy checkpoint. They sat there for nearly an hour, their faces lowered as more German vehicles passed. When a single German truck approached, DeLentile stepped into the road and motioned the vehicle to pull off to the side. He approached the vehicle, saying nothing. He merely raised his hand and fired a pistol into the driver's head. Moving quickly, he pulled the driver from the truck and dragged him into a ditch, where he laid the German beside the other dead soldiers.

"Get into the back quickly."

The pilots hurried into the back of the truck, saw DeLentile close the rear flap, and, moments later, felt the vehicle pull away.

An hour later the truck stopped, and DeLentile pulled up the rear flap and motioned the men off. Samuel looked around and saw dozens of armed men and a few women standing in a resistance camp hidden deep in the woods.

DeLentile stepped forward, unbuttoning the tunic of the dead German soldier, a bullet hole visible above the heart. He dropped the jacket on the ground, and, after looking at it with disgust, said, "You will be safe here until we can get you to the American lines."

Samuel asked, "Where are we?"

DeLentile said nothing as he walked away.

A full moon shone through the trees, where camouflaged lean-tos sprinkled the terrain. The shelters were situated in such a way as to provide a perimeter; sandbags necklaced each position, providing limited protection. The floors were deep enough for the occupants to kneel behind the protective wall, but only tree branches provided overhead security.

The Americans were broken up into two groups, with Samuel and Patterson sharing a shelter with the old man. His name was Girard, and he never spoke. He smoked constantly, his heavy exhalations the only sign he was alive.

Samuel saw thin traces of moonlight breaking through the heavy canopy of branches and heard the distant sound of bombers approaching from the south. "They've got a bomber's moon for tonight's mission."

Patterson sipped coffee from a tin cup, and replied softly, "I wish I was up there instead of here."

After a long pause, Samuel asked, "What do you think they're going to do with us, Wylie?"

Patterson shrugged. "I don't have any idea. All we can do is wait for our troops to land and move inland. Then we'll have a chance."

Samuel turned as the old man struck another match and lit a cigarette. The drone of engines grew louder as the formation of B-25s approached. Seconds later, the ground began to shake as the high explosives began slamming into the earth not far from where they hid.

"Jesus," Patterson muttered. "They're dropping their payload close to our position."

The earth seemed to rise and settle as the terrific concussions continued, moving across the ground, the high explosives marking their track over the terrain.

The woods suddenly came alive with hurried shouts from resistance fighters. The old man jumped from the shelter and motioned the two fliers to follow. The three ran to the far edge of the camp, where others, silhouetted by the explosions, had assembled. Samuel's heart was pounding as he ran through the woods, Patterson following close behind. When the group reached the edge of the wooded area, DeLantile brought everyone together. He knelt, speaking loudly, over the explosions. He spoke quickly, pointing and shouting. The resistance fighters then broke into smaller groups and began filtering off in different directions toward the west.

DeLantile led the Americans into an open field, where they hid in the darkness. Hours later, as the sun slowly rose, the resistance fighter led the Americans along a river, where they stopped near a bridge.

The Frenchman studied the bridge with his binoculars, then turned to the Americans. "The Germans have a roadblock in the middle of the bridge."

"How do we get across?" Patterson asked.

"We swim." His eyes suddenly flashed to the opposite bank. The distance appeared to be approximately fifty yards.

The men slipped quietly along the bank, away from the bridge, until they reached a point where they would be out of the Germans' view. One by one they eased into the water and carefully swam to the other bank.

Reaching the other side, the men moved quickly into the cover of the forest. Since the rain of bombs had begun falling, Samuel had wondered why that area was targeted. "Why did they bomb our positions?"

"The planes have been saturation bombing this area for two days. Every place where they suspect German troops might be in the woods," DeLantile said.

"Our bad luck," Patterson said acidly. "Where do we go from here?"

DeLantile thought for a moment, then rose and began walking through the woods. The others followed, not knowing where they might end—whether they would be safe, captured, or killed by the enemy.

Three days and nights passed, each moment more frightening than the last until they reached the outskirts of Toulon. The immediate problem was obvious. How would they sneak into the city undetected? DeLantile, whose resourcefulness in tight situations had been proven, told the men to wait for his return. He left the Americans in a wooded area and started walking toward the city.

Near midnight, the sound of a truck grinding to a halt on the nearby road brought the Americans to full alert. The only weapons they had were pistols and Samuel's sabre. They quickly fanned out, forming a defensive line and waited. The beam from a flashlight could be seen moving jerkily through the darkness. When the beam stopped moving, Samuel raised his pistol and took aim. Just as his finger was about to close on the trigger, he heard the familiar voice of the resistance fighter break the quiet.

"*Mes amis.* Follow me. Quickly."

The Americans stepped closer where, in the light of the moon, they saw DeLantile. He wore a devilish grin, and the uniform of a German soldier.

46

Two weeks later a telegram from the War Department arrived for Shania, along with a package from Guillard. Both had been delivered to her at the school. She ripped open the envelope and read that he was reported missing in action. She drove to Sabre Ranch, and walked to the cottonwoods, where she opened the package from Guillard, read his letter, and found some solace in knowing that Samuel was seen landing in his parachute.

She whispered to the cottonwoods, "He's alive."

A few hours later, Hannah came home and found her sitting in the grove of trees. She saw the telegram lying on the picnic table. She said, "Is there something you need to tell me about my son?"

There was a slowness in her words as she spoke. "He's missing in action," Shania said. "That comes from the government. But Thomas Guillard saw his parachute open. . . . he's alive!"

Hannah didn't have to think about that even a moment "If he had a parachute, he made it to ground. If he made it to ground . . . he's made it. He knows how to live off the land. Knows how to stay alive. He knows which direction he came from. Which direction he needs to go. And if it's made easier for him, he'll find friends to help him, if not . . . he'll do for himself."

Hannah stood and started toward the house. "He's the grandson of the Sergeant Major, the grandson of Selona, the son of Adrian and me. He'll survive."

When Adrian came home, Hannah handed him the telegram. He read it, turned, went to the window, and stared out. "He's alive. I know he's alive. If he wasn't, I'd already feel it in my heart," he said.

He went into Samuel's bedroom and sat by the two baby cribs where his grandsons slept.

He didn't cry. He didn't moan. He whispered softly, "Your daddy will be coming home. I promise."

Then he did something he had never done before.

He went and sat on Selona's "Remembering Bench," and prayed to God for the safety of his son.

47

Jean-Claude DeLantile slipped quietly through the darkness shrouding the burned-out shops and buildings along the streets near the port of Toulon, ghostlike reminders of the Allied bombings now coming daily to drive out the German occupation forces.

Bullet holes pocked the buildings; windows were broken; businesses and restaurants stood empty after the pillaging invaders swooped into the city, stealing everything they could get their hands on.

But the worst reminder lay along the sidewalks. Young men, their hands and feet bound, executed by gunshot, lay rotting. The smell filled the air. Flies buzzed around the blackened corpses.

Where were the Americans?

That was the question that had swept through the ranks of the Maquis during the four weeks since the invasion at Normandy on June 6. But still the butchery continued.

Suddenly, a loud, gruff voice called, "Halt!"

DeLantile froze.

"Raise your hands and stand against the building." A German soldier approached from across the street. In the thin light of approaching dawn, DeLantile could see that the soldier wore the collar pipings of the Waffen SS: two white lightning bolts.

DeLantile raised his hands. "I have nothing of value," he said.

The German thrust the muzzle of his *Schmeisser* submachine gun into DeLantile's stomach. "Empty your pockets."

DeLantile's left hand was thrust deep into his pocket of his coat. "Nothing, *mein Herr*. I swear to God!"

As the soldier raised his weapon DeLantile's right hand swept the barrel away from his body as a straight razor suddenly appeared in his left hand. The cold steel of the razor flashed in the dawning light. The soldier grasped at his throat. A stream of bright blood pulsed from the German's throat as DeLantile clamped his free hand over the man's mouth.

DeLantile drove his knee into the soldier's groin, heard and tasted the invader's hot breath rush from his nostrils into his face. After what seemed an eternity he felt the soldier go limp, then allowed the body to pitch forward. He caught the German and quickly dragged the body into a nearby alley. There, in the darkness, he tried to compose himself and think.

His mind raced. When the body was found, the Germans would seek revenge. For each German killed by the resistance, twenty French citizens were executed and left to rot where they fell, as evidenced by the bodies in the street beyond the alley.

Then the breeze wafting through the alley brought him his answer—the foul smell of the rotting bodies, butchered by the Germans.

He quickly stripped off the soldier's uniform and undershorts, and using the laces from his boots, tied the German's hands behind his back, and bound the feet.

He whispered to the dead man, "When you are found the rats will have eaten away your face. No one will recognize you, not even your mother. The soldiers will think you're just another Frenchman killed by one of your soldiers."

He hawked and spit on the dead man's head.

Moving silently, he went back to the street, hugging the shadows until he reached a burned-out bakery shop on the bottom floor of a building. Quietly, he slipped through the glass window. In the rear of the shop, a scarred bread case was all that remained. Everything else had been destroyed; even the ovens had been removed. He carefully slid the case to one side, revealing a small trapdoor in the floor. He tapped three times, then twice, then three times again.

The door lowered wide enough for him to drop onto a ladder where another man stood. Together the two men moved the case back over the opening until it was covered. The trap was raised back into the opening and secured by a heavily oiled bolt.

DeLantile followed the man down through the thick darkness until he could feel his feet touch the floor. A light came on from a lantern and he turned to find four men training British Sten machine guns on him.

"Relax, *mes amis*. All is well. My apologies for being late. It could not be helped."

He looked at his brothers—they, too, members of the Maquis—and glanced toward the corner of the cellar where the five Americans sat on the dirt floor.

"The arrangements have been made. You will be leaving tonight, my friends."

Before they could reply, the earth seemed to tremble slightly, then there was a buzzing sound, causing all to suddenly become breathless. They listened in silence as the ground shook from heavy bombs falling from the sky above the city.

Waiting in fear is the most exacting of all tests of a human being, especially in darkness, when the eyes tend to create images that assault the brain and weaken the spirit. Hours after DeLantile arrived, after the lights had been doused, Samuel began to see images of German soldiers storming down the steps, their heavy boots making a cacophony of frightening sounds. Huge dogs barked and snarled, as the men lay cowering in the corner, facing gnashing teeth and the muzzles of machine guns.

When flying he had no real fear since he was in motion, doing something with his hands and mind. Now he could only wait in the darkness and smell the fear. He recalled his father talking about the trenches in the Argonne, and the wait for the whistle signaling them to go over the top. What was it his father had said? He tried to recall, but there was nothing.

Hiding in the cellar for the past two weeks had taken a mental toll on the Americans. They ate, slept, talked in low voices, and waited for whatever would happen next. Bodily functions were relieved in a bucket that served as a communal toilet. The bucket was emptied in the early, dark hours of the morning. Food was brought by other members of the resistance, and, though filling, was meager. All the men had lost weight and were now haggard from the experience.

"Samuel," Patterson whispered. "You doing all right, buddy?"

"This is scary as hell."

Patterson chuckled. "The first time I was shot down, I thought I was going to go insane. But the underground came through. You can usually count on them getting you back if they can get to you."

There was surprise in Samuel's voice. "You've been shot down before."

"In forty-two. Over Belgium. I thought I was never going to get back to England."

"How did you cope?"

There was low rush of air from Patterson. "I thought about home, and all the good remembrances, like everyone else. But what really kept my mind squared away was thinking about all the errors I had made, especially with family. So I made a plan."

"What kind of plan?"

"I thought about how I could take all the mistakes and try to set them straight. Right the wrongs. Ease the pain I had caused. But most importantly, I thought about what kind of person I would be if I ever got the chance to get home."

"Did it work?"

"Yes. Give it a try. It'll make those brain devils stop dancing in front of your eyes."

Samuel gave this some thought. "Do you have them now?"

"No, I'm thinking about the man who is going to return to his loving family."

Samuel leaned against the earthen wall, closed his eyes, and began to make a mental list of the things he had done to disappoint his family. Foremost was going to Tuskegee, and not Southern California. How could he right that disappointment? He concluded that the solution was to make them proud of him when he returned home and followed the family tradition of the restaurant and ranching business. Never to leave again and cause so much worry and concern. He would never leave his wife and children again, casting them into a misery that must seem interminable.

He thought for hours. He was seeing Shania and himself, riding horseback in the desert, each carrying a child in the saddle.

The brain devils began to disappear.

The drone of the bombers could be heard, drawing closer, then the antiaircraft fire began, and the Americans and Maquis could only sit helplessly and listen. The wail of sirens cut the air, even in the cellar, drawing all the men into a huddled group. As with frightened animals, the fear trembled through them, where intermittently, there was heard the mixture of prayer and cursing in two languages.

Suddenly, there was heard the signal at the trapdoor.

DeLantile lit a lantern and hurried up the steps to unbolt the trapdoor. The voice of a woman could be heard talking in hurried French.

DeLantile said loudly, "Come. It is time."

The men hurried up the steps and into the bakery to noise Samuel could only think of as hellish. Smoke filled the street; vehicles ran crazily about, and Samuel froze as he saw a man standing at the blown-out window. He was dressed in a German uniform!

A young woman carrying a light machine gun motioned them along. Beyond the window a truck had been backed to the opening. The woman climbed into the back and the others followed. The man dressed as a Nazi hurried to the cab and raced the engine, then the truck stormed away as DeLantile closed the rear canvas flap.

Inside, Samuel was pressed close to the woman. She had long dark hair flowing from beneath a beret. What amazed him most about her was that she appeared calm. She looked at his sabre, and smiled oddly. She asked in perfect English, "Is that a rapier?"

Samuel shook his head. "No. It's a sabre."

Then he began to feel calm, as if this angel of salvation had washed away the fear with her voice and presence.

The truck jounced and jostled through the streets for what seemed forever, until the noise of the bombing began to fade in the distance. It grew quiet, and the men relaxed; Patterson leaned and whispered something to DeLantile, then laughed aloud. He lit a cigarette and offered it to Samuel.

He took a long drag. "Where are they taking us?"

"Probably to another point along the underground railroad, where they can transport us to our lines."

Samuel looked at him oddly. "Our lines?"

Patterson pointed at DeLantile. "The invasion has begun. Our boys have already come ashore."

A cheer rose up from the Americans in the truck, who hugged and shook hands with the French resistance fighters.

Darkness had fallen when the truck reached a darkened isolated farmhouse. One of the Maquis scurried from the truck and opened the door of a barn, where the truck was driven through just as the door was closed. The men and woman climbed out to a smell Samuel found familiar—the aroma of manure.

The greatest moment came an hour later when two more Maquis arrived, carrying wicker baskets filled with blood sausages, loaves of bread, large, round heads of cheese, and jugs of wine.

They sat and drank together as comrades, knowing that with each passing moment, the oppression of the invaders was coming to an end.

48

The next morning, as the Americans lay sleeping, the quiet was broken by a shout from one of the Maquis. "German soldiers!"

DeLantile looked quickly at the woman, then the other Maquis, and spoke with an urgency in his voice. Three of the men took their weapons and disappeared through the door; the rest took positions near windows. The woman listened intently to DeLantile, then approached Samuel and Patterson. She knelt and folded a map out on the floor. "We are here." Her finger followed a line that led south and east. "The Allies are here. You must travel by night and remain under cover by day."

Samuel looked in horror at Patterson, then said to her, "You want us to leave you? To fight alone?"

There was a gleam in her eyes as she said, "We have been fighting alone for many years. You are too important. You can do more damage to the Bosch with your airplanes than we can with machine guns and explosives. Please. Come with me."

Against their will, and sense of honor, but knowing she was right, they followed her to the truck, which had been backed out. Bales of hay were being moved by DeLantile until he revealed a trapdoor in the flooring. He raised the trap and handed Patterson the lantern and pointed to the cellar.

The woman said quickly, "There is a tunnel in the cellar, behind a barrel. The tunnel leads for one hundred meters to a stream. Follow the stream until it winds beside a rock wall. That is where you begin your journey to your lines."

Samuel looked at the hole. He didn't want to leave these brave people. "Come with us," he said.

DeLantile was pouring kerosene on the hay and soaking the canvas of the truck. The woman shook her head and kissed Samuel lightly on the cheek. "Please. There is not much time."

Patterson started down, followed by Samuel and the other Americans. They heard the door slam closed, heard the bales being restacked, then the groan of the truck as it was driven back in place, covering the trapdoor.

The men sat for a moment in the eerie place, the light dancing off walls braced with stone.

Patterson looked around, and said, "There's the barrel."

Samuel and another pilot moved the barrel. Patterson, holding the lantern, crawled through the entrance, followed by Samuel and the others.

The tunnel seemed to be ancient, but in good condition. They crawled, following the lantern.

They stopped only once, when they heard the chatter of machine gun fire echoing from the entrance. Next came the sound of a tremendous explosion Samuel assumed was the truck detonating.

They began crawling again until they could hear the sound of running water and saw light marking the opening of the tunnel. Once outside, they regrouped and began discussing their next move.

"I say we wait until dark. That'll give us more cover," Patterson suggested.

The others nodded in agreement, except Samuel, who wondered aloud, "What if the Germans found the tunnel?"

The sound of more machine-gun fire was heard. "I don't think they'll find it, Samuel. Our chances are better at night."

Samuel agreed, but was numb, and sickened by the lives that had been sacrificed for his freedom. He realized that he never even knew their names.

*　*　*

The night gave them cover as they moved along the stream until they reached the rock wall, where they knelt and looked at the stars for reference. They followed the rock wall until it joined another. An open field lay beyond; in the distance they could see the faint outline of a clump of trees. Overhead, engines droned—bombers flying night raids. The rumble of exploding bombs grew closer, and the distant sky was lit up by thick white beams from searchlights and the momentary iridescent imprint of flak exploding against the darkness.

The searchlights provided them a solid point of reference. Samuel knelt with the men and made a suggestion based on family history. "My grandfather was a cavalry scout against the Indians in the Southwest. When they scouted, they sent two men ahead a certain distance to look for trouble. When they reached that spot, one man would come back and take the others forward. This would go on and on until they reached their destination."

Patterson spoke for the others. "Sounds like a smart plan. Samuel and I will go first." The others agreed, and they began an all-night overlapping recon that allowed the men to travel quicker and more safely than in one solitary group.

As dawn neared, fatigue set in as they traveled to the east of the bombing targets and avoided the German gun emplacements. They stopped in a tree line, climbed into the branches, and huddled inside their heavy flight coats to fight the chill as the bombing continued to echo through the day.

Once again they watched the constant stream of fighters and bombers streak across the sky, like flocks of geese flying north at the end of winter. To fight the cold, Samuel mentally wrote a letter to Shania, allowing himself some relief from the agony.

He glanced at Patterson and the others, some nodding in brief moments of sleep, then quickly waking, partially from the curiosity created by the air show and part from fear of falling from the tree. The one constant that had been ticking in Samuel's mind, aside from survival, had been the closeness he and the other men had come to share in this time of war and survival.

He finished the mental letter, closed his eyes, and thought about home. His family. His freedom.

49

☆ ☆ ☆

It was late in the afternoon when Samuel, suddenly jerked from his short nap, heard a sound that was both frightening and familiar. He studied the terrain, and in the distance, saw men coming across an open field, walking deployed between rows of lumbering tanks.

"Wylie! Troops and tanks coming from the southeast."

Patterson stared, but his eyes were too tired to see clearly, his brain too fogged to have any precision.

"I can't make them out, Samuel."

Samuel watched, but mostly he listened, until a sound from the past came crashing back from the depths of his memory. "I know that sound, Wylie! I know that sound!"

He dropped from the tree to the amazement of all the pilots. Patterson thought he had lost his mind. But Samuel ran toward a machine whose sounds were as familiar to him as those of his horse . . . or the hoofbeats of the mule he rode in Arizona to beat a tank in a cross-country race. These tanks were like that machine: Shermans!

He ran across the field, waving the sabre wildly, shouting at the approaching column of armor and infantry.

From his position in the tree, Patterson felt his stomach tighten. Then he heard what he feared the most: the clatter of machine-gun fire.

The spray of lead hit Samuel in the legs, wracking him with pain. There was a burning sensation he had never known, and thought impossible. He pirouetted, then stumbled sideways and crashed to the ground.

He lay motionless on the cold earth, clutching the sabre, listening to the approaching tanks and the shouts of the infantrymen. His mind swirled, a dozen thoughts flashed through his mind, all cascading at once, forming a torrential river of confusion.

Then, the pain became too much, and he slipped into unconsciousness.

But the last words he heard were those of a young voice saying, "Christ, he's an American."

Then he heard nothing.

He woke up in a battalion aid station and lay still, taking in the sounds, trying to adjust his senses to the surroundings. He heard murmurs, screams, prayers, and the constant movement of people. When he finally looked around, a sudden chill made him shudder. He saw the wounded, men with blood-soaked bandages lying on stretchers, some with heads covered with thick white gauze, some with arms in slings. He saw a soldier with both legs amputated.

He raised himself on his elbow and saw that his legs were covered by a blanket. He felt a strong burning sensation as he slowly peeled back the blanket and—Thank God!—he released a sigh of relief. His legs were heavily bandaged, and one was in a splint, but they were there.

Sudden relief flashed through him a second time when he saw the curved cavalry sabre leaning against the side of his stretcher. For a moment he forgot the pain. He heard a voice. "How are you feeling, son?"

A soldier stood beside him, on one collar the gold leaf of a major, on the other, a small silver cross.

"I'm alive, Chaplain."

The officer knelt beside him and touched his forehead. "Are you in pain?"

Samuel shrugged. "It hurts like . . ." He caught himself.

The chaplain chuckled. "Like 'hell'?"

"Yes, sir. Like hell."

The chaplain motioned for a medic, who came over carrying a wad of bloody bandages. "This soldier is in pain. Can you give him some morphine?"

The medic nodded and hurried away. The chaplain turned back to Samuel. "There is one bright spot to this situation, Lieutenant."

Samuel could see none. "What's that, sir?"

"You've got a million-dollar wound."

Samuel didn't understand. "What's that, sir?"

"You're going home. Back to the States. Your days in combat are over."

"Home?"

The cherubic smile of the chaplain shone through an unshaven and haggard face. "That's right, so get some rest, Lieutenant . . . ?"

"Sharps, sir. Lieutenant Adrian Samuel Sharps. Three-Thirty-Second fighter group."

"The Colored group?"

"Yes, sir."

"A fine outfit. You should be proud."

"I am, sir."

The chaplain looked at the sabre. "I was told the medics had to pry it from your fingers. A souvenir?"

"No, sir. My grandfather carried it on the western frontier. My father during World War One."

"You've done well by it, son."

The chaplain left, and the medic gave him an injection. The pain started to drift away as the opiate began working on his brain. He felt himself begin to drift into a cloud, as though he were flying his P-51. He thought he heard a familiar voice, then the light in the aid station faded, and he felt no more pain.

He didn't know what time it was when he was awakened by the sudden sensation of being lifted. He looked up to see the chaplain standing with two medics, who were lifting his stretcher.

"Don't be frightened. They're taking you to the rear, where you'll be transported to a hospital ship."

Samuel gripped the sabre in his hand and waved it appreciatively toward the chaplain, then lay back, and felt the cold metal of the scabbard against his face.

Both were going home.

50

✬ ✬ ✬

When Samuel awoke, it was as though he had been cast into the bowels of perdition. He lay on the stretcher in what appeared to be a hallway, with a steel floor, walls, and ceiling, narrow, like a grave, and cold as ice. He was shivering, it was dark, except for a few red lightbulbs in metal cages extending from the ceiling. The glow, the cold, the closeness, the screams of the other wounded made him realize what hell might be like.

He saw something coming toward him in the glow, a whitish creature with a red tint bending to the other men lying on the stretchers that lined one wall of the hallway. The form would bend down, stay a few moments, then move on to the next stretcher.

The nurse stopped by his stretcher and knelt. She appeared red, but he could see that her uniform was actually white.

"How you feeling, soldier?" The voice was soft, angelic. Must be the morphine, he thought, making him hallucinate.

His mouth was desert-dry from the narcotic. "Thirsty."

She left and returned a few minutes later, carrying a towel. "You're scheduled for surgery in a few minutes. You can't drink anything. But you can suck on this wet washcloth." She handed it to him and he sucked until he felt a small amount of moisture enter his mouth. It was wonderful.

"Where am I?"

"You're aboard the USS *Mercy*, a navy hospital ship. You'll be taken to surgery soon, so just lie still and try to rest." She checked an IV that connected his right arm to a plasma bottle hanging from a metal rod attached to the stretcher.

There were more screams of anguish, which seemed to become a catalyst, setting off others throughout the hallway. He saw more nurses appear, with men dressed in white, who began picking up stretchers and carrying them along the hallway. Two men took the handles on his stretcher, and he felt himself rise, and with the suddenness nearly dropped the sabre, which he now clutched with all his strength. The nurse walked alongside him. He looked up and asked her, "Can you do me a favor, miss?" He extended the sabre to her. "My name is Lieutenant Sharps. Can you keep this for me until I get out of surgery? It's a family heirloom."

She took it from him. "I'll put it in my quarters. You said, 'Lieutenant Sharps'?"

Samuel nodded. "Yes, ma'am. Sharps. It's very important to me."

She squeezed his hand. "It'll be safe with me." Then she turned and continued along the line, stopping briefly to tend to the wounded. Samuel's eyes followed her until she disappeared from the hallway.

He was lifted again and taken into the brightly lit surgery room. There was screaming, loud talking, orders being yelled from doctors to nurses; he heard someone begging God.

Two men wearing masks and blood-soaked white aprons stood over him, reminding him of how he looked after butchering a deer for his mother. Then a black rubber mask was pressed to his face, he heard someone say, "Just breathe normally."

The ether made his brain swirl like the propeller on his Mustang; the sounds became echoes. The taste was putrefying.

Then there was nothing.

Samuel woke up in a bunk attached to a wall; an IV ran into his arm, and his legs burned. He rose, and raised the blanket. One leg was heavily bandaged; the other was bandaged and splinted. The pain was unbearable.

He suddenly felt nauseated as he thought of the possibility he would never fly again. The pain rushed from his head to his chest, then to his heart, and for the first time in his life he felt weakened by fear.

A sailor walked by, and Samuel said, "Medic?"

The sailor said, "I'm a corpsman." He looked at the chart. "Lieutenant Sharps?" There was an odd look on his face.

"Yes."

"One minute, sir. I'll be right back."

Samuel looked at his legs. The morphine was wearing off and the pain increasing. The corpsman came along the aisle of wounded, carrying the sabre.

"Lieutenant Wilson left this here. She said you were a Colored officer and that this belonged to you. It does belong to you, doesn't it, sir?"

Samuel nodded. "Yes, she was kind enough to watch it for me while I was in surgery."

The sailor laid the sabre on the bed. "You want something for pain?"

Samuel nodded. He took the sabre and laid it on the other side, between his body and the wall. The corpsman came with an injection, and within minutes Samuel was feeling comfortable.

As he slipped into the narcotized sleep, his free hand closed around the metal scabbard.

He dreamed of home. Of seeing his wife and child. His parents and friends. For the first time in over a year he dreamed of something other than war.

New Challenges

51

* * *

Shania had been riding in the desert, trying to keep her mind off Samuel, when she returned to the ranch late one afternoon in September. She saw John Parks standing on the porch, a worried look on his face. Hannah came out carrying the baby and handed a telegram to her in silence.

Shania slowly opened the envelope, afraid to read the words. A huge smile burst across her face. "He's alive! He's been wounded, but he's back in American hands."

Hannah and Parks broke into tears; Shania took the baby and danced around the yard with him in her arms.

At that moment, Adrian drove up, and, without asking, knew what was happening the moment he saw the commotion: His son was alive.

Two weeks later Samuel's first letter arrived, explaining what had happened, his wounds, and that he had been transported to a hospital in England.

Thanksgiving, Christmas, and the turn of the new year came and went. The war in Europe had taken a definite turn after the German offensive in Belgium failed in December in what was called the "Battle of the Bulge."

Hitler and his monstrous Third Reich were now living on borrowed time.

But the most wonderful day of Shania's life was on the last Sunday in January 1945, when the telephone rang. She answered and stiffened. She stammered, "Yes, this is the Sharps residence." She covered the receiver, and whispered to Hannah, "It's long-distance. From New York."

In a matter of seconds she was prancing about, squealing, then she began to cry. Hannah came to her and asked, "What's the matter?"

"It's Samuel. He's in New York."

Shania motioned for her mother-in-law to be quiet so she could talk. She listened, then said to Hannah, "He's going to Fort Dix, New Jersey, to report in, then he'll be given thirty days leave. He'll have to stay there for three days to complete his processing, then report to Walter Reed Army Hospital for a physical, then he's coming home!"

Shania was fighting emotion and her mother-in-law's excited interruption. Hannah had an immediate suggestion. "Why don't you take the train to Washington and meet him. The two of you can make the trip home together."

Shania had already thought of that. But she had other notions. She covered the mouthpiece, and whispered, "When he steps off that train, I want him to see all of his family waiting, the way it was when he left. Besides, it would take all that time to get there, and we might miss each other. I don't want to take any chances. I've waited this long. I can wait another week."

Hannah understood; she, too, had endured the greatest lesson taught to those who waited for their loved ones to return from war: patience.

Shania had learned that same patience in the long months since their separation, and could make it the rest of the way on sheer determination alone if necessary.

Hannah spoke with Samuel for a few minutes, then went outside. She needed fresh air and the openness of the world to fill her once again.

Her son was home safe from war!

*   *   *

Later that night, when Adrian arrived and heard the full story, he went to his closet and brought out a fresh bottle of whiskey. He went to the porch with two glasses and poured a drink for himself and Parks.

So overcome was she with joy, that Hannah said, "Sweetheart, could you pour me a tiny drink?"

Both men looked aghast at each other, then broke out laughing.

Shania said, "Poppa, could I have just a little? I feel like celebrating."

Adrian poured all four a drink, and the only regret he had was that he hadn't bought a larger bottle.

That night, Shania called her father and told him the great news, and after a half hour of pleading, LeBaron agreed to catch the train the next day and come to Arizona. It would be a family homecoming welcome, just like in 1919, when Adrian returned from France.

She suddenly felt alive again; she knew that all was going to work out for them. The long months of waiting would soon end, and their lives would be back on track.

She walked to the cemetery, knelt by Selona's grave, and whispered, "He's coming home."

Then she went inside and did what she had not done since the day Samuel left: she slept peacefully and didn't cry herself to sleep.

52

Walter Reed Army Hospital, was named for the army pathologist and biologist who had discovered that yellow fever was carried by mosquitoes. Samuel knew the doctor, for Reed had served as an army surgeon at Fort Lowell, Arizona, and on the western frontier for eighteen years and had treated many of the Buffalo Soldiers and their families, including Samuel's father and uncle.

He felt a kinship to the hospital as he limped through the main entrance and found the information center. A sergeant sitting at the desk pointed him to the Colored section of the hospital. There Samuel saw his first WAC—Women's Army Corps—nurses. He knew about them and had heard there were several in Europe, but Second Lieutenant Bernice Fryar was the first he met.

She was thin as a rail, her hair was pulled back into a bun, and her white uniform was so heavily starched the material made a swishing sound when she walked. She led him to an examination room, handed him a gown, and said, "Take off your uniform and put this on. The doctor will be with you shortly." She turned and left, and he could hear her uniform hissing as she walked down the hall.

The doctor read Samuel's medical file. He was tall, heavyset, with skin a deep charcoal. The doctor examined the scars, the bone damage. "Do you still have pain?" he asked.

Samuel sighed slightly, then shook his head. "I get some twinges occasionally, but nothing I can't handle."

The doctor made notes. "Do you intend to remain in the service after the war?"

"Yes, sir."

"I see you're an aviator."

"Yes, sir."

"You may not be able to remain on flight status."

"Why?"

"You'll have to take a flight physical if you want to be reinstated. The damage to the bone and muscle tissue in your right leg was severe. That could create fatigue after prolonged use of foot controls."

"I'm getting stronger every day, Doctor. I don't even need a cane to help me walk. I've been walking—hell—I walked all the way across the Atlantic Ocean."

The doctor smiled. "How did you manage that?"

Samuel said, "Well, halfway across. I walked all the time on the ship. I would walk nearly six or eight hours a day, around the deck."

"I'm sure that was great therapy. But the question will be whether you can take the strain of a prolonged test of endurance."

"I can take it, sir."

The doctor obviously liked Samuel, and asked, "Where's home?"

"Arizona."

"Tell you what, Lieutenant. I'm going to hold off on recommending you be grounded from flight status. I'm going to give you time to get into shape. If you can pass the flight PT test, you'll be back in the air. Otherwise, you'll be grounded."

"That's fair. When can I take the test?"

"Is there an army post near your home?"

"Yes, Fort Huachuca."

The doctor wrote in the file and handed the records to Samuel. "Report to Fort Huachuca in thirty days. The post flight surgeon can give you the test."

The doctor stood and extended his hand. "The Negro community in America followed the Negro aviation squadrons very closely in the newspapers. You men did a fine job. You made your people very proud. I commend you for such a fine job. I do hope you continue to serve as an aviator."

They shook hands, and the doctor left. Samuel hurriedly dressed and left the hospital. He hailed a taxi near the near the main entrance and told the driver, "Take me to the train depot."

Samuel was finally going home.

53

⁂

Adrian could barely think as he sat in his office in Willcox, watching the Southern Pacific refrigerated cars being loaded with beef carcasses from his packing plant. He had done well for himself during the war, and did not feel guilty, as Hannah had often suggested he should. Certainly, he thought, he had made a profit. A large profit. But why shouldn't he? Others had.

The war was drawing to an end, and it was time to start thinking about the future. His son would be coming home a hero, as he himself had been, and would be warmly received by the state of Arizona. A good war record wouldn't hurt Samuel in the future, either in business or politics. The thought of a Colored man in Arizona politics when Adrian was Samuel's age was unheard of. But that was then, and the climate was changing. Arizona was a state with multiple races—Negro, White, Hispanic, and Indian. Tensions didn't run as high on the cultural level as in other states, especially in the South.

He was about ready to call it a day when Hannah walked in, followed by Shania, carrying the baby.

"Well, what do we have here?"

He had not seen Hannah smile so radiantly since the day Samuel and Shania were married.

"We've decided to stay the night in town. That way we won't have so far to drive in the morning to meet the train."

"We can all go out to dinner, relax, and enjoy the evening. We already have the hotel rooms, so no arguments." Shania wore a huge grin as she wagged her finger at Adrian.

He threw up his hand. "I surrender. It's a great idea. I wasn't looking forward to driving home anyway."

Adrian grabbed his coat and hat, and they left, with John Parks following.

Selona had always told Adrian, "Need brings about yearning; yearning brings about dreams." As he sat with his family and Parks in the Willcox hotel restaurant, Adrian looked around the room. He had an idea, had had it for some time, but never discussed it with anyone.

"Hannah, what would you say if you and I went into the restaurant business?"

She paused from eating. "We already are in the restaurant business, dear."

"That's in Bonita. I mean another one. Maybe two more."

"What in the world are you talking about?"

He began laying out his plan. "The war's going to be over soon, and this country is going to be getting back on its feet economically."

"I agree." Hannah said, her words sounding cautious.

"That means jobs. Which means prosperity. That means more time and money for luxuries, such as eating in a nice restaurant, like the kind we saw last summer in California when we took our trip."

"What on earth are you getting at, Adrian?"

"Restaurants. We build one here in Bonita. Maybe one in Phoenix. Jonathan and I talked about this very thing before he left for the service. We've got more than enough money."

"Money? Samuel is coming home tomorrow, and you want to talk money and business?"

"What's wrong with that? There's nothing wrong with making money. I swear, I believe we had this conversation before the war started."

"Yes, and we'll have it every time you go talking about another fool notion."

"Fool notion! I made a success out of my last fool notion, in case you've forgotten."

Shania was feeding Baby Franklin a bottle and lightly laughing. She knew when to stay on the sidelines and watch rather than get into the action.

"I still think it's a good idea. So does John. Don't you, John?"

Parks nodded carefully, not appearing interested in getting caught in the crossfire. "I do believe there's a strong potential for such a venture, Hannah."

Hannah put down her napkin, then looked at him hard. Then Adrian saw something strange happen; something that confirmed his belief he would never figure the woman out. Her hard scowl slowly turned to a soft smile. "All right then, Adrian, tell me more about your plan."

He carefully explained what he had in mind, with Hannah questioning him closely. By the time the restaurant closed, Shania had taken the babies to her room. John Parks had retired to his room.

It was midnight when Adrian and Hannah went to bed. Even after the lights were out Adrian kept talking about his plan. By the time she fell asleep, Hannah had the entire plan memorized.

54

* * *

The moment Samuel stepped onto the platform he realized his life had gone full cycle, from the day he left for Tuskegee, to Europe, and now back home. He still walked with a limp, carrying one bag, the sabre strapped between the carrying handles. The train had arrived early, and he wasn't surprised to see that there was no one to meet him, so he sat on a bench and felt the cool, crisp air against his face.

Since being wounded, he had traveled on an odyssey of sorts, from the aid station to the hospital ship, from the ship to a hospital in England, finally to the United States. For him, the war was over.

The price had been high. He carried a lot of baggage in his heart; the memories of friends and saviors remained with him as painful reminders of the sacrifice that had been required to wage a great war against an evil force.

He took the battered sword in his hands and slid the blade gently from the dented scabbard. His grandfather had carried it onto this platform when he brought Darcy Gibbs's body back when he was killed by Apaches protecting this very rail line. His father had carried the sabre from this station and returned from World War I. Samuel had carried it from here to Europe and now had returned.

"Hello, stranger. Welcome home!" a soft voice said from behind.

He knew the voice and smiled as he stood and turned to see Shania holding little Adrian's hand, and holding Baby Franklin in her arms. Behind her stood his father and mother and John Parks.

He rushed into her arms and smothered her for a moment with kisses as his family swarmed around him. Then he held his two sons in his arms, and through a cloud of tears realized—God! He was home!

The front room at Sabre Ranch had swelled with friends by the time the two cars arrived in front of the house. Teddy Bruner was the first to embrace Samuel. He threw his arms around his friend and their wet cheeks joined; each held the other tightly.

"Welcome home, my friend. Welcome home." He paused and looked at his friend's leg. "I guess we'll both have to miss spring roundup this year."

Samuel laughed. "Hell, no! We're going on roundup if we have to do it by car!"

Adrian removed the sabre from the carrying handles of Samuel's bag. He held the weapon with reverence and slid the blade easily from the scabbard. "You took mighty good care of this, son. I'm very proud of you." Then he extended the sabre to Samuel and nodded at the mantel above the fireplace.

The Sharps rifle rested in its familiar place, above two empty pegs. Samuel took the sabre, and in the silent room, walked to the mantel and placed the sabre on the pegs. He stepped back and smiled, taking in the fullness of the moment. The significance. That these two weapons represented the fabric that bound their family: through good times and bad; through laughter and tears; through war and peace.

Shania slipped her arm through his and leaned her head against his shoulder. Adrian put his arm around Hannah, and John Parks dabbed at the tears in his eyes.

For a long while, not a word was spoken.

55

After everyone left, Adrian motioned Samuel to come to the front porch. They went outside and stood beneath the stars, neither saying a word. They just stared, the smoke from Adrian's pipe the only movement. Adrian stepped down from the porch and walked lazily about, not in any particular direction, like a man with something on his mind but uncertain how to get it said.

"What's on your mind, Pop?" Samuel knew his father's characteristics and knew when he needed to say something uncomfortable.

"What are your plans, son?"

Samuel stepped down from the porch and stood beside his father. "I want to stay in the army, Pop."

Those were not the words Adrian wanted to hear. "I was hoping that when you were discharged you might come back and go into business with me."

"I don't think I'd be much of a businessman."

"I think you're wrong." Adrian couldn't hide the disappointment in his voice. "We're going to build a few more restaurants. Your mother likes the idea. It's the first time she has agreed with me on any business plan. Surprised the living hell out of me."

Samuel grinned. "I remember when she thought you were an opportunist for wanting to sell beef for army rations."

Adrian remembered. There had been anger and talk of war that morning. "She was mighty upset."

"Not as upset as when I decided to go to Tuskegee Institute."

"Grams nearly had heart failure."

"If I hadn't gone to Tuskegee, I'd never have met Shania."

"Guess things turned out for the best," Adrian said. He looked a Samuel's leg. "You going to be able to pass that physical?"

Samuel squatted and picked at the pebbles in the driveway. "I'm going to pass it, Pop. I'm going to get back in the Air Corps."

"Will you go back to Europe?"

Samuel shook his head. "There's so many waiting to go, I'll be sent to a training squadron and train the young guys."

"What about when the war is over? What will you do?"

"I don't know what's in the future, but I want to be a part of whatever happens. The Negro has a place in the military, and that place is getting bigger. I want to be a part of it."

"So now you're a Negro. I remember when being called Colored took long enough to earn."

"The times are changing. I had a white friend from Georgia."

Adrian looked at him quizzically. "So?"

"Yes, sir. From Macon, Georgia. Fine fellow. We sipped bourbon from his flask on the flight line one night and talked about the differences between the races."

"What happened to him?"

"He was with me when we were with the Maquis. I never saw him after I was wounded. But I know where his family is. I'll find him one day and thank him."

"Thank him for what?"

"When I was wounded, I dropped the sabre. He recovered it and brought it to the aid station."

That meant something special to Adrian. "If you ever do see him, tell him I said 'thank you,' too."

"We best be getting inside."

They started in. Adrian said, "Samuel?"

"Yes, sir?"

He stuck out his hand. "You've made me very proud, son. Very proud."

They shook hands beneath the Arizona stars.

It was a good feeling.

56

They had made love all night in the main bedroom in Vina Gibbs's house. He talked about the war, about Thomas, and his friend Wylie Patterson, and even the Maquis woman who kissed him on the cheek minutes before she died so that he might live. He talked about the hatred in the restaurant, the way the Negro squadrons had to fight for the right to fight, and the proud record established.

He talked about his wounds, and the long stay in the hospital in England. "I thought I would never get out of that place," he said.

Then she ran her hand along his legs, felt the thick scars, and whispered, "Do you intend to stay in the army?"

He didn't say anything for a long while. "I like the army, Shania. When this war is over there will be a lot of changes for the Negro in the military. I'd like to be a part of that. If I can still soldier."

"What do you mean 'if you can still soldier'?"

He sighed heavily. "I've been placed on temporary medical leave. I have to take a physical in less than thirty days at Fort Huachuca. If I don't pass, I'll be medically discharged."

"If you pass, can you fly again?"

"The size of the flying service will be cut back dramatically, but I think the political atmosphere will demand that Negro pilots will constitute some of that force. All I have to do is pass the physical."

"What do you think, Samuel? Can you can pass it?"

"I have almost thirty days to get myself in shape. The only problem is the leg. If I can't make the mile run under six minutes, I'm out of the army."

She squeezed his stomach muscles, and he pulled her into his arms. They kissed long and lovingly, then she giggled, "You're strong enough everywhere else. I know you can do it, baby. I just know."

"I hope you're right. The last thing I want is to go into ranching."

She kissed him again, then said confidently, "You'll make it, baby."

He didn't reply. She only heard him softly snoring as she lay staring at the ceiling, wondering what the effect on him would be if he failed.

Shania awoke, ran her hand to his pillow and found it empty. She put on her robe and walked around the house, looked through the window and saw him standing in the cemetery. She quickly dressed, put a shawl around her shoulders, and hurried to him.

He was standing at Selona's grave.

"I wish I could have been here when she died," he said, his voice no more than a whisper.

"You were here in her heart and soul. There wasn't a day that passed that she didn't talk about you."

He looked toward the desert for a time. "I want to go for a ride."

She smiled. "I've dreamed of that since the day you left."

"So have I."

They walked hand in hand to the house. In his old room he opened the closet and retrieved an old, weather-beaten McClellan saddle, took his worn cavalry hat down from the shelf, and went into the front room, where Shania waited.

He reached up and removed the Sharps and the sabre. "Are you ready?"

"What are you doing?"

"A Sharps family tradition. I'm going to find out if I'm still a soldier."

She followed him to the stable in total confusion. They rode to the rim of the canyon, where the men of the Sharps family had traditionally faced a rite of passage. He sat silently on his horse, staring into the deep canyon where he had once made the dangerous ride to the bottom, as did his father, uncle, and grandfather, who was mortally injured on this very spot. He could almost hear their voices as he stared into the abyss.

"Samuel, have you lost your mind?" Shania said. He had not said what he was going to do, but now she knew!

The horse jerked nervously, but he held the reins taut, then patted the animal's heavy neck. "Settle down, settle down. You've done this before."

His hand flashed up; his fingers touched the edge of the brim in a sharp salute. He spurred the horse, stood into the iron stirrups, and leaned back as the horse bolted over the edge and into the red mouth of the canyon.

The pain in his leg was almost unbearable, but he had come here to find out the truth.

Down the horse plunged, speed building as Samuel's right hand held firmly to the reins, checking the power of the animal, while his free hand drew the steel sabre rattling against the saddle. With a smooth movement he extended the blade toward the imaginary enemy that lay waiting at the bottom. As the sun flashed off the burnished blade he realized he was leaning dangerously over the neck of the charging horse. He pulled the reins taut, sat back as far as possible, and distributed his weight evenly, winning for the moment against the forward pull of horse and gravity, against the throbbing pain in his leg.

Down they drove, leaving a spray of gravel and a cloud of dust that rose heavily into the cold air. The deeper he and the horse descended, the thicker the red dust rose until he and his mount appeared as flaming apparitions.

It was only in the final moments of the descent, with his leg throbbing painfully, when the horse dived over the last ledge, and he heard its hooves crack against the hard floor of the canyon, that he yelled, *Charge!*

The canyon echoed with the sound of the horse's pounding hooves, the rattle of the empty sabre scabbard, and the snort of the animal in full charge.

He stood in the stirrups, ignoring the bolt of pain that shot up his leg and into his spine. He leaned forward while extending the sabre beyond the horse's rising and plunging head. At the precise moment he and the enemy would join in battle, the sword flashed forward, narrowly clearing the head of the animal; then he pulled on the reins, wheeling the horse into the opposite direction.

Another scream burst from his lungs as he spurred the stallion to full gallop and again stood in the stirrups, his leg now numb, and extended the sabre. He slashed and cut, parried and thrust the blade at the enemy as though he were fighting a legion of demons.

He rode hard until both he and the horse were exhausted, then reined the animal in and began walking him slowly toward the mouth of the canyon.

He looked up, saw Shania watching from the rim. He saluted her sharply with his sabre, then crisply returned the blade to the scabbard.

What he could not see was her broad, proud smile; Shania knew that he was still a soldier!

57

Hannah decided that, despite the cold weather the night would be the right for the family to gather in the cottonwoods for a bonfire, to begin the process of healing the wounds.

Adrian complained only slightly. "Hannah, it's going to be awfully cold."

"We'll all wrap up in them old buffalo robes you've kept folded away in the stable," she said.

He chuckled, cautioning her, "We might smell like horses by the time the night's over."

She laughed softly. "We've smelled like horses before. Besides, horse smell is good smell. Isn't that what Selona used to say?"

"She did, and she was right." He put his arm around her waist. "I remember when I came back from France. We stayed all night in them cottonwoods under those buffalo robes. You smelled like lilacs the next morning."

She giggled. "Go on with your foolish talk. You start getting romantic on me, and we might not make it to the cottonwoods."

He kissed her lightly on the lips. "It's been too long since I've kissed you, Hannah."

"Don't be so long in doing it again, next time. I thought you had some business in town before the gathering."

He sighed, grabbed his hat, and started for the front door. Before leaving he took a ladder and went to the cemetery, where he propped it against the wrought-iron fence. Hannah watched through the window, knowing what he planned.

It was a good plan.

Samuel and Shania returned from their ride around noon, both laughing and tickling at each other's ribs as though playful children. Shania was radiant, looking full of life after suffering so many months of loneliness. Samuel's leg ached, but he ignored the pain, her laughter balm enough for the moment. The pain would go away, but she would always be with him.

They rode in slowly, walking the horses; all the while Samuel looked around, reconnecting himself to his home. He felt a sense of loss as they passed the cemetery. Something seemed to be missing. Then he slid from the saddle and walked, each step a little less painful, for the strength was returning.

When Hannah heard what he had done, she looked at him incredulously. "Have you lost your mind? What if you'd have fallen on that bad leg?"

Samuel put his big arms around her and held her close. "I didn't fall. I had to find out, Momma."

"You forget the Sergeant Major was killed doing that on a bad leg."

"The Sergeant Major was nearly seventy years old."

Hannah recalled that day in 1918, when the Sergeant Major's horse returned with an empty saddle.

"Blamed foolishness is what it was. For both of you."

Shania came in carrying Baby Franklin. Little Adrian toddled behind her. Samuel picked him up, and the four went into the sitting room. Hannah looked through the window toward the cemetery and smiled. She knew what Adrian was up to, and it made her feel good.

That afternoon Samuel went to the cottonwoods and split wood and began building the logs for the bonfire. He had a good pile built when he saw his father's car pull into the front drive. He picked up the ax and started toward the car. Adrian opened the trunk and said, "You want to grab this for me son and give me a hand?"

Samuel looked into the trunk and could only shake his head in awe and great appreciation. He put his arms around his father and hugged him as tears streamed from his eyes. "Welcome home, son," Adrian said.

They embraced long and deep. A father and his son. An old soldier and a young soldier. Survivors of war!

"Come on," said Adrian. "Let's go put this where it belongs."

Samuel reached into the trunk and removed the heavy metal object and followed his father to the cemetery.

The sun was just going down when another branch of the Sharps family arrived. Benjamin and his family had driven from Tucson. He was not in the service, having suffered from asthma all his life. They would stay in the Gibbs house, where he had grown up.

Samuel started the fire and the family gathered around as the flames began to roar. Hannah looked at the Reverend John Parks, and asked, "John, would you say a few words for those who are not here with us?"

Parks spoke openly from the heart. "Friends, we are here to welcome home one of your family who has served with honor and valor for a cause important to all humankind. We are all grateful that he has come home safely to his loved ones. In these times it is difficult to speak of those who have returned, and will return, without thinking of those who will never return. But they are with us in spirit."

From somewhere within the group, a voice began to hum, then the words from "Amazing Grace" began to rise from the gathering, lifting above the fire toward the heavens.

Then, almost as if on cue, their eyes turned to the metal object Samuel had removed from the trunk. Which Adrian had taken to town to be altered that morning.

Hanging above the archway to the cemetery, not two, but three sabres were joined together to form a trident.

EPILOGUE

Vietnam

✴ ✴ ✴

The Tiger Force recon team slipped through the dense foliage like ghosts moving through walls, touching nothing as they worked their way carefully toward a large opening, where a small village was visible. The monsoon rain fell in windswept slants, nearly obscuring the tiny ville near the Ia Drang Valley in the Central Highlands. The village, nothing more than mud huts with thatch roofs, was divided into two sections, with a community gathering place between the two.

That was what Corporal Franklin LeBaron Sharps was studying through his binoculars. Like his father, he was tall, with deep ebony skin and broad features, which were now twisted in a mask of fury. Private John Dawes eased to his side and whispered, "What's the plan?"

Franklin whispered, "You take Kirkwood and Burkett and cover the back door. I'll take Marion and Elliott, and we'll go in and scope out the ville."

Dawes nodded and turned to Private Burkett, whose white face was covered by camouflage paint. He motioned with one finger toward thick jungle near the south end of the village. Then they dispersed without making a sound.

Three more LRRPs appeared wearing tiger-stripe fatigues carry-

TOM WILLARD

ing rucksacks laden with explosives, ammunition, and other equipment vital to a long-range recon patrol unit.

The night suddenly turned gray as a loud crash of thunder preceded a finger of lightning, highlighting the three LRRPs as they moved from the jungle. When Franklin reached the first hut he looked right then left, removed his bayonet, and showed it to the other two. He carefully locked the bayonet on the muzzle stud, then switched off the safety on his M-16 rifle.

Franklin slid along the edge of the hut, his heart pounding. He peered into the hut and found it empty. A small cook fire was smoldering, with only a slight wisp of smoke, telling him the owners had been gone for some time.

As he started toward the second hut there was a loud "squeal!" as a frightened pig shot past him. His heart was now racing, so he knelt and tried to calm his nerves by breathing in long, deep breaths. When he had settled down, he continued his sweep.

He quickly checked the second hut and found it empty. As was the third. One by one each hut was checked.

The three joined up on the farside of the first section and started forward. Franklin held up his fist and pointed. Marion and Elliott squinted, and through the rain saw the hooch. He motioned them forward, raising his weapon at the ready to fire.

Ten yards away, beneath the poncho hooch, four Vietcong soldiers slept in hammocks, their Kalashnikov AK-47s lying across their chests. On the ground lay several empty bottles of Bamiba beer.

John took aim, as did Marion and Elliott then shouted, "Let's rock and roll!"

A startled Vietcong awoke just as John opened fire with his M-16 fusillade. The jungle came alive with the thunderous roar of the weapons, as the hammocks swung wildly, bullets tearing bits of tissue and bone.

Within seconds the four VC were dead, their blood running onto the wet ground, forming rivulets of red that ran onto the jungle boots of the LRRP soldiers. Smoke drifted lazily upward, then flattened as the humidity and rain seemed to want to deny it access to the sky.

Marion stepped forward and kicked one of the dead soldiers in his hammock. "Sleep on that, sucker!"

Franklin pulled a knife from his harness and cut the rope attached to one end of the hammock of a dead Vietcong. The VC's body spilled onto the ground, his face in a pool of his blood. "That's for my dead brother, Adrian, you son of a bitch!"

He stood there breathing heavily, smelling the gunpowder, the death, and loving every moment, as he had each time before when he avenged the death of his brother. Then he knelt heavily, and said to Marion, "Check them out for papers. Money. Anything. You've got two minutes, then we move. We'll hook up with the others at the back door."

He looked around, knowing there was still one piece of work left. He walked off, reloading a fresh magazine, as Marion and Elliott began searching the bodies. "Wire the bastards!" he said.

Marion checked the first body, found nothing, then took a hand grenade, pulled the pin, and placed it in the VC's armpit, rolling him carefully onto that side. If the body was turned over by other Vietcong, a loud surprise would be waiting!

When Franklin reached the open area he felt sick at the sight before him. Dawes, Burkett, and Kirkwood stood looking at two Vietnamese children. "Are they still alive?" he asked Dawes.

Dawes tossed a cigarette onto the ground. "Barely."

Franklin looked at the two children suffering before him. "Charlie sure gets pissed when the locals step out of line."

The two small children appeared standing, but weren't; their small feet dangled inches from the ground. Their tiny bodies were held by bamboo poles planted in the ground and shoved up their rectums. The little girl, squirmed pitifully, then closed her eyes. Blood and excrement slowly oozed down the pole.

"How you want to do this?" asked Dawes.

"Can you do anything for them?" asked Franklin.

"Yeah, but you ain't going to like it. Only trouble, there ain't enough morphine to do the job right." He hawked and spit with disgust. "Otherwise, they're going to suffer. Can't get a chopper in with this weather. Besides, it wouldn't matter. Neither one's got a snowball's chance in hell. They're just living on minutes."

Franklin looked at their faces, then lifted the girl from the pole as Dawes lifted the boy from his stake. They laid them on the ground, side by side. Franklin knelt and ran his hand along her face, pushing back her matted hair. He was surprised to see a brief moment of gratitude, as though she knew what he would do to relieve her torturous misery.

Franklin stood, as did Dawes, and lowered his M-16 to her head. Dawes did the same to the boy.

Both pulled their triggers at the same moment the earth shook with thunder and lightning forked through the sky.

Afterword

What the Negro serviceman knew could not be denied following World War II became a reality on July 26, 1948. In Executive Order 9981, President Harry S. Truman, without the consent of the U.S. Congress, declared that the armed forces could no longer continue, or maintain, a segregated military.

The order stated in part: "It is hereby declared to be the policy of the President that there shall be equality of treatment and opportunity for all persons in the armed services without regard to race, color, religion, or national origin. This policy shall be put into effect as rapidly as possible, having due regard to the time required to effectuate any necessary changes without impairing efficiency or morale."

The contribution of the "Tuskegee Airmen" cannot be properly assessed solely on the basis of missions flown, enemy aircraft shot down, battle-damage evaluation, or decorations. In the final analysis, a higher assessment is required to appreciate fully the contribution of these valiant aviators, support staff, and administrative personnel.

For decades the United States government refused to acknowledge the military services as a social proving ground. The military, however, has proven over the years to be exactly that. The military was the first major American industry to address the issues of racial and gender equality, and homosexuality. With hard-and-fast rules regarding these areas, the barriers began to fall, and an important change occurred.

To say the "Tuskegee Experiment" was a success is an understatement. From the ranks of these valiant men came great military and political leaders, scholars, physicians, educators, attorneys, and common men. However, unlike ordinary men, they were not allowed the luxury that others in similar endeavors enjoyed: the luxury of failure.

How many statisticians kept a hungry count of the number of white pilots who washed out of flight training? How many squadrons were placed in an impossible combat situation and given a poor rating for lack of combat aggressiveness when they never had the opportunity to engage the enemy?

The contribution of the "Tuskegee Airmen" is finally coming to light in the United States, a page of important history that has sat in darkened silence or been completely ignored. History books in junior and senior high schools, colleges and universities, are now revealing their story.

For this author, it has been a privilege to write about these valorous men, who fought and died for freedoms I have enjoyed all my life, while they were denied those same freedoms most of their lives.

I have had the privilege of knowing some of these men and their families, and that has been the greatest thrill in writing this novel.

You are my friends and my heroes, and I thank you for the honor.

Tom Willard
Author, *The Black Sabre Chronicles*